AMOR
Fati

Selam ♡ Happy Reading!

AMOR
Fati

by

SELENA
GUTIERREZ

Amor Fati
By Selena Gutierrez

Copyright © 2021 by Selena Gutierrez.

Cover Design by Jena Brignola
Editing by Kay Springsteen
Formatting by Jill Sava, Love Affair With Fiction

Charlotte

It was a high school crush.

The typical shy cheerleader crushes on the rich star football player story.

Until homecoming night when our fates were bound together.

Then he disappeared.

Now, years later, the universe brings us together and I fall in love with a man who rescued me all those years ago.

But life isn't all sunshine and rainbows.

No, the real world is filled with bloodshed.

And I fell in love with a monster.

Lorenzo

One fateful night I saved her, and she called me her savior.

And wasn't that a joke because I was anything but...

I was a monster.

Who spilled blood in the name of family and gladly did it in order to keep them safe even if I damned my soul in the process.

And she was the light that kept me sane, but I would rather admire from afar than damn her soul in my world.

DEDICATION

To anyone who has ever thought about starting something that sounds impossible and is holding back. My advice to you... DON'T HOLD BACK! You don't know what awaits you on the other side. Blast your favorite song, put some sunglasses on and enjoy the ride.

*To my mother for pushing me to do this.
Mom somehow you knew this was going to turn into a beautiful passion. Without you this book wouldn't have come to life.*

*To my best friend Ale...
girl you are the real one! Always responding to all my messages at any time of day with my crazy ideas, read anything and everything I sent you and calmed me down when I would panic about releasing my words into the world. For always hyping me up and giving me the courage to keep going.*

PLAYLIST

Check out the music that inspired Amor Fati!

Into the Past
Familia
Renegade
Secrets
Bow
Talk to My Skin
I Got You
Snitch
Do I Wanna Know?
Blame It
Let Me
Let's Not Play Games
Killing In The Name
FRZZN
Speechless
Worship You
Monster
Human
Prisoner

Let You Down
BEBÉ
Umbrella
Black SSea
Not Afraid Anymore
Criminal
Love Is a Gun
Ordinary Life
Teenage Fever

PROLOGUE

With bloody hands, I raised both guns and fired three rounds in front of me.

"Come on! You wanted me? I am RIGHT FUCKIN' HERE!" I roared out into the dark warehouse as the rest shot off rounds.

Her screams came from the far left. "Look out!"

BANG! BANG!

Searing pain radiated from my left arm, and the warm blood seeped through my shirt as I fired another round, my anger intensifying. My blood burned with the need to kill, curse, and damn anyone who hurt her.

"Get to her now!" I yelled behind me as I ran ahead.

Shooting whoever the fuck got in my way. My arm dripped blood, and the agony spread, but the pain was nothing compared to the rage that was running rampant through my veins.

War had arrived, and I was heading into battle headfirst to defend what was...

MINE.

Finally coming into contact with her, my fury and horror spread.

I took cover the best way I could, dragging the chair with Charlotte on it with me.

She was tied to that chair, dried blood caked her once pink lips, bruises marred the body I had spent hours worshipping, and a knife was sticking out of her delicate arm. Her green eyes were barely visible from the tears that ran down her face. "*Amore,* I'm sorry I'm going to get you out, okay?" I worked on freeing her as shots were being fired around us. I shielded her with my body and once she was untied I took her in my arms, covered her with my body as I ran behind the crates.

"Stay down!" I warned her, hoping she could hear and understand.

Through the tears, she just nodded, holding her left arm.

Loading my gun, I peeked out, then shot more rounds as bullets flew by our heads.

"Thought you were a smart man, Rizzi. Come on." He laughed.

That sound made my blood boil even more.

"I thought you were loyal, you fuckin' *rat!*" I shouted, firing off two shots his way.

"HAHAHA tell me...what would you do for the one you love?" he yelled.

"NOOOOO!" Charlotte screamed and tried to move.

CAZZO!

I ran and jumped in front of Julian firing four rounds. *BANG! BANG! BANG! BANG!*

My body hit the ground with a jolting *thud*, and I gasped for air.

Another shot rang out.

"SHIT!" Julian dropped to his knees, holding his shoulder.

"Enzo!" That was Dante. Then I saw him, Alessio next to him.

"Awwww... isn't this cute?"

I felt blood come up.

This was it.

Born into a life surrounded by blood, and now I was dying surrounded by it.

Everything around me slowly faded. Voices grew distant.

They say when you're about to die you get one last memory. I saw her beautiful face. The way her smile brightened a room. How her green eyes sparkled in the light and how her long waves framed her face.

My angel, my love, my world.

"S-save..." Between gasps blood spewed from my mouth, and I begged, "Get ou-ut... tell h-her I-I lo-love her."

BANG.

One last shot was fired before my body fell into the darkness.

My demons were welcoming me home with open arms.

Per Sangue Rizzi Vivo e Per Sangue Rizzi Muoio

ONE

Charlotte

Where it all Began

Why me?

Seriously, why in the world was I doing this again?

Oh right— I fuckin' put myself in this position.

Out of all my bright ideas, which were very few, according to my father. I had to go ahead and follow in my mother's footsteps, cheerleader. I'd thought we would bond over it, which never happened. Now here I was close to performing, about to puke my guts out on my navy-blue shell uniform top, all because I wanted to bond.

And to make matters worse, I was up front because, according to Coach Ramirez, "Your smile is contagious."

Gee, you would think that would boost my confidence.

It fucking didn't!

Bile rose in my throat. My hair wasn't helping. My ponytail was so tight I didn't think I would need a facelift later in life.

Taking some deep breaths, I wiped my sweaty palms down my skirt. It was a matching navy-blue V-notch skirt with a white and sparkly silver stripe on the side. One thing I did love about cheer was the uniforms. I had dreamed about wearing one since I could remember.

"Come on, Charlotte, you can do this!" I said to myself eyeing Katherine and Ava, my two best friends, who were currently stretching. Why in the hell did they not look nervous? All they were worried about was if their hair bows were straight, if their smiles sparkled, and if their skirt wasn't too long.

Yup, you heard that right.

Too long.

Looking away from them, I poked my head out of double doors of the gymnasium, out to the stands trying to find our other best friend Isabella, Ava's twin. I spotted her off to the side of the stands speaking with Mrs. Hollis, no doubt about our government project. Sometimes I wondered why I couldn't have been like Isabella and enjoyed my studies better than cheer? Don't get me wrong, I loved cheer. It was performing I couldn't get past.

Even after two years on varsity, anxiety got the better of me every single time. Thank the heavens it was senior year and would be over soon. Sure, I'd miss going to practices, football games, all the fun moments that came with the cheerleader life. All except performing.

Continuing to look around, I tried to see who was going to sit directly in front of me while I danced, hoping it was no one I knew. But it was hard to tell, since a group of people blocked my view.

I was literally moving my head side to side, trying to get

a better look, pretty sure I looked stupid at this point because my head was the only thing sticking out from behind the door. The group finally walked away as I was about to release my pent-up frustration on them, but the moment they did, a chill ran through my body.

Oh, hell no!

No, this could not be happening! Of all people, why *him*?

He was supposed to be sitting with the rest of the football team at the top of the bleachers like the fucking king he believed he was.

But of course, he did whatever the hell pleased him. It was his fucking kingdom and we were mere peasants. He was sitting there in his navy blue football jersey that fit him like a freakin' glove, talking to his cousin Dante who was sporting a cocky grin.

Those two ran the school.

The popular, rich boys, who everyone wanted to be friends with and every girl wanted to sleep with.

Yes, even me.

I know, cliché, right? Crushing on the hot football captain. But trust me, a girl would have to be dead not to notice him. At seventeen, he was six feet three inches and packing muscle no teenager in high school should. His deep dark brown eyes saw everything. And he had jet-black hair that I just wanted to run my hands through. Oh, and let's not forget the forearm tattoo that gave him the extra bad boy effect. I couldn't quite decipher what it said since it was in another language. Except for that one time during our government class when he had stretched out his arm to reach for the stack of papers that I was able to read one word. I wouldn't have known how to pronounce it, just that it was like the word family.

But it didn't matter that I couldn't' read it. A tattoo on muscular arm? Who wouldn't find that sexy?

He was the kind of man normally found on the cover of GQ.

The one you wanted posters of to hang on your bedroom walls.

But unlike in the movies, this cheerleader never dated the football player. Aside from not being his type, I was always reminded by my friends that he was the last boy I should crush on. He was a man whore, who could have any girl by the snap of his fingers and couldn't care less about her feelings.

I watched how he sat around his friends and carried himself, all high and mighty but there were moments where I saw a hint of something else. Like an actual human who actually cared and not what he projected.

"Char, hello…Charlotte?" Ava's voice has me pulling my head back in. She was standing next to Katherine, who wore a huge grin on her face.

Oh no, I had seen that grin before; her evil brain was working. The one that usually got us into trouble. I loved her. I mean, who wouldn't? Half the student body was obsessed with her five-foot five-inch toned body… tan skin, hazel eyes, light brown hair. Girl had a lot going for her. But when she got that grin we all knew to prepare ourselves because she meant business.

And as my luck would have, Ava was sporting the same grin.

Welp, there went my backup.

"Katherine, is there a reason your grin is as big the Great Wall of China?"

"Okay, first of all, remember I said to call me Katy, and second, why do you always get so nervous?"

"Well…" I didn't know about the other times, but I know the reason this time. Brown eyes, dark hair, nice sports car, football captain. Ring a bell? You probably had one in your high school as well. "Oh, Katy, come on just tell me what is going through your mind so I can get back to holding in my puke."

Literally.

"Char, don't exaggerate. I just wanted to do something we always do when one of us needs cheering up. Come on, you should know this."

Ava's arm nudged me. "Yeah, come on, Char, ready?"

How could I possibly forget? We had only been friends since we were five years old and were obsessed with princess dresses. But we were missing…

"I'm here, I'm here! I didn't forget!" Isabella yelled as she rushed through the double doors, book in hand with an outfit that looked straight off Gossip Girl. How she made a plaid skirt, chunky sweater and white sneakers work was beyond me.

Isabella had it all. Brains, style, beauty. Hell, her and her twin sister Ava looked like they had been created in a lab. Both at five feet six inches with curvy bodies that had every guy in our school begging to be controlled by them. Not to mention their blue eyes, dark blond hair, high cheek bones and cupid's bow lips. They might have been identical twins but Ava was the wild one. Always more outgoing, free, and didn't take crap from anyone, just like Katy. And Isabella? Well we were more alike; shy homebodies and always stuck to what we knew.

A smile curved my lips as I looked over at my three best friends, the girls I had grown up alongside and shared everything with. Aside from our differences we always seemed to get ourselves into some kind of trouble.

"Okay, come let's get this over with." I tried to sound bored, when in reality this calmed me down every single time.

We smiled at one another we stepped forward, linking our hands, and then together we recited, "In the good, the bad, worst and the truly horrible. Together always, forever, until the beating stops." Then we touched our necklaces. Four hearts in a line attached to one another, each one representing us. A necklace we got when we were fifteen, after the horrible car accident Katy was in, one where she lost her father and where we almost lost her. We've been inseparable ever since.

Innocent, unaware of the troubles the world brought.

Of how cruel it can truly be.

"Hey!" Isabella turned to hug me. "You got this! I know you're nervous but believe me when I tell you, You. Are. Amazing. Go out there and show them how special you are!"

"Thanks, Bella."

It was funny how we were all friends but there was something about Bella and me, we understood each other. Like we shared a brain. Same could be said for Katy and Ava. I guess each group of friends has a person you get along with most.

Then, no later than twenty seconds after Bella left, Coach Ramirez was calling us into formation.

Dammit.

I was stuck in front of the line all while Katy and Ava moved toward the back, and all because I happened to be a couple inches shorter.

It was a blessing and a curse to be five feet two inches tall. I could wear any heel I pleased and still maintain my petite style, but I got stuck in front for everything else. That and never being able to reach anything in the top cabinet.

The doors opened.

I said a prayer.

Squeezed my pom-poms and took a deep enough breath to know that I wasn't going to puke and walked out.

I was so distracted trying to take deep breaths with a big smile plastered on my face that I probably looked like the Joker at this point. I forgot all about who I would be in front of.

The crowd cheered, as we took our places. I bowed my head closing my eyes waiting for the music to start, taking one last deep breath.

It was quiet for a second before the music blared through the speakers. At the first note, I snapped my head up.

Locking eyes with *him.*

Lorenzo Rizzi.

TWO

Lorenzo

Those green eyes were going to be the death of me one day.

Damn if Charlotte didn't take my breath away in that moment I don't know what did.

I swear those eyes felt like they stared into my very soul and saw the very demons that haunted me.

During class I couldn't even concentrate on what was being taught, not that I was really going to pay attention. I really didn't need to be there. The only reason I was in school was to play football, the only thing I really had chosen for myself because the rest of my life was basically decided for me.

Run the Rizzi Dynasty alongside my cousin Dante, my second.

That didn't mean a man couldn't admire an angel like Charlotte.

Man, she was beautiful.

God gifted her small frame with all the right curves, a perky ass, long dark brown hair, legs that a man could only worship for days. But my favorite features about her? Her angelic face. Big green eyes that I swear sparkled every time she smiled, full lips, smooth skin. She even had this small birthmark on her right cheek that was barely noticeable, but I saw it.

I saw all of her.

Aside from a few hellos, side glances, and the few times we got put into the same group for a project in class I hadn't really talked to her. She was like some forbidden fruit that I desperately wanted to bite but couldn't.

My life was too dangerous.

I clenched my jaw at the memory of my mother, the price she paid for loving my father.

Thank God for my cousin Dante, because if he weren't there to keep me in check I would have leaped at the chance to claim her. All I could do was admire her from afar, the way she would put her hair in a bun with a pencil when she was about to take an exam, take deep breaths every time she was about to present in class or perform with the cheerleaders, or the way she would wait for her friends at lunch with Oreos and her nose stuck in a book.

But watching her perform, that would always be my favorite pastime. She was gracefully moving throughout the gym floor, doing kicks and flips like it was nothing. I swear my heart stopped the moment she was thrown in the air for a front flip.

"What the bleacher do to you?" Dante murmured next to me.

I ignored him.

"Oh man, you got it bad." He looked down at my hands

that gripped the bleacher even tighter at the sight of another flip. "Shit you want my coffee? It's Irish."

"Shut up, Dante," I said through clenched teeth.

He leaned in. "Look, you said you didn't just want fuck her and leave her, and you know that she can never—" He was cut off by a scream.

"Yeah girls, come on!!! WOOOO Char, Katy, and Aaavaaa!" Isabella, Charlotte's best friend, shouted from the front.

Dante gaped. Fucker had it bad for Isabella; ever since they got paired together in French class.

My brows scrunched. Why the fuck was he taking French? We were Italian.

I elbowed him. "You were saying *Stronzo*!" Asshole.

"*Cazzo*." Fuck. Dante muttered under his breath and ran his hands through his long dark hair. "Okay I think we both know we can't ever go there. They'd be running for the fuckin' hills if they found out who we really are."

And they would.

People at school just thought that the Rizzis bled money, and no more than the top one percent of Boston. Ever since our fathers had paid for the new football field, new computer labs, donated a shit ton of money to the school library and gifted us the latest most expensive sports cars every few months the moment we turned sixteen.

People wanted to be us, be friends with us, girls threw themselves at us.

To them we were just some rich kids who didn't have a care in the world except for racking up our parents' credit bill and partying.

Hah, if only they knew.

Our family ran a successful construction company but

that was just a cover for our other "side businesses," as we called them. The ones we were groomed to take over one day. Together Dante and I would run everything and everyone with the Rizzi name and because of who we were to become, we couldn't just bring anyone into the fold, no matter how perfect we thought they were.

Or how much we desired them.

"Only admire from afar." That was what our fathers told us. Why?

Because not everyone was cut out for the Mafia.

People thought after watching a couples movies, or some TV shows, or reading a book they were ready to be part of our world. But all they saw was money, drugs, girls, and good times. Not the reality of what it really was. How you never forgot the smell of blood from your first kill, the way a head blows when you put a bullet through it, or the feeling when you had to torture and then kill one of your uncles because he played around, threatening he would go to the Feds and talk.

And in our world you didn't play with those things; that was a threat to our family.

Dante and I had spent four hours the night before torturing an uncle who had taught us how to swim, an uncle for whom we cared.

But he had put our family in danger.

Our fathers told us it needed to be done, and then left to the docks to deal with an MC biker gang who wanted to steal our shipment of drugs.

For generations, my family has run Boston, and while many have tried to take us down, no one has been able to dethrone us. And it is going to be my job with Dante at my side to ensure that no one ever will. So last night, before I put a bullet between my uncle's eyes, I said. "*In nome della famiglia.*" In the name of family. And when our fathers got home, stained shirts and split knuckles, we drank wine and went over family business.

Like it was normal for their seventeen-year-old sons to kill someone. And, in reality to us it was; we had both been made by the age of fifteen.

So while I watched Charlotte wave her pom-pom in the air after her dance, I let my eyes travel up her body, admiring each curve until I reached her catlike eyes that were watching me, observing me.

Was she aware that she had pulled her bottom lip between her teeth?

For a few seconds I held my stare to hers, clenching my jaw. I was reminded of my dad's words. "The ones meant for us are those who are willing to pull the trigger." Something I knew she wasn't willing to do. So I turned my gaze away from her, acting unaffected, talking to the girl in front of me.

I reached for Dante's coffee the moment I no longer felt her eyes on me. "Give me that shit." I chugged it down while he chuckled and pulled a flask from his backpack.

We might be playing our homecoming game tipsy, but as long as it got Charlotte Frizzell off my mind I was cool with that.

THREE

Charlotte

The day following the homecoming game, came the event every girl in that school waited for: the homecoming dance.

The girls and I were getting ready at Katy's house. Pep rally was behind me, so my nerves were calm again. Of course we won the game; we have some of the best players. Lorenzo had made the winning touchdown, and if he weren't already being treated like a king he would be now.

Along with Dante, who was vying for class manwhore. He too looked like a GQ model with blue eyes, muscles and a half sleeve of tattoos.

The untouchables, the kings, the ones all the girls fawned over. And once they took over Rizzi construction...well all of that would just double.

Yesterday had been surreal. While we were performing, I hadn't been able to keep my eyes on Lorenzo. But hell if I didn't feel his eyes staring at me, raking my body with what I could hope was lust. Damn near made my knees buckle during my dance. Then during the game, I could have sworn we made eye contact again after his winning touchdown. But of course, I was wrong because two seconds later Ashley, class whore, was all over him and by the looks of it he enjoyed it.

"Hey Char, pass the eyelash curler." Ava called out from across the room, snapping me out of my thoughts. I was sitting at the vanity applying eyeliner.

"Yeah sure, catch!"

Katherine came out of the closet in her glittery dark blue short V-neck dress and caught my gaze. "Hey, I saw you talking to Caleb after the game. You know he has been eyeing you for a while, right?" She wiggled her brows.

"Omigod he has such dreamy eyes," Bella added.

Nothing compared to Lorenzo's chocolate brown eyes. "Oh, it was nothing." I shrugged. "He wanted me to be his date for tonight, but I'm going with you girls so I said no."

Katherine let out a giggle. "No wonder he looked like a sad puppy when I passed him in the parking lot. I gave him my protein bar thinking it would cheer him up and all he said was, 'these are Char's favorite' and handed it back to me."

The room fell silent as I looked through the mirror at the twins who were zipping up each other's dresses. You would think those girls were really different when you saw them but in that moment Ava and Isabella couldn't look more alike, biting the inside of their cheeks, holding back their laughs.

Yeah, it didn't last long. We all laughed so hard my cheeks hurt and my eyeliner was threatening to run.

"Okay, okay let's hurry up and get ready. We have a dance to get to." Ava looked around. "Hey, have you guys seen my earrings?"

Isabella reached into her bag and handed her the long silver earrings and asked. "Hey you think you could clasp my necklace? And Katy, you almost done with the lipstick?"

I looked at them through the mirror as they all helped each other and smiled applying my own nude lipstick. They were more than just my friends; they were my sisters. And while I had two older brothers I would always love these girls like family.

I stood and walked over to them. "Okay, Katy, let me finish zipping up your dress. Isabella your left heel isn't strapped, and Ava... Damn girl! That red dress fits was made for you! Honestly, you all you look amazing!"

We each smiled at each other and Bella said, "Charlotte... always hyping us up. You look beautiful as well. I knew that blush laced dress was you."

"Awww, I love you guys! Now hurry we have to go!"

We finished getting ready not knowing what the night would bring.

Not prepared for what was to come.

FOUR

Lorenzo

Pink was all I saw.

I bit back a curse.

God that woman couldn't be any more perfect.

The sway of her hips while she danced had me clenching my jaw until it hurt. And still my cock was hot steel pressing urgently against my zipper.

She and her friends hadn't stopped dancing since they had arrived.

"Hey, you want a drink?" Dante handed me his flask.

"Nah man, someone has to get us home."

"Yeah well, I'm drinking until that stupid black strapless dress stops calling my name."

I gave him my best good luck with that look. Poor sucker almost choked on his own tongue when he saw Isabella.

Hell, I wasn't any better.

I literally choked on my punch when I saw Charlotte in that dress that hugged her curves like a second skin.

No one in that room could compare to her and if she were anyone else I would have already been all over her.

I looked around the room, it was nearing the end of the dance and when I turned toward the girls they had started heading out. "Let's go," I barked, watching the girls.

"As long as we can keep drinking at your house."

"Just don't pass out naked by the pool again."

"One time!" Dante made a face. "I was bruised for a week from my mom's ass whooping."

We both laughed. Italian mothers were not to be messed with.

Walking out, I saw the girls approaching Katy's car. It was near my BMW all the way at the end of the parking lot. The only ones left back there.

They had been too distracted laughing to notice a convertible red mustang pull up next to them.

A random guy started asking them something, and I got a bad feeling.

So did Dante, because without a word, we picked up our pace.

Good fucken thing because one of the three assholes got out of the car and grabbed Charlotte's arm, tugging her hard against his chest. Katherine, Isabella, and Ava tried to help but another two guys got out of the car and pushed them back as Charlotte tried to shove away from her captor. But he only dragged her in tighter against him as he backed her up into the car. His grimy hand ran up her thigh and under her dress.

"Get off of me!" she said in a shrill tone, but he just laughed and gave her ass a squeeze. Her scream was masked by his dirty mouth.

All I saw was red from that point on.

I might be known to be a player, but I never forced myself on a girl.

"Hey! Let her go!" I yelled out as I ran toward them, Dante right behind me.

"Oh yeah? And what's the Great Lorenzo Rizzi going to do if I don't?" the asshole spat out.

Well, damn... it was a guy from one of our rival schools.

"You asshole! Let her go!" Katy shrieked.

From the corner of my eye I see her trying to bypass one of the guys holding her.

I narrowed my eyes and glared. "I said let her go before you fuckin' regret it." I lowered my voice to a menacing level. "Don't make me repeat myself."

Charlotte looked at me with pleading eyes. He hadn't stopped running his hands over her body. Ripping one of the straps of her dress, revealing her nude bra.

"What, you defend this bitch?" He released a harsh laugh.

Charlotte fumed at the comment, and before I snapped, she turned and spat in his face. I almost clapped at her fierceness but I stopped when he slapped her so hard across the face she would have fallen to the ground had he not had a grip on her.

Her friends gasped loudly, but they were still being held in place by this guy's friends.

Charlotte's eyes welled with tears as the asshole drew back his hand ready to strike again.

Oh, fuck no! I was going to fuckin' kill him; no one touched what was mine.

Mine?

Did I just think that?

Before I knew what I was doing I reached behind my back

and grabbed my 9mm. I didn't have to look behind me to know Dante had done the same. Only difference his pointed at the other two, and like a scared little bitches they ran off leaving the girls safe with my cousin.

With faces full of panic at the sight of our guns.

"Look, you piece of shit you have about two seconds to let her go before I shoot you in the kneecaps!" I aimed at the *stronzo.* Asshole.

"Oh, like you're such a bad ass."

I took a step forward and shoved my gun at the arm that held her breast.

He immediately shoved Charlotte away and raised his hands. "What now? You gonna shoot me?"

With a sob, Charlotte ran to her friends.

"No, shooting you would be too easy."

He didn't even see me coming because I had him on the ground in two seconds flat, landing punch after punch. Feeling the rage flow throw my veins. Consumed by the demon within. And I allowed it to flow freely every time my hand connected with his face.

The girls' cries were distant.

Adrenaline coursed through my blood.

As I turned into the monster I was trained to be.

Every punch filled with rage and vengeance.

His blood coated my fists and his face no longer looked like him, but I couldn't stop.

I didn't want to.

Until I felt a hand on my shoulder.

A calming warmth ran through me, bringing me back down from my rage. Like a ship when it reels in its anchor, letting it know it's time to go. Or in this case stop. I looked back and was met with big green eyes filled with tears and what I could only assume was fear.

Charlotte had met a piece of the monster I was, and she feared him.

Now if she only knew the truth.

"Lorenzo, please stop, please."

My heart broke to see that the very thing she feared in that moment wasn't the asshole who'd felt her up but the one who was trying to save her.

Slowly I stood, never taking my eye off her. "Dante, call it in."

"Already did. I'll give you a moment while I talk to the girls." He pulled the girls to the side. Pretty sure giving them the whole speech about how they can't say anything about what happened, blah blah blah.

I, on the other hand, couldn't speak. Which never happened to me. I was trained to get myself out of any predicament. When coach caught us smoking weed under the bleachers, well I just mentioned his affair and, *boom*, done. But this... fuckin' blank.

"Charlotte, I—"

"Thank you." She barely got the words out.

"What? No, wait. I shouldn't have reacted that way. It's just when I saw him hit you, I-I lost it. No man should ever touch a girl...w-woman...like th-that." Hell, I was even stuttering.

What the ever loving hell?

She looked at me for a couple seconds and then did something I didn't expect.

She took a step forward kissing my right cheek. And I was hit with the sweet smell of coconut. "Thank you, if you and Dante weren't there I have no idea what would have happened."

She held the side of her dress that was ripped. "And about the guns…I um promise I won't say anything and I'll talk to the girls and make sure we are on the same page."

I stood there, silent. Opening and closing my mouth. Wondering what to say next but I kept coming up blank.

What the hell was wrong with me?

Cat got your tongue, Lorenzo?

Meow, bitch!

A throat cleared behind me. "Clean-up is here," announced Dante, "and I talked to the girls and offered to take them. They're shaken a bit up. They're leaving Katy's car here. I'm taking one of the SUVs." He looked between Charlotte and me.

Not taking my eyes away from her I piped up. "As long as you're good to drive, I'll take Charlotte home. I-I mean if that's okay with you."

"Yes," she said softly.

Great.

Let's hope I find my balls by then.

FIVE

Charlotte

I hugged Lorenzo's sweater tighter around me. He had given it to me when we got into his BMW. I gladly took it; anything to block away that other asshole's smell.

I wanted to shower a hundred times over.

I had been forcefully touched, slapped, and had my dress practically ripped off me. I wiped away the tear that escaped my eye and hugged myself tighter. I never thought that this would happen to me, and if Lorenzo hadn't had been there I don't know what would have happened.

Just thinking about it made me go into panic. I inhaled the musky scent of cologne that clung to the sweater, instantly feeling comfort.

From a fucking sweater.

After everything that happened and what I saw I didn't know what to feel, think or do. I did know one thing.

I felt safe.

Because of Lorenzo.

Even though he and his cousin had pulled guns. Which I knew wasn't normal but right now I couldn't think straight.

I looked over at Lorenzo, his eyes so focused on the road in front of us. He was gripping the steering wheel so tight I thought it might come off. It was dark, but I was pretty sure I saw his jaw clenching and unclenching, that strong jawline.

Even angry he was beautiful.

"Hey, you okay?" he asked for the millionth time. "Are you cold?" With a click of a button my seat warmed up.

"Yeah, just tired." Lies. Slowly I touched my cheek; it still stung from the slap.

"I'm sorry," he said, reaching over, gently running the back of his hand over my cheek.

"Stop please, stop apologizing, it wasn't your fault. You saved me." I turned to look at him. "What's going to happen to the guy? Are you going to…kill him?"

Why was I asking this? Lorenzo wouldn't kill someone.

Right?

Well, he did carry a gun.

He cursed under his breath. "No Charlotte, he is going to the hospital and it will be made sure he doesn't remember what happened tonight, then he will go back to his normal pathetic life." We came to a stop, and he looked my way. "Don't worry, he will never come near you again."

"How do you know?"

"I just know." He sounded pissed.

I shouldn't have been asking questions, and I decided it was best to leave it at that just as he pulled up to my house.

Thank God my brothers weren't there or they would check who had brought me home.

I don't think they would have liked to see a guy dropping me off while I had a ripped dress and a bruised cheek. I was the baby of the family, overprotected always. Not to mention one was in the army and the other was in the police academy.

Lorenzo turned off the car and came around to open my door.

"So I guess chivalry isn't completely dead. Are you going to walk me over to my door next?" Inwardly I winced.

Smooth Char, very smooth.

His lip twitched. "Well I was but since apparently it's not impressing you, you can walk there on your own." He stepped away from the door, and I just sat there unable to move because he had said *impressed.*

Was he trying to impress me?

"Need a little help there?" He smirked, and heat rose to my cheeks.

"Nope, just trying to see if you were going to take it one step futher, carry me out of the car and up my four steps." Was I flirting?

Really after what just happened? But I couldn't help it. One minute I was panicking after nearly being… no I didn't even want to say it. And the next I was flirting?

His lips twitched, almost smiling, then the smirk got sexier. Pretty sure I was blushing. Which surprised me after everything.

Before I knew what was happening he stepped into the car, unbuckled my seat belt and wrapped his arms around me.

I shrieked when he picked me up, thinking I would fall. I gripped his forearm in a bruising manner. "Don't worry…I got you,." he whispered, inches away from my face.

I gulped. "Promise?"

"I promise." The tone in his voice let me know that he spoke the truth. That while his eyes held on to mine under the night sky, I knew I was safe with him. The danger that arose earlier was practically nonexistent. And without removing his eye from mine we walked toward my blue colored front door. Unable to explain what I saw in them. "You alright there?"

"Yeah. I'm really not fragile, you know. I'll be okay." I squeezed his arm as he approached the steps and hoisted me closer to his body.

What the hell? I loved this! I wished he would never put me down. "Thank you for keeping me safe."

He froze on the second step.

Not even kidding, right foot in the air and everything.

The look I received from him made me nervous and drove me to bite my bottom lip.

It was one of those expressions that you didn't know whether you just fucked up or maybe you should just run.

Cursing he took the last two steps and gently set me down. He weaved his hands through his hair. "Charlotte, I will never be safe, not in the way you expect, at least."

"But—"

"Let me finish. I need to get this out. You are a beautiful, amazing, kind and… fuck… you're perfect!" He inhaled sharply then blew out the breath. "Any guy would be lucky to have you. To give you moments full of laughter and memories. But that? That's not me." He leaned down and kissed my cheek.

I watched him walk away.

Confused by his words. What the hell did he mean but that?

And maybe I should listen to him, but I couldn't. I didn't want to.

I shook my head and yelled out. "Hey I'll see you in class on Monday?" It came out more of a question than a statement.

With a stoic look he simply responded. "Goodnight, Charlotte." Then he got in his car and drove away.

I slept in his sweater, dreaming of him and how I would see him in class Monday morning.

On Monday, I spent a little extra getting ready only to arrive and find his seat empty. Not just that day but the days, weeks, and months to follow as well. Neither he nor his cousin came back to school after that night, and I was left wondering why.

Was it my fault?

If saving me had cost him something, what door had it opened instead?

Why had he told me that with him I wasn't safe?

The sting of what he'd said that night hurt far worse than the slap from that asshole.

As much as I tried to move on, I couldn't. Lorenzo had been a part of me that day, and damn him if he didn't feel like he could keep me safe, because all I had felt with him that night was safe.

In my eyes Lorenzo was...

My Savior.

SIX

Lorenzo

8 years later

BANG!

"Dante! Dante!" I shook him. "Hey, hey stay with me! Fuck!" He just groaned.

Three more gunshots rang out to my left.

BANG! BANG! BANG!

We had come to an empty warehouse to meet with one of the small gangs that sold our drugs. And found ourselves in the middle of an ambush.

Big mistake.

Dante had gotten shot twice and was losing a lot of blood—fast.

Antonio, my most trusted associate, and I pulled my cousin behind a wall, while our other men covered us.

"Antonio, where the fuck is the car?!" I shouted.

"Just outside, boss. We just have to get to that door over there."

I did the math, and it would be a fuckin' mission to get out of here but I also had to get Dante out and without getting shot again.

FUCK!

"Alright, help me get him up. Have the others cover us." I barked out orders at Antonio while he helped pick up Dante. "You better shoot motherfucker, because if another bullet touches a hair on Dante's head, it's your fuckin' life! *Capire?*" *Understand.*

"Enzo, get out of here." Dante groaned, trying to pull away.

"I'm not leaving you! *Non abbandoniamo la famiglia, se moriamos moriamo insieme!*" *We don't abandon family, if we die we die together.* "Alright? Now let's get you out of here and find you a good looking doctor to heal you." At that he smirked.

Bastard.

I gave Antonio the signal to go on my count.

"Can I have two?" Dante tried laughing but ended up cursing over the pain.

"I'll make sure they have them ready for you."

He gave me a thumbs up.

I held back my laugh; he was a complete manwhore.

I gave the signal and ran out from behind the wall, firing my gun blindly, while trying to hold Dante on one side. A bullet grazed my right shoulder as I fired off two rounds finally making it to the doors and pushed it open. One of our associates was in the driver's seat, the other on lookout and my cousin was close to passing out.

"Dante! Keep your eyes open, stay with me!" I slapped him across the face. "Don't you dare close your eyes…YOU HEAR ME? Stay awake!" If he died I'd make sure to go down to hell and drag his soul back and kill him again for thinking he could leave me alone in this.

I applied pressure on his wounds, one on his shoulder that looked clean through and through and the other on his side that was bleeding fast.

"Antonio, call over to Mass Gen right now. Tell them to meet us at the private entrance, and I want extra men there guarding every single entry, exit…if it has a door I want a guard!"

He immediately started barking out orders on his phone.

I looked down. Blood was everywhere. My once-white shirt was now crimson.

"What the fuck happen tonight?" I demanded of Antonio once he was off the phone. "I want names yesterday!"

I was going to kill whoever thought they could mess with my family. We had gone in there to clear a few things up, but apparently they were out for blood. And if blood was what they wanted—well good luck, motherfuckers.

They would be drinking their own blood by the time I was done with them.

We pulled up to the hospital, our own private entrance with the doctors and some nurses waiting for us.

No one else used this entrance except for us. I had recently donated a lot of money to the hospital and remodeled it a bit. It was a good investment and we had twenty-four-hour access to it. Shit we even had doctors on our payroll, which made things a lot easier when it came to these sorts of things. The occasional gunshot wound, stab wounds, the accidental whoops my hand slipped and I broke one of my idiot associates noses kind of things.

The doctor opened up the back passenger door. "Mr. Rizzi, let go of him, we got him from here." Reluctantly, I allowed him to move my hand, and Dr. Whatever his name was pulled Dante onto the gurney. "Mr. Rizzi, you should get your shoulder checked, go into one of the rooms, I'll send a nurse and will come find you when I have news."

I stare him down, fighting the urge to point my gun at him. What the fuck was he still standing there looking at me for? He needed to be saving Dante's life not telling me what to do. I clenched my fist. "Go save my cousin's life, don't worry about me," I gritted out, heading for one of the rooms.

The room was bright and smelled like antiseptic. The only sound came from the buzzing of the fluorescent light.

Leaning back against the wall, I took a deep breath and stared at my hands that were covered in Dante's blood. The metallic smell coming off them had the bile rising in my throat.

My hands started to shake.

I had seen my fair share of blood, but this…this was my family's blood on my hands.

Slowly I slid down the wall, head between my knees.

Tightness in my chest.

Couldn't fuckin' breathe!

It was my fault he was here!

Idiot had pushed me out of the way when a shot was fired. Fuuuuccck!

I tried to take a deep breath, but I barely took small gasps of air. The smell of my cousin's blood invaded my nostrils. It felt as if someone had their hands around my throat.

I was choking.

My cousin who was as close as a brother, my best friend, the one person who always stood by my side was currently lying on an operating table all because he took a bullet that was meant for me.

It was me who should be on that table not him.

NOT HIM!

The tightness on my chest was to the point where I couldn't even think straight. I had forgotten where I was.

Until a hand laid on my shoulder. Why did it feel so familiar?

The moment I looked up, my heart stopped. I was dreaming because there was no possible way.

It couldn't be. It was always a dream. The face I dreamed of every time I had killed, tortured, and threatened someone. The only face that brought me back from it all.

The lost anchor.

I inhaled a breath.

God I could even smell the sweet coconut lotion.

Reaching out I put my hand over it to see if I was dreaming, if it was my mind playing tricks on me.

But it wasn't because I felt the warmth beneath my palm.

And Charlotte Frizzell was really kneeling in front of me.

SEVEN

Charlotte

No amount of training could have prepared me for this moment.

Nursing school had taught me how to get a patient's breathing under control when they were having a panic attack, but I froze.

About to have a panic attack myself.

I was not prepared to come face to face with Lorenzo.

Years later.

Eight years, to be exact, since that night. The night when he'd disappeared and all I was left were my dreams about a savior who'd promised he had me.

How wrong was I?

I ran my gaze over him.

Dammit, couldn't he have at least gained some weight or suffer from early hair loss? He was handsome before, and now he looked like the sexiest man alive. Even through his stained white shirt bulging muscles were evident. Definitely bigger than before.

Get a hold of yourself Charlotte!

You are a professional. An RN for crying out loud. You can produce a normal sentence.

"L-Lo-Lorenzo? Wh-what are you doing here?"

So much for being professional, and stuttering, Char? Really? That's what I got? Seriously, what else is he doing here? He's at the hospital for a reason! Well… I didn't really know why. I mean he was in the private wing of the hospital. I had only been working at this hospital a couple of months when I got assigned to this unit. They told me my ER skills were better served here with the gunshot wounds, knife stabs, broken ribs, and…

The wheels in my head started spinning.

Gunshot wounds…him and his cousin…homecoming.

Lorenzo stared at me while his breathing evened out. Okay, good sign. He just continued to stare at me like I was some kind of ghost while I tried to remember why I was sent into this room.

Then I saw the blood on his hands. Realized that was what stained his shirt.

Right, I was sent in here to clean a possible gunshot wound.

Wait, was Lorenzo shot?

Why?

How?

A flashback came to me from minutes earlier…a gurney rushing by with a patient bleeding out, and when I saw his face it had reminded me of Dante but I thought it was all in my head. Apparently it wasn't.

I wanted to ask what had happened, but I was here to do

my job and not ask questions beyond those of "How much pain are you in, and where were you hurt?"

"Lorenzo… I mean Mr. Rizzi, if you're starting to feel better I would like to examine your injuries. Please stand." I got to my feet, going to wash my hands and grab a pair of gloves.

He rose. "I already told Dr. Davis I'm fine; it was just a small bullet graze. I don't need your help so go help where help is wanted."

My eyes widened, and my jaw worked soundlessly as I tried to find words.

"Leave!" he barked and tried to move his shoulder but winced. He clearly was not okay. I tried to take a look, but he shoved away. "What I just say? Get away from me!"

What was his problem? The Lorenzo I knew had never been an asshole. Then again, I never really did know him.

Never got the chance.

Just before he side stepped me, I gripped his shoulder. "Look, small or not, I have a job to do. So, remove your shirt so I can disinfect your wound unless you want your arm to fall off."

He cursed when I gave his arm a squeeze.

"Don't worry, I'll give you some pain medication so you can endure the process." His eyes bore into mine, trying to intimate my steady gaze, but I lifted a brow showing him I was not kidding.

Even if shivers were running down my spine.

"I can handle it," he responded through clenched teeth.

"Then sit up on the table so we can get this over with!" My tone might have come out a bit harsh but I could care less at this point. I went into the cabinets grabbing what I needed and then turned my attention back to him almost tripping over my own two feet.

He sat there, shirtless. Abs that went down to a V-cut, and arms so muscular I might break my poor needle if I tried to inject him.

I wanted to run my hand along his abs to see if they were real or photoshopped. And not to mention the tattoos that seemed to cover him. His right arm was a complete sleeve, writing ran down his left side, his chest was covered in beautiful designs that intertwined with each other.

"Are you just going to stand there staring or are you going to do your 'job,' as you call it?" he snapped, turning his gaze away from me.

I bit my tongue instead of telling him off. God the man was gorgeous!

Asshole but beautiful.

Again, couldn't he have gotten fat?

Up close, I inspected the wound; it was a pretty big bullet graze that ran across his shoulder. And since he insisted on no pain medication I proceed with saline. Cleaning the wound and then moving on to the alcohol. Once the alcohol-soaked gauze touched his skin, he hissed fisting his hands.

Oh, let's have some fun big boy.

I grabbed another clean alcohol-soaked gauze, this time pressing a little harder down to wipe. I was preventing an infection not giving a facial, so what was a little pressure, right? He tensed but made no movement... mmmm maybe he *could* handle pain. I swiped a little to the left of the wound with more pressure and then back down.

"*Cazzo*! Fuck!" He drew back slightly. "Are you trying to rip my skin off?"

I held back my smile. "Oh, do you want that medication now?"

"I'm fine," he snarled. "But Jesus, do you treat all your patients like this? I feel sorry for them if you do."

Now that pissed me off.

Yes, I had been a little rough on him, but that was only because he was being a dick. And one thing I did know was that I was good at my job or else I wouldn't be here.

"Only to assholes like you!" I snapped, and as the words left my mouth I mentally slapped myself. It was unprofessional, but I was seriously getting annoyed.

He raised a brow.

Angry, I let out a breath. If I liked my job I had to tuck my tail between my legs and apologize. No matter how bitter it tasted coming out. "I'm...sorry, I didn't—"

"You did." He turned toward me, our faces inches apart.

Unable to mask my annoyance, I stared him down, waiting on his reaction.

But his expression remained impassive, giving no hint of what was running through his mind. Then, he added, "Don't ever apologize for speaking what's on your mind."

I could only stare, confused.

"How about a deal? You get me an update on Dante, don't rip off my skin and maybe...just maybe I'll play nice." He smirked and winked.

My knees almost gave out.

That smirk had gotten sexier; it could have a girl undressing in less than five seconds.

Dammit, body, don't betray me now.

I licked my suddenly dry lips. "Fine, but criticize my job again, and I will personally peel your skin off." I turned to grab some bandages to wrap his shoulder.

He chuckled but agreed and my knees?

Weak! Even the way he laughed was affecting me, and I had only been with him for fifteen minutes.

Wrapping his shoulder was harder than expected. With the burn of his eyes boring into me, along with my hands touching his body, keeping my focus on the task at hand was hard. I tried averting my eyes from his but it was nearly impossible not to look at him. Every time I glanced his way, his eyes were on mine, holding my gaze until one of us tore away.

Even with the gloves on, my hands burned every time I touched his skin;.

Clearing my throat, I removed my gloves as fast as I could. "Alright, we're all done here. You can wait in the waiting room; I'll come find you when I have news."

I walked out before he could say anything else and practically ran to the closest room I could find, which just so happened to be the supply closet.

I wasn't proud of what happened next, but I needed to relieve some stress the only way I could at work—by kicking some boxes. I might have cursed a couple times and probably the day he was born. I took a couple of deep breaths, touching my necklace. Oh, the girls would not believe this. I had imagined seeing him again before but in my mind it had gone a lot different. Never thought he would be such a dick!

"Ugh, the nerve on the asshole!" I kicked a box.

After a couple more kicks, maybe a few more curse words, I fixed my hair and walked out feeling much better. Well, at least until I ran straight into a rock-hard chest.

One with a delicious spicy scent I wanted to bathe in.

"You know I always thought of my birthday more of a blessing than a curse." Lorenzo peeled me off him and lifted a brow.

Son of a bitch!

"I... I... Well, you see...um, well..." My cheeks must be cherry red at this point. "It's been a long day, and if it makes you feel better it wasn't just about you."

Liar.

"Mmhmm...well I'm heading to the waiting room now."

"Okay." I was walking away when I heard him call out.

"Hey, Charlotte."

"Yeah?" I didn't even bother turning.

"Don't get lost in any more supply closets."

Yup...deserved that.

EIGHT

Charlotte

*H*ours later, I watched Lorenzo from afar. He sat in the back row of the waiting room in clean clothes, phone pressed against his ear. And by the way he ran his hand down his face I could tell it was a hell of a phone call. The stress was apparent even from fifteen feet away. I also noticed three guys in suits spread throughout the room.

The one by the door watched me as I neared and tapped the open door with the back of my hand.

Lorenzo stood at the sound, saying something into the phone before hanging up.

Up close, I could see the bags under his eyes, the tensing in his jaw, and his hair looked like he had run his hand through it more than a couple of times.

"Hey, so Dante is out of surgery," I said approaching. "Everything went well. The doctor will be out soon to talk to you about his recovery."

Lorenzo let out a breath, mumbling something I didn't catch. His face instantly appeared relieved, but the stress he carried was still evident.

I caught myself leaning forward, wanting to comfort him. It was an explainable pull I felt toward him. "I, um, have to go check on other patients."

"Yes, I understand."

I had already started for the door when his hand took hold of my wrist and slowly traveled down to my hand. When I turned back, he gave my hand a small squeeze. "Thanks, Charlotte."

Unable to respond verbally, I gave him a small smile.

The rest of the night I couldn't get those deep brown eyes out of my head, and those muscles haunted me while I charted on my patients. I bit down on my bottom lip every time I imagined running my hands down his muscular arms.

Ugh, I hated this. Only a few moments together, and I couldn't get him out of my head.

"Hey, Charlotte," Tani, one of my co-workers, called, snapping me out of my daydream. "You mind taking over room 1506? I really need a break."

"Sure, no problem." We constantly helped each other out when one of us needed a break so this was nothing new. Taking the tablet from her I headed toward the room and stopped dead in my tracks when I saw the name on the chart.

Ohhh no… Ah, hell! That was what I got for always being so helpful.

I knocked on the door before walking in.

Dante was lying in bed; all bandage up, with a big smile plastered on his face. Yeah, he was high on morphine and wow! The past eight years had been kind to him as well. Then again, what did I expect? We were only twenty-five. And Dante had muscles on him that looked like he could crush me in half, even with his wounds. Those muscles were covered in tattoos. On his chest, shoulders and his arms which trickled down to his fingers. Normally, I wasn't so much about the ink, but fuck those Rizzi men made them look good.

"Mr. Rizzi, how are you feeling?"

"Much better now that you're here." He wiggled his brows. "Hey *cugino*... Cousin! I thought you promised me two hot nurses." He smirked then squinted. Tilted his head, squinted again, eyes widening.

Three... two... one...

"Charlotte? Charlotte Frizzell?" He rubbed his eyes. "Enzo, are you seeing her too? Or am I seeing a ghost?" He kept rubbing eyes and opening them wide as though to make sure it was me. Then he proceeded to pinch himself. "Ouch!"

I couldn't hold back my laugh. "It's me alright. Glad someone wasn't rude after seeing me, unlike others." I shot Lorenzo a look.

All while Dante spoke a hundred miles an hour. "Ohmygod! Others? What others? Duuude don't be rude! Say hi! Charlotte, what are you doing here? Wait, are you my nurse or myyyyy nurse." And it was like his eyebrows had a mind of their own the way they flew up and down. "Waaiit..." He pointed between us. "You two already—"

"I ran into her earlier." Lorenzo stood, walking over to him. I busied myself taking Dante's vitals and checking the monitor and the IV lines.

"And you waited this long to tell me? You've been in here for..." He looked up at the clock and squinted. "Okay so I can't remember how long but helllllooo I think I should know when the girl you have—"

A thump sounded, and when I turned to see what it was, Lorenzo looked away while Dante rubbed the top of his head, cursing.

"Dante, are you feeling okay? Do you have any pain?"

"Well, I was going to say something before I was so rudely interrupted by this *stronzo*! Asshole." He pointed to Lorenzo, who gave him a murderous glare. "Soooooo… you're a nurse now. Are you a baaad nurse?" Clearly he was striving for a seductive voice.

Ha! It sounded anything but, more like he needed a nap.

"Only sometimes." I winked, and his mouth dropped open as I typed a few things into the tablet. Then a hand touched my elbow. Dante was grinning like he was a five-year-old entering a toy store after being told he could get anything he wanted.

"Yes?"

"Damn, Char, you got even more *beeeauutifuller* since high school."

I smiled and kept myself from laughing at his newly created word.

"Dante!" Lorenzo snapped as he eyed the hand that was still on me. "Get your hand off her," He added through gritted teeth.

Now, what was his problem?

"What, you jealous, Enzo?" Dante went on. "Come let me talk to this beautifuller girl here." He wiggled his brows again, but this time his eyes looked like they were closing.

"Okay, buddy, I think maybe some sleep will do some good. See you in a few hours."

"Ahh, come on, Char…" He yawned as I helped him lie down. "Enzo, ask the pretty girl out, it's the least you could do because if I'm right, which I know I am, you still think about her every night…"

I froze mid-pillow fluff and glanced up at Lorenzo at the same time he looked at me.

"I would know." Dante's voice was fading. "I dream about Isabella, God that woman curves haunt my dreams."

Wait. What?

"Isabella? My best friend Isabella?"

His eyes shot open. "Shiiiiit…" was all he got out before closing his eyes again.

NINE

Lorenzo

*N*ice fucken going, Dante!

Charlotte and I were left awkwardly staring at each other while his loud snores filled the room.

I opened my mouth, closed it, cleared my throat instead.

What the hell could I possibly say?

"Sooo um, he was a little high on the morphine. It's probably best we let him sleep it off." She bolted towards the door.

"Charlotte—"

"I'll check on him in a few hours." She opened the door so fast it almost smacked her across the face. Not that I blamed her.

Dammit, Dante!

If he hadn't gotten shot I would have shot him myself in that moment.

Fanculo!

I ran my hands through my hair, sat down only to get back up again and look out the window into the night sky. It had been a fuckin' long day. Between the meeting, the ambush, Dante getting shot, running into Charlotte, and now this, I needed a vacation. HA! Vacation wasn't a word in my dictionary.

I think the last time I went on "vacation" I had been sixteen. Dante and I traveled Italy thinking we were about to party it up for the summer; instead, our fathers had sent us for training with our uncles.

I looked over to Dante, who was snoring like a polar bear. I hated to admit it, but he was right—just like how Isabella haunts his dreams, Charlotte haunts mine.

When I say haunt what I really mean is calm them.

I thought it was just a high school crush, but I never got her out of my head. It was like an obsession.

One that probably would get me on a special segment of Dateline.

But we learned a long time ago that it's better for us to only see them in our dreams than to bring them in. Especially after that night.

After dropping off Charlotte at home I had gone home where Dante was waiting for me outside with a look that said nothing and everything at the same time. Together we walked into my dad's office, into the belly of the beast. And with one look from my dad, I knew I wasn't walking out of there same again.

The memory of it all was forever embedded in my mind, replaying it like it was just yesterday.

"What the fuck were you thinking, Enzo!" My dad yelled

at me while Dante and my uncle stood to the side. Our dads were spitting fire after hearing what happened. "You think you a boss now? Huh? Pulling a gun on school property, and in front of witnesses!"

"Papa, they were hurting her, and if I didn't step in they would have—"

"I don't give a rats ass what they were doing Lorenzo! You know we leave no loose ends! You're fucken lucky the boys that got away have family who frequent our clubs and have pending debt. They're being dealt with, but as for the girls—"

"NO! Don't you dare touch them!" It was the first time I yelled at my dad. I was in his face, challenging him.

My blood boiled at the thought of someone touching Charlotte. I didn't care if he was my father. I would rip his hand off if he thought he could lay a finger on her. I saved her and I'll be damned if I let anyone else hurt her.

His head snapped back—shock registering in his eyes. Even my uncle looked surprised. If I was being honest so was I.

I had never yelled at my father. Not only was he my father but he was my boss, the Boss of the Rizzi family.

Respect was always a given.

But in this moment I didn't give a flying fuck.

A look at my cousin let me know he thought the same and would go down fighting alongside me. He fisted his hands as he tried stepping forward but was held back by his dad.

"Hmmph, so it's like that, is it Enzo? Alright, well since you think you can handle yourself and believe those girls won't say anything…"

"THEY WON'T!" I roared. My hands balled into fists I was ready to use.

My father smirked and called Dante over, pushing him down

to his knees. My uncle stood in front of him drawing his gun. My cousin held his head high, ready for what was to come.

Bile rose in my throat. We were promised until high school graduation but we fucked up. No, scratch that. I would fucken do it again if it meant saving her.

Slowly I knelt on the dark hardwood floor beside Dante.

Head raised, eyes connecting with my father and fear out the window.

Imprinting this moment into my memory forever.

The moment I surrendered to the life I was born for.

The fires of hell rose, ready to take hold of my soul. Prepared to drag it to hell where it belonged. From this moment on, my life was no longer mine but belonged to the family.

And the king was about to crown his prince with a bloody crown.

With the cold rim of the gun pressed at my forehead my Dad said the word that would finally seal my fate to my family. "Choose. Death or Family?"

There was no choice to make. No questioning what my decision would be.

My choice was and would always be family.

Until the day I died.

That night, Dante and I walked out of that office forever changed. Three years after that night, on my twentieth birthday, we took over, and while blood was always spilled we changed the way our fathers ran things. In the last few years, we created more legit businesses to cover for our dealings. Business that brought in revenue and didn't look suspicious.

Of course, we still kept our construction company, underground fights, clubs, and we still loaned money, but we had a new system that didn't have us acting like the guys in movies, asking for payment with a bat. Even if I did carry a bat in my trunk.

You know, for emergencies…. like when I had to let one of the club managers it was wrong to steal our cases of liquor for his personal under the table sales.

I rubbed my face with my hands, thinking back to Charlotte. Years ago I had made a promise to myself to never look for her, and yet here she was again. Working in the hospital wing I had rebuilt. As if the universe had worked its forces and brought us back to each other.

With a quick text to Antonio, to a guard to Dante's room, I slipped out in hopes I would find her.

I was walking by the nurses' station when I spotted Charlotte looking at her phone then tapping her fingers rapidly across the screen. I wondered who she texted; did she have a boyfriend?

And just the thought of that possibility had me trigger happy.

I watched her from eight feet away, feeling a gravitational pull toward her. And maybe she felt it too because for a moment she froze, slowly glanced up and green eyes locked tight with mine.

I could stare into those glorious eyes forever, forgetting it all.

I took steps toward her and didn't miss the way she sucked in a breath.

Her throat cleared and the connection between us was broken. "Did you need something?" Her tone coming off with a sass.

"Just wondering if you're on break."

"Yeah, why?" She crossed her arms putting up an armor between us.

"Thought maybe we could go for coffee." I nearly laughed when her face went sour. I guess she was still upset about earlier.

"You want to go to coffee with me? After you were a dick to me?"

"A dick?" I lifted my brow. "Not so professional, is it now?"

She smirked. "You said don't ever apologize so…" She shrugged it off and I felt my lip twitch. I liked her sass.

"Touché." One step toward her, and her sweet scent invaded my senses. "Well how about a cup of coffee as my apology?" Lips pursed and eyes squinted, she seemed to think about it. To be honest it had never been this hard to get a girl to say yes to me. Hell, they threw themselves at me, but Charlotte no; she was a different breed. From the looks of it she didn't fall easily to anyone.

But I wasn't taking no for an answer. Not after all this time.

"Or do you hate coffee?"

"No not at all, but—"

"Oh, there is a but." Hands in my pocket, I stepped closer. "Come on, I'm pretty sure you were grabbing a coffee on your break."

"Actually…." She stepped back, looking away from my face. Her armor fell and was replaced with embarrassment. "I wasn't really heading to grab a coffee. It was more of a milkshake kind of break."

Why would she be embarrassed to say she wanted a milkshake? Jesus, most girls just wanted a black coffee with no sugar because they were afraid to eat. "Ahhh, well that does sound way better, but can we throw a burger in the mix?"

Charlotte smiled and I inwardly groaned, god that smile could start and end wars. "So that's a yes to my invitation?"

She rolled her shoulders back, standing up a little straighter. "Only if you promise not to be such a freakin' di—"

Dr. Davis passed by at that moment, and her face was coated bright shade of pink.

I couldn't hold back my smirk. "A dick?" I asked.

The doctor choked, and her face couldn't get any brighter. She waited, maybe to be reprimanded for using foul language toward a patient. But the moment I saw him open his mouth I gave him a look that said, *do it and I'll have* you *fired.*

Instead of delivering a reprimand, he cleared his throat and said, "On break, Nurse Char?"

She nodded.

"Well, have a nice break. Mr. Rizzi." He bowed his head and kept walking all while she stared at the walking figure confused.

She turned to me but before she could say anything I cut her off. "So the milkshake?"

"Oh, ah… yeah. I know a place around the corner, let me just grab my bag."

While Charlotte grabbed her bag, I texted Antonio, letting him know I would be gone for a while and told him to hold off the two men he wanted to send. I had my gun. I could protect her.

Wow, that brought back memories.

"Ready." Charlotte lips looked plumper and shinier than before.

Making me want to run my tongue over them. "Let's go."

TEN

Charlotte

The waitress's jaw nearly unhinged when she came by to take our order and laid eyes on Lorenzo.

Yeah, girl, you and me both.

But he seemed completely unbothered as she just stared at him while he ordered us our cheeseburgers, a chocolate milkshake for him then pointed at me. "Oh, um, a cookies and cream milkshake please, ah…" I checked her name tag, "Jordan."

She didn't even bother looking my way. It was like I was painted on the damn wall and it ticked me off that she was so interested in Lorenzo. It made me want to pull her jet-black curly hair.

What the hell was wrong with me?

Lorenzo was nothing of mine, so why should I care if Jordan the waitress stared at him like he was the juiciest piece of meat in the place.

"Still like Oreos, huh?" Lorenzo noted when she left.

I let out a small laugh. "Borderline obsessed is more like it."

He chuckled, and it rumbled through me like a wave. "So how long have you been working at the hospital?"

"A couple of months, not too long. I worked in the ER before getting transferred to the private wing. They said my trauma skills would be better used there."

"Trauma nursing, you enjoy it?"

"I do, keeps me busy and the cases I see are interesting. I guess all the stories my brother told me about the field got me interested in it."

"You have a brother? Is he a nurse as well?"

"Two brothers actually, and no he's in the army but he tells me stories about the nurses and doctors out there."

Our milkshakes arrived, and I was thankful it was a guy delivering them and not Jordan. Taking a sip of the creamy goodness. I eyed Lorenzo. So many questions about me, now it was my turn. "So, what have you been up these past eight years, aside from getting shot at?"

Mid-sip, Lorenzo choked.

Holy crap, it was a joke.

He pounded his chest a couple times before croaking out, "Well, I don't get shot at every day, just every other day."

Now I choked, eyes wide, and my mouth dropped open.

"I'm kidding," he said quickly. "And to answer your question, I run my family's construction company and my own clean energy company along with other small businesses."

"Wow, sounds like you've come a long way, Mr. Homecoming football champ," I said before I could stop myself.

I winced, certain he felt what I was feeling because we just looked at each other and I knew.

No words needed to be said.

I knew he was apologizing or wanting to explain.

But I didn't need it nor want it. It was a long time ago; I was over it.

Yes, it took time to get past what happened to me but slowly it became a thing of the past and in the end it only made me a stronger version of myself. I learned to defend myself so no man would ever treat me that way again.

He opened his mouth to say something but was interrupted when the waiter came by with our food. My heart pounded against my ribs as the noise from the plates hitting the table filled the silence between us and his eyes bore into me. He held it there even a few seconds after the waiter left. "Hey after that night—"

"You don't owe me an explanation, Lorenzo. It was a long time ago." I offered him a reassuring smile.

He nodded, making the air around us a little bit lighter.

"So I remember you having a group of friends. Katherine, Ava, and Isabella."

I let out a laugh. "Ah I see what you did there, trying to get the inside scope on Isabella for Dante?" I lifted my brow. "But if you must know, she's my roommate and works for a big tech company after she graduated from MIT."

"Wow, so she did good for herself."

"She did." Swirling my straw, I decided to ask the question I had been wondering about before I lost my nerve. "Soooo, about what Dante said when he was high on morphine. You really dream about me?"

I had to know if I was the only one dreaming. Or if…

possibly we dreamed about each other.

"Aren't you curious? And like you said, Dante was high so anything he said could be his wild imagination."

"Key words being 'could be.'" I bit off my fry and stared him down.

ELEVEN

Lorenzo

How the hell was I supposed to answer her question when she bit into the fry like that? I was officially jealous of that fry! It had touched her lips, something I had desperately wanted to do since I saw her come out of the lockers with that shiny lip gloss.

"Let's not focus on Dante's choice of words while he was high. Why don't we enjoy these burgers, and I'll tell you about some funny stories about Dante when we were younger."

She thought about it for a second. "Alright, but they better be funny." She picked up her burger and sank her perfect white teeth into it.

Cazzo! Fuck.

I couldn't even have a simple meal with her without wanting to pounce. Charlotte looked beautiful in her dark gray scrubs, long brown hair in a ponytail, very little makeup on, not that she even needed it.

While we ate, I told her stories about Dante, as promised. Both of us laughed so much to the point of crying. She told me about her brothers; Colton was in the army and currently on deployment, Julian was a detective for the Boston Police Department alongside her friend Katherine, who was dating Colton.

Her brother and best friend both detectives?

Fan-freaking-tastic.

She told me about the twins, Ava was at a marketing firm and would always get them into the hottest parties in the city, and when she got back to Isabella she laughed again. Dante was going to shoot himself after I told him what he'd said. Especially about Charlotte.

Thank God I got her to drop the subject.

Once we finished eating and the check was brought, Charlotte tried to reach for it but I snatched it and lifted a brow. "I thought we agreed it was my treat."

"Fine…and it looks like you made an impression." She pointed to the back of the receipt and giggled.

I turned the check over and what do you know, it read. "Hey handsome, call me some time, we could have some real fun —Jordan." Along with a phone number.

"Well, she is going to be waiting for the call a long time because the only girl I'm interested in, is sitting right in front of me."

The giggling stopped abruptly. Charlotte was about to say something when her phone dinged. Pulling it out she looked down at it. "Sorry, I have to get back."

"Yeah no problem, we can pay this up at the front." We slid out of the booth and made our way to the front cash register.

Oh look, little miss Jordan came over to charge us, fuckin' great.

I reached in my back pocket for my wallet, and pulled out my black Amex card.

She took the card, sending me a secretive smile as her fingertips brushed mine. Then looked down at the card. "Lorenzo Rizzi." Her eyes literally twinkled. Exactly how every girl did when they saw my last name. "Would that be all or did you need *anything* else?"

Seriously! I side-glanced Charlotte, who was standing right next to me looking down at her feet, her demeanor seeming intimated.

Ohh, there was no comparison at all!

"Actually, there is." I wrapped my arm around Charlotte's waist, pulling her closer. "I think you owe my girlfriend an apology. That note was not meant for me, was it?"

Jordan's mouth dropped open. "Oh noo… I…um… So sorry, yes that was not meant for you." She quickly swiped my card and handed it back with my receipt, and then ran away.

Once outside Charlotte spoke up. "Lorenzo, why did you just—"

"She was rude, and I wasn't about to let her disrespect you like that." My hand was still on the small of her back feeling the electricity course through my palm. "Besides, I probably stopped her from doing that ever again."

"But I'm not your girlfriend, you could have easily asked her out. You have to admit she was pretty."

"Really? I didn't notice." Green eyes and pouty lips are the only thing I'd seen. We continued walking back toward the hospital with my hand still on her back. Both of us completely silent.

I could feel her eyes looking over at me every few seconds while we waited for the elevator to arrive.

Once inside she turned to me. "Thank you for dinner, Lorenzo, I really needed that milk shake if I want to make it to the end of my shift."

"You're welcome. What time are you off today?"

"In about two hours but I put in extra hours so I have another four to go. So, I'm off at midnight."

"You always work nights?"

"No, I'm on the day shift, but a coworker couldn't make her shift and I was called in."

The elevator doors opened just as I said, "Well lucky for us they did."

She gave me a small smile before we got off, and I walked her over to her lockers.

"I'll see you later when you come in to check on Dante?" I asked.

"Actually, Tina is his nurse. I have to attend to my other patient but I'll be in tomorrow morning so I'll check in on him then. I have questions." She laughed.

I laughed along even if on the inside I all I wanted to do was to shoot my cousin. "That'll go over well. Wait, you worked all night tonight, and you still come in tomorrow? Don't you sleep?"

"Well tomorrow is my regular shift, but I won't come in until ten a.m. since I stayed late today. So, I'll see you tomorrow… I mean if you're still here."

"I'll be here." I leaned down, catching her sweet coconut scent again and placed a kiss on her smooth cheek. "Goodbye, Charlotte."

TWELVE

Charlotte

*D*umbstruck!
My entire drive home all I could do was think about dinner, the small kiss, and how his hand felt on me.

The rest of the night I avoided the hallway that led to Dante's room because I didn't want him seeing the plastered smile I had on my face. Although Tina noticed, even made a certain comment that made me turn cherry red.

Dinner had been good, really good, actually. Wait till the girls hear about this, well Isabella first. We were roommates and I hoped she was still up, which she usually was. Always up late working but I enjoyed coming home and sharing our day together, uh expect when her boyfriend Levi was there. Now that man was an asshole times ten!

Our apartment was only fifteen minutes from the hospital

and it was nice. I only lived here because Isabella already had the place and let me live here for cheap when I was in my last year of nursing school. The girl made crazy money and could afford a luxury apartment.

It was a two-bedroom apartment with large windows in the living room that overlooked the city, walnut wood floors throughout the apartment, a kitchen with a chef's stove. But the best part: we each had a walk-in closet.

I hung my jacket on the coat hanger, took off my Adidas and walked down the small hallway into the living room where Isabella sat on the couch with a big bowl of popcorn and wine. Her go to snack when she would fight with Levi. "Hey Bella, what are you doing up?"

"Hey, I just finished up some work. Want some wine?" She was already pouring a glass.

I grabbed the glass as I sat down then took a big gulp tugging my feet under me.

"Ohhh, I thought I had a long day." She eyed me. "Should I grab another bottle?"

"I think we're good, but you might want to take a sip of your wine before—"

She chugged before I finished. "Okay, I'm ready!" she said while refilling her glass.

I threw my head back, laughing; we couldn't be truer friends if we tried. I took another gulp of wine before I told her about Lorenzo, without telling her what happened to him or Dante because well HIPAA and I liked my job. Also left out the whole she haunts Dante's dream part but I told her about dinner and the kiss on the cheek. Her eyes nearly popped out after every detail.

"What?!" she exclaimed around a mouth full of popcorn.

She swallowed so quickly I worried she'd choke. Then, "I'm shook! Like what are the odds he would come in tonight, especially after all this time? Did you ask him why he didn't come back to school?"

I shook my head. "I didn't want to pry." I didn't tell her of the pain I saw in his eyes when I'd made my comment. Changing the conversation, I asked, "So, are you going to tell me the real reason you're still up with popcorn and wine?"

She shook her head, and I made a don't you dare lie to me face.

"We had another fight." She sighed. "But it's nothing. I'll be okay."

I could tell she was lying.

This had been a constant thing between her and Levi. Always arguing for no good reason, just because he was a real dick. If he had a bad day, he usually took it out on her.

"Hey, you know I'm here when you're ready to talk about it, right?"

She nodded, staring down at her phone, probably a message from Levi because her face went sour.

"Hey, I have an idea, why don't we have Katy and Ava over Saturday night? We can have a movie night with tons of wine."

She cheered up instantly. "YES! You also need to tell them about Lorenzo! They are going to flip! Are you seeing him tomorrow at the hospital?"

"I don't know yet." I hoped I did.

We stayed up a few more minutes before each heading to bed. I rushed through my nighttime routine and went into my closet pulling out a box from underneath my coats. Smiling when I saw the gray sweater with our high school logo on it. The very same one he gave me after that horrible night. It had been a while since I had seen it, but after tonight it only seemed fitting to pull it out. Pulling it over my head I got into my warm bed.

I was exhausted.

But chocolate brown eyes and tattooed muscles invaded my dreams.

I felt like my head had barely touched the pillow when the piercing sound of my alarm was soon invading my ears; the alarm clock I had set for eight a.m. I had about two hours before work… I thought about sleeping in, but then I would be running around like a maniac getting ready for work. Instead, I got up, brushed my teeth and headed toward the kitchen to grab some desperately needed coffee.

But I was still half asleep because I stubbed my pinky toe on the edge of the door frame.

Way to start my morning.

"Fuuuuuccckk!" I jumped around, acting like it would ease the pain. It was one of those pains you feel on every nerve, every hair, and makes your eyes water.

God, I hope Isabella left the coffee pot on, because there is no way I'm making it through today without a cup or two.

"Morning, sunshine! Loving your word of the day." Bella said from the kitchen with a box of donuts. Wine last night and donuts today…something was wrong. "Donut for your pain."

"Glazed?" I eyed the box.

"Got you two."

I grabbed my coffee and sat next to her at the kitchen table. "Soooo, any dream about sexy v-cuts last night?" She bit into her donut and wiggled her eyebrows.

I giggled. "You're horrible."

She laughed, reaching for another donut.

I slipped my coffee watching her. "Hey, you okay?"

She just nodded.

"Promise you'll tell me when you're ready?"

"Promise. I have to go get ready for work. Big presentation coming up and it's killing me! Hey, we are still on for Saturday, right?"

"You'll do great and yeah I'll text the girls today and pass for the wine after work."

"Great!" She went into her room and called out. "Bring tequila."

"Okay, wait, what? I thought we quit tequila!"

Lorenzo

After spending the rest of the night with Dante at the hospital I went home to shower and grab him a few things.

I couldn't stop thinking about her. Those green eyes and plump lips. I wanted to taste and claim them, until she was begging me for more.

It was wrong.

She couldn't ever be part of my world.

It was too dangerous.

But dammit if I wanted to be a fuckin' selfish bastard for once in my life.

The family had always come first since I was seventeen,

even younger. For once I wanted something for me because I wanted it not because it benefited the family.

Reaching for the long-sleeved shirt in my closet I glanced down at my forearm, "*la famiglia e' tutto,*" —family is everything—was written in cursive. In the mirror my family crest on my chest stared back at me.

Reminders of the life I was bound to.

I finished getting dressed, grabbed Dante's stuff, and headed downstairs to my office. I had gotten some work done when I got home. Aside from our family dealings we still had many legit businesses that needed my attention, and numbers for our energy company weren't adding up. "Antonio!"

"Yes, Boss?" he asked, walking into my office.

"What the fuck is this? Figure this shit out and don't tell me it's what I think it is."

Antonio stared down at the files, just as confused. "I'll let you know what I find. Oh, Dante woke up and is asking for coffee." He chuckled. "Asked for the usual."

"Of course, he did." Dante's coffee usually came with the number of the cute barista he would take home later that day. "You would think getting shot at would give him a new perspective on life." I grabbed my car keys.

"Knowing him he is going to take it as a sign to drink more coffee." He laughed. Antonio was not only my bodyguard but a good friend. He had been with us for years, and became part of the family, one of us. Even has our family crest on his forearm.

"Fuckin' Dante. One of these days it's going to bite him in the ass."

"I think he likes that shit." We laughed before going back to business. "So, we have a lead for yesterday's events. Someone was feeding them inside info."

"No fuckin' shit! Get me names." My jaw tensed. "I'm going to be at the hospital most of the day. I'm taking my laptop so call me if anything happens." I left Antonio to work only stopping for Dante's usual on the way.

Minus the phone number.

I pulled up to our entrance at the hospital thirty minutes later, grabbed my gun from the glove compartment and tucked it in behind my jeans. Throwing the keys of my G-wagon to one of our guys as I headed to Dante's room.

"You got my usual?" He nodded to the cup holder holding three coffees.

"What kind of cousin would I be if I didn't? Hell, I even got you two," I handed him one but pulled it back before he grabbed it. "You know what? On second thought, I don't think you can have coffee."

"Like hell I can't! I need that shit, I couldn't sleep after the morphine wore off."

I smirked. "Realllly, Isabella haunting your dreams again?"

He froze and I was loving it; payback's a bitch, *stronzo.* Asshole.

I snapped my fingers as if I had just remembered something. "Oh, that's right you know I forgot to tell you, yesterday when you were high in morphine you were very…" I waved my hand in the air. "keen on sharing… and you might've confessed to Charlotte you dream about her best friend."

"FUCK ME!" He ran his hand over his face then turned towards me. "So, I didn't dream of Charlotte working here? Wait, from my dreams she is hot and—"

"Watch it!" I growled.

"Oh shit! You still hold a flame for her?" He laughed but ended up coughing from the pain. Giving him the finger, I handed the coffee. "Who's the extra coffee for?"

Ignoring him, I walked out, and right as I turned the corner, I spotted Charlotte standing behind a computer with her brown hair in a bun with a braid on one side. She wore black scrubs, and from my angle... they hugged her ass just right. Walking over I set the coffee in front of her. She looked up and smiled.

God, that smile.

"Hi. Thank you, you really shouldn't have... you bought dinner yesterday."

I shrugged. "I thought nurses loved coffee. You know, the whole twelve hours and everything." I sipped my own. "So what time are you off today?"

"We do." She smelled the coffee, as if just smelling it would give her energy. "And I'm off at eight today since I pulled so many hours yesterday."

"Good, you need rest. So, are you going home after?"

Would it be too forward to ask her out to dinner again? Looking at her standing there in those tight black scrubs had my mind working overtime.

All the things I could do to her.

Until she was screaming my name and begging me for more, but I knew Charlotte was more than just a girl for sex.

She was meant to be worshipped.

For hours.

How could you want someone so badly that you wanted to risk everything just for one moment because a lifetime wouldn't be possible?

One moment that you would save forever and look back on its years from now and know it was worth it.

Just one moment.

THIRTEEN

Charlotte

"Well, aren't you a curious cat today? And if you must know, I am not. I have to stop at the store to grab some wine for girl's night Saturday."

God I sounded sixteen telling him about girls' night. At least now we were twenty-five and could drink.

"Nice. Celebrating anything special?"

"No, just wanting to hang out together." Damn, staring at him was not hard at all; looking away was the problem. He wore tight black jeans, a grayish brown long-sleeved Henley pushed up at the arms letting the tattoos show. Before I started drooling and imagining very vivid scenes of him… "Hey, I was just about to go check on Dante."

"Well, he's up if you want to go right now."

Walking over to Dante's room was complete torture, the spicy masculine aroma that radiated off him smelled so damn good, I wanted to spray it all over my bed. When we got to the door, he placed his hand on my back and opened the door leading me in. That one small move sent goosebumps all over my skin. I shivered and then felt the loss of his touch when he removed it.

"Hey, Dante, anymore morphine?" His face was a look of pure panic. and I had to bite my cheek to keep from howling like a hyena.

"No, I think we're good." Cough.

Oh, not so fast, I want details.

"So, I'm going to check your wounds and see how they are healing. Sit up for me please." He sat up as I grabbed my gloves. Checking him I asked, "So how did you sleep last night? Any pain?"

"Morphine wore off but nothing too bad that I couldn't handle...I have my ways to control pain." He winked.

Mmm... I knew what his methods were. I looked over at Lorenzo who must've read my mind because he wore that sexy smirk of his.

"Really?" I set his bandage back and pulled up his hospital gown. "Is it all those dreams about Isabella?" He froze, closing his eyes, and cursed. I tried holding my laugh but failed miserably, practically choking. Dante was red with embarrassment and Lorenzo padded his shoulder. Dante gave him the finger cursing him to hell.

"Um I... Char, see you... I didn't mean... ugh. Oh for fucks sake, why did I ask the doctor for extra morphine?" He released a string of curses in what I could only assume was Italian; I knew that much about them.

"So, it is true?" I lifted one eyebrow.

"NO! I mean... FUCK! I mean, have you seen her?! *Bellissima!*"

Beautiful, that word I also knew.

"I haven't seen her since high school but…" He looked heavenward. "She was fuckin' perfect. I can only imagine what she… damn… I need to shut the fuck up."

Okay now that was sweet, and I had to give it to him. Isabella was a fuckin' knockout! She had the beauty and brains…what more could you want! "Yes I see her every day and she is pretty perfect." I took off my gloves and grabbed my tablet and typed in a few things. "Especially when she is in her silk shorts." I looked up through my lashes.

"S-silk sh-shorts?" He tugged on the neck of his hospital gown. "Is the air o-on? Fuck… kill me now." He groaned and closed his eyes, still looking heavenward mumbling a prayer. I looked over at the monitor and his heart rate had gone up. I bit my lip to keep me from laughing but I couldn't help it.

"She also has a matching cropped tank top."

He groaned. I was going to end up giving him a heart attack.

"Fuck it! Get me the damn morphine!" He made the cross motion over his chest.

And me? I was close to crying from laughter.

Then I made the error of looking at Lorenzo. My knees knocked together, and I choked on my laugh.

Forget Dante getting a heart attack—I was ten seconds away from passing out of lust!

His eyes had gone darker and his side smile had me pressing my legs together.

DAMMIT!

Now Dante was chuckling all while doing the air cross motion my way.

"Okay so I…" I cleared my throat. "I'm going to get going,

I'll be back in here a few times to check on you." Damn, it was hot in here. Was I sweating?

"Thanks, Charlotte." Lorenzo's voice sent shivers down my spine.

"Mmmhmm… P-push the button if you need me." I walked toward the door talking over my shoulder. "And Dante…your secret's safe with me."

"I owe you one, Char!"

When I got to my workstation, I almost downed my coffee in one sip. It was cold compared to the heat running in my body right now. Was I imagining things, or was Lorenzo was looking at me like a lion looks at an antelope?

I messed with Dante about Bella, but I felt the same way. For a long time, Lorenzo had been part of my dreams, he was always the one who came to my rescue when the nightmares came and I woke up in a panic.

Since that night I had developed panic attacks, they didn't happen often, but when they came on I just remembered how I felt next to Lorenzo, safe. Something that he said I would never be with him. But he was wrong, because in his arms that night I'd felt invinsable. Nobody I dated ever came close to giving me what he had. What was it about him?

I need a drink or two—maybe a whole bottle of wine.

Thank God for Saturday. I pulled out my phone and looked for our group chat *Ride or Die Tribe*; yeah, it was weird but ehh! Who cares?

> Me: Girls night Saturday Night our place. I'm buying the wine.
>
> Bella: Don't forget the tequila!
>
> Ava: I'm there, I need some girl time. Wait tequila? You okay twinsy?

Katy: Whoa tequila! Remember what happened last time? I am so there, though!

Katy sent a GIF of a girl taking a row of tequila shots. No wonder her and Charlotte's brother Colton dated, they were made for each other. He was on deployment; she was stressed but thankfully she had my other brother Julian keeping her distracted with work.

Katy: I haven't received a call from Colton this week so I need it.

Bella: Will tell on Saturday. DON'T FORGET THE TEQUILA! Katy, I'll drink with you, and he will call soon. Oh, and Char has some juicy gossip.

She followed it with a frog, a tea cup and fire emojis. Freakin' Isabella.

Me: BELLA!

Me: Katy he will call soon, you know how it is.

Ava: Aww doll, he will call soon. Okay, since you guys are getting the drinks I got the snacks! Spill the tea Char... Or tequila. I am ready to hear this!

Katy: Thanks guys. WHAT!! Char spill now! Hey Julian is jealous, asked if he could come to get out of his blind date.

Me: You will have to wait! Damn what number is that now? Sixth blind date in three weeks. Laughing emojis and no he cannot!

Bella: Damn Julian! Okay guys I need to get back to work...see you Saturday.

Ava: Suck it up Julian. See you guys soon.

Katy: Bye got to get back on this homicide case, wish me luck.

Me: Good luck, see all of you Saturday.

Setting my phone down, I stood and went to check on a

couple patients, even took a trip to the ER to help out a bit. By the time my break rolled around I just sat in the nurse's lounge and ate some fruit I had brought in. I just checked in on Dante really quick before I was back to the ER.

Lorenzo was on a call outside so I hadn't seen him, which I was grateful for because who could concentrate with a beautiful face like that.

The rest of the day went by pretty much the same; I checked on my patients and Dante. Well, I tried because I felt Lorenzo's eyes on me, sending shivers down my spine. And when I got off work he walked me to my car, opened my door and gave me a kiss on the cheek, closer to my lips than before.

Leaving me in a daze.

Making me forget what I was going to buy at the store and ending up with just tequila, which I didn't happen to notice until I was already home.

God, he was making me crazy!

I hadn't seen him for two days.

Two days and I couldn't get him out of my head—not that I ever had.

But at least then I didn't walk around like a complete idiot sporting a smile, creeping people out.

He was slowly tiptoeing his way into my head, consuming my thoughts, imprinting himself in me until I only ever thought about him.

It was scary.

I thought talking to Bella would help but she wasn't home by the time I went to bed and she was gone the next morning when I woke up. When I texted her asking if everything was all right, she just responded, "Fine, I have lots of work." Whatever was bothering her would soon be known.

At work I sat at my station finishing up some charts and decided to go check in on Dante, hoping to run into Lorenzo and all his sexiness.

"Hey Char, are you heading into Mr. Rizzi's room?" Dr. Davis fell into step with me. I still felt embarrassed from the other day, but he had been acting normal around me, I would even say nicer.

"Hey. Yes I am. Did you want me to change anything in his treatment?"

"No, he's fine. Actually, I need you to set up his discharge papers for tonight." He gave me his orders and left while I stood there, overwhelmed by disappointment. It was great Dante was feeling better, but my mind went to Lorenzo.

It felt like homecoming all over again.

Was it wrong of me to wish that Dante was in the hospital for longer just so I would see Lorenzo?

Would this be the last time I saw him?

Would he leave again with nothing but a simple goodbye?

So many questions I wanted answers to.

And why did I care so much? I needed to stop acting like a teenager who got all giddy about seeing her crush.

It had been years and I was sure he had a life to get back to.

FOURTEEN

Lorenzo

I wanted to walk over to her and slam her against the wall ever since that day.

A woman who could mess up Dante, a ruthless killer, and have him stuttering in less than two minutes.

My kind of woman.

When I walked her to her car that night, I was close to slamming her up against it. Every time she smiled, my hand twitched to run my thumb over her bottom lip. When she walked by I admired the way her scrubs molded to her perfect figure.

She was a fuckin' goddess.

I couldn't even hold back my desire every time she walked into the room.

Like right now.

"Hey Char! How's it going?" Dante asked as she walked in, wearing black jogger scrubs.

I watched.

Admiring her like I had been since yesterday, even when she thought I wasn't looking. Lurking in the shadows—like a total creep!

Dammit!

"Busy. So, I heard Dr. Davis saw you earlier."

"Yeah, he was in here not too long ago."

Her face shuttered, expression grew guarded. Something seemed off by the way she took in his response.

"Is everything alright?" I asked, approaching them.

"Yeah, it's more than fine actually. I just got the green light to get started on your discharge papers. You can be out of here tonight. Dr. Davis thinks it's better for you to rest at home." Her smile couldn't be more forced.

I knew it was safer at home for Dante but I would be lying if I said I wasn't disappointed. I was already thinking about stabbing my cousin just to stay another day.

"Thank fuckin' God!" Dante expressed happily but I guess he saw my face. "Hey Char, do you make house calls?" I smacked his shoulder. "Ouch! You know I got shot, right?" He rolled his eyes. "I meant if I need help or have… uh, questions." He smiled at her. "Can I call you?"

"Oh, um… yes, of course. I'll give you my number but if you're in extreme pain come in." She pulled out her notepad and wrote her number. "Here call me if you have any questions. I'll get started on the paperwork and be back when everything is ready."

"Thanks, Charlotte." I looked at her for a few seconds before she left. I hadn't noticed I was still looking at the door until Dante cleared his throat.

"Soooo here you go!" He handed me the slip of paper. "A

thank you would be nice. I knew you were too pussy to ask for it so you're welcome."

He wasn't wrong.

Not that he needed me to say it out loud.

An hour later she was pushing Dante in a wheelchair to my waiting G-Wagon, with our men guarding the perimeter.

"Wow I didn't know CEO's had a bodyguard let alone ten." She took in the scene and helped Dante stand.

I was loading up Dante's bag. "Ha yeah well…" What could I say, someone tried to kill us soooo…

At least she hadn't seen the gun tucked in my jeans.

Then again she'd already seen me point a gun at seventeen.

"Hey, thank you! Take no offense when I say I'm glad to be going home. It was nice seeing you again," Dante said leaning in for a hug.

He touched her, and my hand twitched. I almost reached for my gun and shot him again.

Aw hell, I sound like a maniac.

I would for sure end up on a dateline where the family members said things like *"…and he was so protective of her I had no idea he killed for a living."*

"Never." She smiled. "No more getting shot at, okay"" Looking over at me…her smile slowly faded.

With one look, Dante was in the car, leaving us alone.

I made my way over to her, a little too close because her head tilted up. Her big eyes were full of questions.

Reminding me of that night.

Merda! Shit.

"Thank you for everything and sorry again for being an asshole when we first saw each other."

Nodding, she pulled a strand of hair out of her face,

looking down. Leaning back on her heels, her voice was low as she said, "No problem, it was my job to help."

Her job? I knew she felt something just as I did. So that was a lie. With my index finger I lifted her chin. "I hope to see you soon." I kissed her cheek, right on the edge of her outer lip.

Her breath hitched, and she pulled away. "Don't make promises you can't keep." She turned, grabbed the wheelchair and walked away.

I guess I deserved that, but she didn't know the reasoning behind the last time.

Pulling out of the hospital I turned to Dante. "Hey can you—"

"Already made the call. Antonio is on it." He smirked. *Stronzo.* Asshole.

He knew what I wanted even before I did, even though I was well aware that he wasn't just asking Antonio to investigate Charlotte but Isabella as well. I didn't bother telling him I knew.

We drove the rest of the way home in silence with music filling the space. I stared out at our city as we passed at least two new construction sites that Rizzi Construction was heading.

"Is this one of the ones we got approved?" Dante carried that evil smirk he was known for.

Yeah, the only reason we got it approved was because he threatened the politician who was holding it back from us. The asshole was planning on using it for his own personal gain instead of for the people. And sure while we profited off it, we brought wealth and benefit for the young. One thing I promised when I became boss was to make my city better for future generations. Because where politicians made promises after promises to help and didn't do shit I actually did something. I might be a villain, but I'd rather be that than a lying scumbag who only used people for their benefit.

What is the saying, a wolf in sheep's clothing? That was a politician to me.

"I think after that possible leak about his secret family, Lopez won't be stopping any of our contracts," I responded. Which only made my cousin chuckle and turn up the volume on *Bitch Don't Kill My Vibe* by Kendrick Lamar. Enjoying the ride through the city my family built.

And then a call appeared on my console, releasing a string of curses from my cousin. The number that appeared was only used for family business. I answered in my business voice. "What?"

"Boss, we got material coming in, needs your attention." Which was code for they had found the motherfuckers.

"I'll be right over." I hung up and looked over at Dante. I didn't need to ask him twice if he was coming; he had that fire in his eyes.

The same one I was sure mine carried.

Nobody messes with family, especially when we are trying to make things better for everyone. It pissed me off. Making them richer and they still dare challenge us.

We pulled up to one of our warehouses. Ours but under a different name because it was where Rizzi Family business was handled. "Dante, let me handle this. You—"

"Hell no! I'm going whether you like it or not... *Insieme per sempre.*" Together Forever. He barely winced as he adjusted his injured shoulder.

Sighing, I handed him the extra gun. "Just don't shoot them as soon as I open the door. We need answers."

"Okay, that was once and I was hungry." He hopped out of his seat, adding, "Plus they had it coming."

How he didn't look like he was shot two days ago was beyond me.

Then again, it wasn't the first time he had taken a bullet, or even the second. Growing up we had to learn to endure pain, learn to thrive on it, "mind over matter" my father would say.

There was no room for being weak.

Walking in, we saw two guys tied up to metal chairs, and by the looks of it one of them had put up a fight because his left eye was swollen shut.

Antonio shrugged. "Eh, what could I do?"

Dante walked over to Bryson, aka Mr. Swollen Eye, the leader of the crew we had met up with at the empty warehouse a couple days ago. One look and he spit over Dante's white Nike's. Yeah, he was definitely dead. "I thought I fuckin' killed you."

My cousin leaned in and laughed. "Well, I guess your aim is shit! Care for a lesson?" He waved his gun in the air.

"You couldn't even shoot me that day. My guess is you're a cheap shot," the guy challenged.

Big mistake. Dante smiled, aimed and... BANG! Shot him in the foot. BANG! One in the arm. "And that's for ruining my shoes, bitch."

And as he screamed in pain, Dante shoved the gun in his mouth.

The guy next to him, Vise, his second, yelled out a string of curses, annoying me. I shot his kneecap. "You either shut the fuck up or I'll show you how good of a shot Dante can be. Unlike me, he will draw out your death slow and painfully. You'll beg for it, so start talking."

Dante took a few steps back and laughed. Sometimes it scared me how much he enjoyed this. *Cagna,* bitch, was laughing like the fuckin' joker.

But I knew. Just like me, every life we took was like a piece of our soul darkened. A candle that was slowly dying out. Through the years we learned to mask it and made it seem like killing was our favorite pastime.

"Now... who sent you?" I looked down at him like the worthless piece of shit he was.

"Wouldn't you like to know?" Swollen Eye said.

Dante, not liking the response, released the power of his fist. Showing him that even though he was shot, weakness did not touch him.

Vise laughed. "You're so busy trying to go straight that you don't even see what's going on!" Dante stopped punching as I walked over and got eye level with him.

"Who the fuck told you I'm trying to go straight?" Now I was laughing like the joker. Where were these idiots getting their information? The guy gave me a look of pure panic. "My family built this city. What makes you think I would ever give it up? What you think you and your little crew can run this city?"

"Better than you can, bitch!" Bryson yelled.

"Idiota." With a laugh, my cousin's fist flew.

I pulled my switchblade from my pocket and stuck it in Vise's thigh. He screamed when I moved it around, pretty sure I was touching bone. I gave no fucks. "Who is feeding you lies?!"

"Fu... AHHHH... FUCK YOU!" He barely got it out.

"We'll never talk! You hear me?" Bryson yelled over Vise's groans. "Fuck you and your family!"

I pulled back the blade from Vise and impaled it in Bryson's arm, leg, rib, and finally left it in his thigh.

"Fine, don't tell me but answer me this. You think you were smart to double cross me? I am the fuckin' boss to the strongest Family in Boston *Cagna*!" Bitch. "I run this city, and you think a little nobody like you is going to overthrow me and take over?" I laughed in his face, making him furious. "You are a worthless piece of shit who got greedy and tried to steal from the hand that feeds you—" I released a low laugh. "How"d that work out for you?"

He paled.

"Pray to whatever god you pray to because you're about to meet your maker." I stood with Dante beside to me. "Meet your judge, jury, and executioner." We turned, walking five steps forward before turning.

"Go to hell, Rizzis," one of them yelled.

Guns raised, I smiled. "Already there."

BANG! BANG! BANG!

Clean shots to the head, with an extra.

"Get a little excited there?"

"Dude got on my nerves." Dante shrugged walking out.

"Antonio, call cleanup, and meet us back at the house," I said as we walked out.

"Got it, boss."

In the car, Dante was the first to break the silence. "You need to make the call."

"I know." I hit the steering wheel pressing down on the gas, twenty over the limit. "*CAZZO!*"

I was livid! My body felt like it was on fire. My mind raced a million miles an hour, adding another name to my list of kills.

We killed because it was necessary, not because we were bored. And this time it wasn't just for anyone; they had messed with my cousin, my blood.

I would gladly do it a hundred more times, letting my demons drag the remainder of my soul to depths of hell. I was already there anyway.

My mind flew to Charlotte.

This was why I had to stay away and keep her safe. If my enemies found out about her they would use her against me.

But how could I stay away from the one person who brought me back from hell, even when she wasn't there?

Her face alone in my head brought the wave of calm.

Long ago she'd believed I was her savior; little did she know she has been mine for a long time.

She was my light.

Reaching over to the console I hit call log, never thinking I would have to make this call.

Dante blew out some air into the tense air.

It rang once.

"*Figlio.*" Son. "This better be important. I'm in the middle of something."

"Hello to you too, Dad."

FIFTEEN

Katherine

"Are you sure this is the right address?" I asked Julian looking at the empty warehouse. Not one car in sight.

"This is the address they gave." He turned off the car and we got out.

The station had received a tip early this morning that a murder had been committed here, and we were assigned to it. I had moved up to detective last year. Was it a little weird working with someone who was my boyfriend's younger brother and best friend's older brother? Maybe, but he was a good friend, and Colton didn't mind him looking out for me. Plus he was like a brother to me.

"Alright, well let's check it out."

Before going in we pulled our guns and flashlights. Holding my gun in one hand and my flashlight under the gun with the other, waiting for Julian's signal to go in. "Boston PD!" Julian called out once inside.

"Clear! Clear!" we both said after we saw nothing. With practiced movements, we tucked our guns back in our holsters, keeping our flashlights out.

"Looks like whatever happened here is long over by now," Julian said.

I pointed my flashlight to the floor and saw some blood. "Mmm, not really. Take a look at this."

"Well, whoever it was is long gone by now."

"I'll look into who owns the building and see if anyone has filed a missing person report," I said

After flashing our lights around the space, we headed out once we found nothing I called in forensics to come in and take a look.

"So, girls night." Julian put on his aviators once we were outside. He was handsome, with short, dark brown hair, hazel eyes, and cut muscles. Nothing like Colton of course. But he was easy on the eyes. I don't know why he wanted to get out of his blind date.

"Oh, come on, why do you agree to these dates if you want to get out of them every time?" I laughed, getting in the car.

"Some of these women are crazy okay? Not my fault."

"Then tell me again why you agree to these things."

"It's Saturday night, and a man gets lonely."

I burst out laughing. He was far from lonely.

"So, you think my baby sister will mind if I crash girls' night?"

"She'll have your balls."

Charlotte

Damn Lorenzo.

"I hope to see you soon." I heard his words in the shower. Had he really meant it?

Also, what was up with all the guys in suits standing guard. It was like the president came to town. I thought about why they had been there—gunshot wounds.

They also had a private entrance to a wing they funded.

It was there, in plain sight. I just chose to ignore it and push it as far back in my mind as I could.

Why?

Because it's easier than to face the reality of things.

I don't know how long I had been in the shower before I finally got out, dried my hair and put on a bit of makeup. I was putting on my blue jeans when I heard the doorbell ring.

"I'll get it!" Bella yelled. Must be one of her amazon packages. "Um…Char. You might want to come out here!"

"Be right there!" I walked out of my room "What ha—" My eyes went wide.

"So, I guess we won't have to go to the store anymore."

There on the kitchen counter sat a big basket filled with bottles of wine beautifully set along with wine glasses, candles, flowers, and even a charcuterie board. "Where did this come from?" I asked looking over the basket.

"Oh, there's a card." Bella smirked, handed it and leaned over as I opened it.

"Here's a little extra something for girl's night. Enjoy your night, you deserve it after the week you've had. PS. I do mean to make good on my promise. -Lorenzo" and his phone number attached at the bottom.

"So, what's the promise?" Bella wiggled her brows.

"Nope not until girls' night! Isn't that what you said when I asked about Levi?" I lifted an eyebrow.

"Good one. Coffee?"

"Mmhm. that's what I thought." I followed her into the kitchen, thinking about how in the world Lorenzo had gotten my address?

Lorenzo

My dad and uncle were flying in from Chicago. They had been living there since we took over to work alongside the five families. Mostly with the Agosti family.

"What time do they arrive?" Dante asked, grabbing some coffee.

"The jet just landed so they should be here soon." I eyed him. He winced just bringing the mug to his lips. "Aren't you supposed to be taking it easy?"

"I did… yesterday. With everything going on, I just can't lay in bed. Plus, it doesn't even hurt that much, a couple of painkillers and good to go." Taking a seat, he winced again.

"Yeah, I can see those painkillers working their magic already."

"Shut up!"

I got the finger.

"Antonio, get back with the info on Char?" He nodded over to the file with her name and looked it over. "Address." Which I used this morning. "Phone number, which you already have, you're welcome by the way." He grinned. "Where she went to school, info on her parents and brothers..." He kept reading. "Wait...one is a detective and the other is in the army?"

"Yup." I avoided his stare.

"And, ahem, you waited to tell me, why? You know her brother could investigate us, right? You know we don't have all the new detectives in our pocket yet."

"Leave it alone, Dante."

"Your call." He looked over file some more.

"What did Isabella's file say?"

For a moment he was silent, avoiding eye contact. "Attended MIT, works at a fancy tech company, has a twin sister, which I knew. Also has a boyfriend, who apparently works with her—lucky bastard," he muttered into his coffee.

"Chin up, buttercup." I padded his back.

"No, no, no. Don't ever, and I do mean never call me that again." He made a face when we heard a car pull in.

"Let's get this over with." We walked over to the entrance to greet them.

My uncle immediately went to Dante, giving him extra attention and then smacked him across the head for getting shot. Apparently he taught him better than that.

After getting settled, we all went into the office.

"So, tell me what's going on?" my father asked, his voice slightly accented. "What's this I heard about Dante getting shot and its by one of the gangs we do business with."

"*Ratto.*" Rat. Saying it like ripping off a Band-Aid.

My father let out a string of curses, knocking back his

drink in between the words.

"What?! In our *famiglia*?" Uncle Giovanni's voice is a bit more thick in accent. He spent more time in Italy than my father. "*Che diavolo!*" What the hell.

Dante and I told them everything we had so far and who we were looking into plus our kills from yesterday.

"Okay, so lay out the cheese and exterminate the fuckin' *ratto*!" my father spat out.

He was currently pacing the room, about to burn a hole through my mahogany wood floors, running his hands through his mostly silver hair. Even at fifty, my father was a scary motherfucker; still built, a tattoo that peeked from his neck collar, and eyes that pierced deeper than a knife. People said I was his twin.

"Do whatever you need to do." Uncle Giovanni pointed to Dante and me. "*Proteggere la famiglia a tutti i costi!*" Protect the family at all costs. "If blood needs to be spilled then it shall be spilled. Get Roberto on it too, he is our most trusted captain. Been with us for years. He will know where to start."

I nodded, understanding what needed to be done and I would do it without a hesitation, all in the name of Rizzi. I would go down fighting and in order to do that I need to let the demons in.

Let them take over my soul.

I just hope one day my savior will be my side when all this is over.

To bring me back from it all.

SIXTEEN

Charlotte

We were tipsy.

Mmmm maybe a little drunk… or… a lot.

Sprawled out on the kitchen floor waiting for the homemade cookies to be ready. Bella and Ava had decided to make their grandmothers famous chocolate chip cookies while we sang to 'Blame It' by Jaime Foxx and T-Pain.

Since I could remember it had been our go to song every time we drank a little too much.

Lazily leaning against a chair, I chugged some water in some sort of effort to sober up, which I doubt was happening. Katy was lying on the floor with her legs propped up on a chair, Ava was leaning against the kitchen cabinets while Bella laid her head on her sisters' legs as she patted her head in comfort.

We had about three bottles of wine and some tequila shots.

Katy and Ava's jaws just about dropped when they saw the

basket, then they immediately asked for details. I spent an hour telling them about my run-in with Lorenzo. Then we jumped into Katy freaking out about my brother, which started to freak me out, but I tried my best not to show it. In an effort to get Katy's mind off Colton, then Ava asked about Levi.

That's where the real drinking started.

We stopped the wine.

Tequila… tequila… and… more tequila!

Bella told us how she and Levi both had big presentations coming up at work that would determine their futures at the company. And he was being a real jerk, putting her down, trying to steal her ideas, throwing hints at her that she was only there because her boss thought she had a tight ass. Asshole was just jealous because she was smarter than him.

"All I'm saying is if you don't do something I will pretend to be you and kick him in the balls," Ava hissed; she had always hated Levi.

"Fuck that! Let me plant some drugs on him and arrest his ass," Katy countered.

"I'm chopping his dick off!" Wow I really did sound serious—then again, I would. None of us could stand the asshole.

Isabella sat up giggling and hiccupped. "Thanks, guys, it's just hard, you know. We've been dating for a year now and.." She sighed. "Okay, enough about me, Charlotte are you going to call Lorenzo to *thank* him." I didn't miss how she said thank.

I chugged water, delaying my answer.

"Char, how you described him… all muscles and tattoos." Ava closed her eyes, clearly imagining him and I was ready to chuck my water at her. "I would be constantly dreaming of jumping his bones."

Oh I have, especially in the supply closet.

Laughter erupted between the three of them while I slapped my forehead when I realized I had said that out loud, then joined in on the laughter.

"Call him Char! A simple thanks is all… or a start." Katy smirked. Throwing my phone at me. I barely caught it before it hit my face.

When the hell had she grabbed it?

"What no! I'm drunk and it's late!"

"Too bad, it's already ringing."

"WHAT!" I looked down. "SHIIIIT!"

His voice popped up. "Hello? Hello…"

"H-he-heyyyyyy… it's, um, Charlotte." I stood up fast getting dizzy.

"Charlotte." Just the way my name rolled off his tongue sent shivers down my spine and I bit my lip. I must have blushed because the three drunkies were trying to hold in their laughs.

Yeah, it didn't last very long and I was laughing along with them while I ran out of the kitchen.

One of them even whistled.

DAMN TEQUILA!

He chuckled and my panties got wet. "I see girls' night is going good."

"Hah, yes it is…um, hey…th-thanks for the basket. It was very kind of you."

"You're welcome. I can hear you guys put it to good use." He said just as Bella yelled out that the cookies were ready. "Drunk baking?"

If he kept chuckling I was going to have to change my underwear. Fuckin' alcohol…always made me…well..

"Hungry…we got hungry and well cookies sounded good." I was failing at trying not to sound drunk.

"Mmmmm… warm cookies, good choice."

I gulped. The way he said warm had me thinking dirty, dirty thoughts.

Dammit! I opened my mouth only to close it back up.

"Charlotte, you still there?"

"Warm, I-I mean, yeah, still here." *Imagining you with a plate full of warm cookies.*

"Okay well, um, if you aren't doing anything tomorrow would you like to grab some brunch?"

"No, I'm not busy!" *A bit eager there, Char.* "I mean yeah that sounds nice."

"Great, pick you up…around eleven?"

"Yeah that works. Wait! Let me give you my address… ummmm." I looked around as he chuckled. "I might have to send it to you. I forgot where I live." I slapped my forehead. *Idiot!*

Another chuckle. Definitely need new underwear. "Charlotte, I sent you the basket, remember? I have your address."

"Right!" Which reminded me, how the hell did he get it?

"I won't keep you from your friends any longer. See you tomorrow… Bye, Charlotte."

"Bye, Lorenzo." Back in the kitchen, all eyes were on me. "Ummm… I think I have a date tomorrow."

Their eyes popped out.

"Pass me a shot!" I said breathlessly.

Isabella poured, I knocked it back while they started planning outfits for my brunch.

And then the rest of the night was a blur… except for an

image of Lorenzo holding a warm plate of cookies… naked. And a trail of crumbs that led down to his…

Buzz… Buuuzzzz… Buzzz

Jesus. what's that noise?

Buzzzzz.

Groaning, I rolled over sending my body into thin air and with a shriek I landed on my ass with a thud.

"OUCH!"

I did not land on the floor.

Groaning I opened my eyes. I guess I passed out on the couch with Katy on the floor next to me.

"OUUCCCHHH! Char, I love you but get your butt off me." Somehow, I managed to stand. "God, is the room spinning?" Katy held her head at the sound of the chime again.

Wincing, I looked around. "Whose phone is that, and where are the twins?"

We went into the kitchen, where Katy's alarm was going off then in search of the twins; finding them in Bella's bathroom.

And it was a perfect picture. Katy snapped a few photos. By the looks of it, Isabella felt sick and laid by the toilet with Ava to her left inside the bathtub with one hand holding a plate of cookies and the other holding her sister's hand.

"What happened yesterday?" Whispering, I stared in the mirror and took us in. Messy hair, makeup smeared, Katy's shirt was on backwards, and I'm pretty sure we all reeked of alcohol.

Groaning from the floor Bella answered. "Tequila, that's what happened. Why did I ask for it again?"

"Because of that asshole of a boyfriend you have. Oh, and we kept drinking when Char announced she had a date with Lorenzo." Ava spoke with her eyes still closed looking heavenward.

"Oh, that asshole." Bella spat so fast it caught us off guard. We couldn't help it, we all started laughing so hard to the point of tears. Katy helped Ava out of the bathtub, and I helped Bella up still laughing, and then I froze, almost dropping her on her ass.

"Char!" She gripped the towel rack.

"SHIIIIT!" We all winced at my voice. "What time is it? Lorenzo is coming at eleven." I need to do my hair, my makeup, brush my teeth, no wait…I need to shower first and then… God, my head hurt. How much did I drink last night? Katy was right, the room was spinning.

"It's ten. Go shower. We'll get your outfit ready." Ava pushed me toward the bathroom.

"Maybe I should cancel. It's—"

"NO!" they all yelled in unison, causing me to wince and the rest to groan.

We were definitely way past hung over.

Isabella pointed a finger in my face. "Don't you dare. Hung over or not, you're going or else I'm giving you more tequila."

"Nope, I'm good." I ran my ass into the shower. Washed my hair, scrubbed my body, and then brushed my teeth at lightning speed. Wrapped in a towel, I walked into my room where Katy was holding the blow dryer, Ava my makeup, and Isabella gestured toward an outfit laid out on the bed.

Rubbing my eyes, I did a double take. Somehow they had managed to change, take off what was left of their makeup, and looked casually put together as if they hadn't all just been ready to give the sun a middle finger. "How long was I in the bathroom?"

"Five minutes too long, now get over here." Katy tugged my hair one way and then the other while Ava applied some light makeup, with some extra concealer. Thank Jesus! Once my hair was semi-dried, waves were added to go along with my natural long wavy hair, all while I sipped on the coffee Isabella brought.

Still feeling hungover as hell.

I prayed I didn't puke.

"Okay, hurry and get dressed." Isabella threw me a pair of dark blue jeans with small rips at the knees, cut off right above the ankle, a brown sweater that hung off one shoulder a bit. She didn't throw me the beige suede booties because they would have smacked me in the face. Then one look in the mirror, and—

Damn, I looked good…even hungover. One last brush of my teeth to get rid of the coffee taste, and I almost puked.

Oh God, don't throw up, Charlotte.

I walked out to the living room where the girls were, all smiles, coffees in hand.

"Dang, we did good!" Ava's whistle is cut off by the knock at the door.

"And just in time." Katy winks, and butterflies erupt in my stomach.

I freeze, unable to turn toward the door.

Come on Charlotte it's just a date. You've been on dates before, this is no different. He's a regular guy taking you out.

I could hear Bella greet him at the door then their footsteps down the hall.

The closer they came, the more my heart picked up speed. I could tell he stepped into the living room by Katy and Ava's gasps.

"Good morning, ladies." His voice came off firm and rich.

I turn and know those piercing chocolate eyes have already sucked me in, and I am totally and utterly screwed. "Lorenzo."

SEVENTEEN

Lorenzo

"You look beautiful." The light coming in from the window gave her an angelic glow.

"Thank you, it's really thanks to them." She nodded her head over to her friends, who were on the couch watching.

"Well thank you, ladies, for making her look even more beautiful than she already is. Fresh chocolate croissants?" I handed Ava the box, smiling when I noticed she was grinning from ear to ear. "Ready?"

"Yeah." We say our goodbyes and took our leave with Charlotte in front of me.

I try my best not to look at her perky ass in the tight jeans but found myself noticing the sway of her hips and her long legs.

This was going to be a long brunch.

Charlotte closed her eyes as the elevator began its descent. "Fun night yesterday?"

"Oh, you have no idea." She giggled, pretty sure from remembering last night's events.

The door opened and I guided her out. "I believe I have an idea after last night's call."

Pink tints her cheeks at my comment, and we walk out to cool air; summer was ending and it had started to get chilly already.

"How's your morning been so far?" she asks once we are in my G-wagon.

"Good, I went to church this morning with Dante," I answer pulling into traffic.

"You and Dante go to church?" The shock in her voice almost makes me laugh.

Everyone was always surprised when I told them we attended church. But well... we needed to confess our sins somehow—maybe even one that was committed right before entering. "Don't look so surprised. I'm a very religious man." I pasted on my best serious look.

"Really!"

I laugh. "No, but I grew up going, and well, I am Italian. We don't mess with God's day— only if necessary." I give her a wink.

She giggled internally. "I respect that." The rest of the way, she asked how Dante was and we chatted a bit about her work.

At the restaurant parking lot, I hopped out and went around to open Charlotte's door, giving her my hand to help her out, but she slipped on the door step. I caught her by the waist.

With her hand on my chest, she looked up, lips slightly parted.

A hint of minty breath hung in the space between us.

I wanted a taste.

"Seems I still may be a little intoxicated."

"Thankfully for us, you are." I gently moved a strand of hair away from her face, my thumb itching to run over her soft, plump lips. Instead, I straightened her up, taking her delicate hand in mine and walked toward the restaurant. "I reserved a table for us outside if that's okay with you."

"That's perfect. I love this weather." She beamed when we sat under a tree with the leaves ready to change color.

Our waiter offered us some mimosas, and she quickly nodded. "Yes please, maybe it will cure this hangover."

"I'll have one too," I said with a small chuckle. "So, I take it the wine basket was put to good use?" I asked once the waiter left.

"Oh, the wine was amazing." She beamed. "Now tequila shots are a completely different story."

"Tequila?"

She nodded. "If you had seen how and where we woke up this morning—"

Our waiter came by with our drinks, accidentally tapped one of the water glasses.

She winced. "Remind me never to drink tequila again."

"Only if you tell me how you guys woke up. I *am* curious now."

And she did and only paused mid-story when it came time to place our orders.

After a quick review of the menu, we ended up deciding to share a plate of French toast. Oreo topping, of course.

Then she picked up her tale again. By the end of the story, I was laughing so hard just by seeing her reenact their faces.

"Tequila for you." She laughed.

"Well then." I lifted my drink. "Here is to tequila and laying off it for a while."

She smiled. "Cheers."

Sitting there with Charlotte, sharing stories, laughing, and enjoying a beautiful view felt like the rest of the world around us didn't exist.

It was just us two, no one else in that restaurant existed.

There was no worry about my family, work, whatever hell was approaching. Nothing but her smile.

Her laugh.

The fuckin' way she made my heart skip a beat every time she smiled.

Sharing a meal with me. To her I was a normal person and not the boss to the Rizzi family. Where other women saw me as just a bank account or a good fuck, she saw *me*.

Just Lorenzo.

"I didn't know we were playing hunger games." She lightly hit my fork with hers. I had been trying to distract her from getting the last piece of French toast. I tapped her fork back which she dodged and picked up the last piece. "Too slow!" She smirked, holding the piece French toast in the air.

"Tsk that's what you think." I tried to take it from her, but she quickly put it in her mouth leaving a little whipped cream on the side of her lip. Acting hurt, I put my hand to my chest but then leaned in. "But I think I have the last bite." Getting even closer, I couldn't help seeing the specs of gold in her eyes. "Right here."

She sucked in a breath as I swiped my thumb across her bottom lip, pulled back and licked the whipped cream off. "Mmmmm…"

Her jaw dropped open. "Ah-aah… wh-wh…" Our waiter

came by before she could finish. He picked up our plates all while she chewed on her lower lip. I inwardly groaned. I wanted to be on the other end of that biting.

I handed my card to the waiter and when he left she opened her mouth to speak but was cut off by the ring of my phone.

I cursed mentally then forced a smile. "I'm sorry I have to take this call."

"Yeah, go ahead."

I stood and stepped to the side, where she couldn't hear but I could still look at her, and seethed out, "What?"

"We have a problem." Roberto said.

Merda. Shit.

Charlotte

I wanted to jump his bones!

The way his thumb swiped my lip and then when he licked the whipped cream off… I wished it were his tongue that had done the cleaning.

Was I still drunk?

Maybe that mimosa hadn't been a good idea. Alcohol always made me a little too happy.

And hot apparently.

He stood there, staring at me with what I could only describe as lust, and my body was responding. Heat spread through every inch of me, making me squeeze my thighs together.

I sipped some cold water, hoping I cooled down.

"Work." He sighed as he approached the table.. "I swear I can never catch a break…is it okay if we cut our date short?"

"Yeah, it's fine." I stood, trying to suppress the disappointment that speared through me. "I beat you at French Toast hunger games so…" I offered a shrug and we headed for the exit when I felt him behind me about to open the door. Leaning in, his lips brushed the top of my ear. I bit my cheek to keep from moaning.

"Rematch? Extra whipped cream." His voice was smooth, rendering me speechless. And all too soon his lips were gone, leaving me at a loss until his hand was on my back walking me to the car.

There wasn't anything that he did that didn't make my knees buck.

"Extra whipped cream… will you lick your thumb again?" I asked once in the car.

Before I could buckle my seat belt, he leaned over.

"Hell no!" And then his lips were on mine. Licking my bottom lip, prying my mouth open. A hand on my right hip and the other on the side of my face.

My hand on his left cheek feeling the light stubble he carried.

His kiss was filled with intense passion. It was warm, tender, and sweet all at the same time as his tongue parried with mine. My core felt the heat of it all as he tightened his hold on my hips. A small moan escaped when he pushed me back in the seat deepening the kiss. Then tugging my lip lightly before pulling away.

Panting, neither of us able to speak, we remained still for just a moment. Then he roared the car to life. Our heavy breathing filled the space around us.

I ran the tips of my fingers over my wet lips. "Lorenzo…"

He reached for my hand and brought it to his lips without taking his eyes off the road. "I'm making good on my promise. I hope to see you soon and more often. I like you Charlotte…a lot."

"I like you too, Lorenzo, and it is not just for your muscles," I joked. That's what I did when I was nervous.

"Dammit, and here I thought it was." He smirked.

FUUUUCCCCKKKK!

Turn on the A/C!

Throw me in an ice bath, anything.

"There is a charity event that my company is hosting this Saturday night." He kissed my hand. "I'd like it if you would accompany me."

"I would love to. What is it for?"

The rest of the way home, he told me all about the charity that funded schools in poor communities, providing new computers, building libraries, and granting scholarships to soon-to-be graduating high schoolers. I thought it was amazing that with his influence he decided to help others in need and gave others who wouldn't have an opportunity for college a chance to attend.

When we got to my apartment, I felt like a giddy teenager when put his arm around me and walked me to my apartment, only to spin me around and back me in the door. And let me tell you, having a sexy guy pressing you up against the wall… basically every girl's fantasy. "You know, after I've tasted you there is no way I am letting you go."

My heart skipped a beat and I slid my hand against his cheek. "Then don't." His lips were on mine again. Dropping my bag on the floor, I wrapped my arms around his neck. His hands ran up and down my waist as he pressed his huge body onto me.

The world around us was lost.

I forgot we were in the hallway and was five seconds from undressing him until I heard a throat clear.

We jumped back like two horny teenagers whose parents had just caught making out. Only it wasn't my mother, but someone a lot worse… my brother.

Shit!

"Julian?" I could not describe the horror washing over me even if I wanted to. "Wh-what are you doing here?" I was still panting. Pretty sure my lipstick was smeared.

"Picking up Katy… crime scene." He focused over to Lorenzo, stretching out his hand. "Hi, I'm Julian, Charlotte's older brother. Well one of them." They shook hands as I panicked. "So, you two looked, cozy." He didn't appear happy. Then again, he had just witnessed his little sister practically dry humping.

But Lorenzo didn't seem intimated. "Lorenzo, and well, you see your sister." He put his arm around me.

I stifled the urge to stiffen beneath his touch. What the hell was he doing?

"She is amazing," Lorenzo continued, "and is making me completely crazy for her."

My heart fluttered.

"I see she feels the same way." Arms crossed, Julian eyed Lorenzo up and down then chuckled. "I'm just messing with you. I'm the cool brother. As long as she's happy. If not, I'm sending Colton."

I let out the breath. "Gee thanks, Julian! How very considerate of you. Come on, let's check if Katy's hangover passed." I opened the door, letting my brother in. "You want to come in, or do you have to go?" I asked Lorenzo.

"Dante's waiting… next time." He leaned in and kissed me… lightly this time. "But I do want to see you again this week. I'll text you."

I just nodded my head yes because I didn't want to pull away from his lips. They were unlike anything I had ever felt.

When I finally made it inside, laughter was all I heard.

"Julian just told us Lorenzo passed his CPR exam." Katy laughed.

Isabella just giggled behind her hand. "Guess we don't have to ask if it went well."

"Oh, by the smoke left in the hallway, I'd say it went better than good." Julian smirked.

I smacked his shoulder. "Julian! That's so embarrassing."

"Hey, I wouldn't have interrupted, but you guys were kinda blocking the door I needed to get through. Be thankful it *was* me and not Colton. He would have thrown ice water on you. Plus, the scared one should be *me*… No brother should see his little sister…" He made a face and then more laughter erupted as I joined in and covered my face.

Given how scorched my face felt, I must have been crimson red.

Once everyone left, Isabella hounded me for details, and when I got to Lorenzo's invitation to the charity event we found out her company was taking part in it as well. We even agreed to go shopping Tuesday morning. After a few more minutes of chatting, I finally escaped to get some rest.

Whipped cream, soft lips, and brown eyes created a blissful dream.

Until I saw Lorenzo pulling a gun, just as he had the night he saved me, only this time he actually killed my attacker.

EIGHTEEN

Lorenzo

"*Fuck!* What do you mean you don't know what happened?" I ran my hands through my hair as I paced back and forth in my office. "What the fuck is going on, huh?"

Roberto had gone to meet with one of our groups that handled loans. We loaned money to businesses and families but didn't collect how it had been done back in the day. We had modernized it in a way that didn't have the FBI breathing down our necks. Not that I didn't have some in my pocket, but still. According to Roberto, the group we had put in charge of it was asking for a bigger cut and more territory. Things went sideways and it cost the life of a good associate.

Worst of all…

Now the cops had a crime scene with his body, which was fuckin' unacceptable for countless reasons. One of them being we had a code we lived by.

A blood oath had been given. Protect the family, his life for ours if need be, and in return that same honor was bestowed on him. It made my blood fuckin' incinerate that he'd been left behind.

I shot up a prayer for him... *Per Sangue Rizzi Vivo e Per Sangue Rizzi Muoio.* For Rizzi blood I live and through Rizzi blood I die.

"Lorenzo, we will get a handle on this." Roberto tried to help.

"Really? When?" Dante was spitting fuckin' fire.

I gripped my leather chair. "Why would you go with only two men after everything going on? And why wasn't I aware that the meeting had gotten pushed up?" My head was spinning. After an amazing time with Charlotte, I come home to this!

Evil never stopped lurking.

Roberto sighed. "Your fathers gave the green light, and since you were out I didn't think it was necessary. I thought I had it handled—"

"And look where we are!" I stared over at Dante, who was flipping a knife in his hand, as I spoke to Roberto. "Next time, remember *you* answer to *me*, not to my father anymore!"

"*Inteso.*" Understood. "I will check in with you from now on." He might be twenty years older and one of my father's best friends, but I was the boss now, not my father. Even if my father did have influence on the older generation.

I turned to my cousin once Roberto left. "Any word from our contacts at the station?"

"Yes, and you aren't going to like it." He clenched his jaw. "He was the one we used to lease the warehouse we used that day. It was anonymously tipped off and traces of blood were found and collected. Now they find said owner dead. Guess who the detectives on the case are."

Now the evidence didn't worry me, we had cops on payroll that would make that disappear. But what was a bitch was who was assigned to the case. Julian had said they had been called to a crime scene earlier.

"*Figlio de puttana*!" Son a bitch. I leaned forward on my desk pinching the bridge of my nose.

"We have him registered as working for Rizzi Construction," Dante added.

"Was cleanup sent to his office?"

"Antonio is on it. He should be arriving soon." He leaned back in his chair and changed the subject. "So, I take it by the skip in your step that everything went good today?"

"I don't skip!" I had walked weird because of my hard-on, though. "I invited her to the charity event."

"Wow, Lorenzo Rizzi has a date. Usually you just get a girl for your bed."

"Yeah well, Charlotte isn't just any girl."

He smirked. "Couldn't agree anymore." He stood and walked out.

"Hey, Dante."

"What's up?"

"Isabella looks good—heard her boyfriend is a dick."

He rubbed his chin. "An asshole is better than a killer."

Dante's words pounded in my head the rest of the day. The possibility of bringing someone innocent into our world was dangerous. My own mother had lost her life all because of it… all because she fell in love with my father.

I feared history would repeat itself.

I knew it was wrong to pursue her.

Kiss her.

Give her hope on the possibility of us.

Because the moment she knew the truth about me she would be running for the hills. Away from the monster.

But I'd meant what I had said. One taste of her lips, and I was obsessed. Letting her go wasn't in the cards, and I would do anything to protect her.

To keep her from losing her innocence.

Keep that light that shined so bright in her. The very one that always brought me back.

By the time we were done with everything I was fuckin' exhausted, but I picked up my phone and texted Charlotte. After the day I'd had, I needed to see her.

> Me: Dinner tomorrow? I'll pick you up from work.
>
> Charlotte: You cook? It's okay I can drive, just send me your address.
>
> Me: Um... does my chef count?
>
> Charlotte: Hahaha, no but it'll do. Text you tomorrow, I have to be up early for my shift. Goodnight, Lorenzo.
>
> Me: Goodnight, Charlotte.

Charlotte

Work had been a fucking nightmare. The hospital got a surge of patients, all drug users who had gotten a bad batch of drugs. Most of us were reassigned to the ER to cover all patients.

Thankfully, I was off now and starving. I hope Lorenzo had carbs.

Yes carbs!

Any other girl would say salad, but me?

Give me all the bread, pasta, and Oreos! I'll run that shit off later.

I grabbed a quick shower in the lockers before heading over to Lorenzo's. Thank God I had done my hair that morning and put it in a messy bun or else it would have looked like a wild lion's mane instead of waves. I applied a little makeup and got dressed in my white long-sleeved bodysuit, jeans, and suede beige boots.

I'd be lying if I said my stomach wasn't doing more and more flips the closer, I got to his street. I was a nervous wreck! I had just got them under control when I pulled up to the gates of his house… forget house.

Cue panic attack.

It was a freakin' mansion!

The gates opened before I even pushed the button outside, and I drove through with my mouth opened the whole way in. And after slapping myself out of it, and I do mean literally, I got out of the car where a man in a suit scared the living shit out me and asked for my keys.

He was huge with more tattoos on his neck and one on his eyebrow than I thought was possible and black eyes that would give nightmares. Accepting my keys, he said, "Right through there Miss. Frizzell. He's expecting you."

I ran toward the door, but before I could knock it swung open.

"Charlotte! You made it." Dante smiled and pulled me into a hug and stepped aside to let me in. "You okay?"

"Are all your security guards like they can be part of the American horror story tv show?" I looked back toward the man who was chuckling.

"I see you met Antonio." Dante laughed. Which honestly made me feel a bit better. Never judge a book by its cover, right? "Dang, you clean up good. He's going to skip again."

"Who... Lorenzo? He skips?"

"Says he doesn't but he totally does... especially after seeing you." He smirked. "He's in his office." He pointed me down the hall as he grabbed his jacket. "I'm heading out, I'll see you Saturday."

"I'll see you there. Oh, and Dante, please take it easy... you're still healing."

"Always do." He winked and left. I walked down the hall and stopped to look at some of the pictures on the wall. I focused on one of Dante and Lorenzo in their high school football jerseys laughing toward the camera. It took me back to high school when all the girls quivered as they walked by sporting their jerseys and cocky smiles. Some things never changed... only now they wore expensive suits.

"That's one of my favorite pictures of us... before we became adults and learned about the real world." Lorenzo stood leaning against the door frame.

"The world isn't always as it seems, is it?" I stopped in front of him, even with my high heel boots he still towered over me.

"No. It isn't.'" He brushed my lips with his. "You look amazing. Come." He grabbed my hand and led me to the kitchen and pulled a wine bottle from the fridge. "Wine?"

"Please!" I let out a laugh. "Sorry, it's been a long day. I was in the ER all day. I guess there was a bad drug on the streets today because a lot of people overdosed."

His eyes flickered with something I couldn't define. "Overdose? Do they know what drug it was?" He handed me a long-stem wine glass containing red wine.

"It was a cocktail of some sort." I took a sip of the wine and instantly got hit with the most delicious flavor of cherry. I licked my lips. "The authorities were alerted, so I guess they should find out where it came from soon enough."

Lorenzo nodded and finished his glass in one gulp. I guess I wasn't the only one who had a long day at work.

NINETEEN

Lorenzo

Those overdoses were no accident and I sure as fuck hoped it wasn't our drugs. I sent a quick text over to Dante.

Cazzo!

"Hey, need some help?" Charlotte stepped into the kitchen. Even after a twelve-hour shift from hell she looked good. If she was an option for dinner, I'd pick her and devour all of her.

"Sure, can you grab the salad bowl and some forks from that drawer?" I pointed. After a few more minutes we sat down in the dining room, and I watched her take the first bite.

"Oh, sweet Jesus, is that homemade?"

"Only way to eat pasta."

"I don't think I'll ever be able to eat regular pasta again."

A smile tugged at my lips. Most girls would shy away from carbs, but not her and I loved that.

"Just warning you, save room for dessert." I sipped my wine.

"Is it a homemade pasta desert?"

"No, but I am pretty confident you'll like it." I winked as she giggled and asked about my day, actually sounding like she cared.

It had been a while since I had a normal conversation with a girl without ulterior motives. Anyone who I met and took home for the night always saw me for my money, my power, or my favorite reason: my body.

Women seldom saw me past the money, muscles, and tattoos. It was like some fantasy they all had.

While it was fun and all, I just wanted someone to talk to, to forget about the shit day I was having.

"So how are your parents? Do they live nearby?" she asked. It was a normal question someone you go on a date with would ask, but I hated it.

Not because of the secret of my family but because of the memory of my mom.

Her death was something I couldn't share with Charlotte.

"My dad lives in Chicago, and my mom died when I was nine."

Charlotte's face immediately paled. "I'm so sorry. I didn't kn—"

"No, it's okay. It was a long time ago."

She reached across the table and grabbed my hands, giving them a squeeze. The small smile on her lips eases the pain from the horrible memory. But it swirls in the back of my mind, a permanent part of me. How the Irish gang had sought revenge for the son of their boss that my family had killed. The shot was meant for me, a son for a son, but my mother was quicker and pushed me toward my bodyguard, leaving her defenseless. I can still feel the burn of my cheek against the hot pavement as my body was pressed down by my bodyguard, watching how three bullets pierced my mother's small frame and how the blood seeped through her white pantsuit.

I would never forget the look on my father's face when we arrived home with my mother's near lifeless body while I clutched her hand for dear life, apologizing for not protecting her. We tried saving her but it was like she only held on until she saw my father's face. She had looked at him, smiled and whispered, "*finché non ci incontreremo di nuovo, amore mio*" Until we meet again, my love. Then she closed her eyes and died in his arms.

I blamed myself for her death. If she had just gone to lunch with my Aunt Mia and not come to pick me up from school like I'd begged her to, she would still be alive. At nine years old, I was ready to sacrifice myself for her, and she had not allowed me to do that.

"I know it's painful, you don't have to tell me how she died." Charlotte's quiet words bring me back to the present.

I look at her and I wish I could tell her, to share every detail with her, and to anyone it might seem weak, that these were emotions a boss should bury, but I believed that everyone deserved that one person to share their all with, to share anything no matter how painful.

I wondered if Charlotte was it.

I lifted her hand to my lips, pressing them to her inner wrist. "Thank you."

"We all have things that pain us." She let out a sigh. "My parents couldn't wait for me to leave for college. They left me the day before high school graduation to travel the world. Something they always dreamed of but never could because of us, and they never missed a chance to remind us. That's why my brothers and I are so close. Colton was always a better father than my own, despite the fact he's only four years older."

Her eyes watered, and it pissed me off that a parent, someone who was supposed to love her, could do that to her and her brothers.

"They left me, without so much of an explanation as to why. Just that they had a life to live, one we had ruined."

It hurt her, and I hated seeing her in pain.

They said the mafia was cruel, but my parents, my uncles, and those around us showed us love despite what they did for a living. Shit, my dad and Uncle Vanni, Dante's dad, made us watch someone being tortured when we were ten, but even then they showed us love.

"Love isn't a weakness, especially for family," My Uncle Vanni would say. "It's the one thing that keeps you going, when everything around you is bleeding red.

My hand rose to her cheek. "They don't deserve your tears. You are a light anyone would be lucky to have." I swore that in that moment that no one would hurt her like that. Her parents were pieces of shit, and if I ever met them I would gladly tell them where to shove it. Hell, I'd even torture them with a smile on my face. So they would at least feel an ounce of pain that Charlotte felt.

Leaning into my hand, she smiled, blinking back the tears her parents didn't deserve.

"How about some dessert to forget about the sourness of our lives?"

She let out a teary laugh. "I don't know… I think you're hyping up this desert a bit too much."

"Oh, I think it will satisfy you perfectly." I turned, slid my hand between her legs, grabbed the front of her chair, and pulled her toward me, inches away from her lips. "Are you ready?" I grazed her lips with mine, not kissing her, but just enough to have her shiver at my touch. Before she went in for the kiss, I stood and stepped into the kitchen. Was it a tease? Hell yes, and my dick fuckin' felt it! But her laugh was worth it, and I returned with a plate of French toast with Oreo crumbs and extra whipped cream to make up for it.

"Nooo... you didn't!" Her eyes were no longer full of tears.

"Oh, I did... rematch?"

"You're on. Grab your fork before it's too late."

Yeah, she didn't pick up her fork.

With her fingers she picked up a piece, wrapped her lips around the golden brown bread with cream and took a bite. It was the sexiest bite I've seen—my dick jumped.

"Want a bite?" She held a piece in front of my lips.

Smirking, I took the rest of the piece in my mouth, her fingers included. Sucked them and pulled back kissing every finger. "Delicious." Her eyes were huge. "I did say I wasn't going to lick my thumb next time, never said anything about yours."

"Uh...w-well...THAT WAS HOT!" We were quiet for a second before, laughing.

Her laughing rolling through me like a warming wave.

I refilled her glass of wine. "Lorenzo Rizzi, are you trying to get me drunk?"

"Of course not."

She pressed her lips together. "You're lucky it's so delicious, and I can't stop drinking it. But before I have another glass, can I use your restroom?"

I pointed the way and watched her sexy swaying walk from the room. While she was in the powder room, I checked my phone for any updates.

Dante: It's ours. Taking care of it right now.

Me: Merda! Need back up?

Dante: No enjoy your night. I have this covered.

Me: Keep me updated.

"Everything okay?" Charlotte asked walking back into the kitchen.

"Yeah, it was just Dante, being nosey. Want to watch a movie?"

"Sure." We grabbed the wine and headed to the theater room. "Okay, when you said watch a movie I thought you meant on the sofa in the living room—not a home theater." She looked around the room that had big reclinable couches in the back row with a huge sectional sofa in front. She sat on the sofa and leaned back. "This couch is softer than my bed."

"Mmmm, wouldn't know." A pillow smacked my face, making me chuckle.

"Oh, I've never seen that one." She pointed to the screen when the Godfather popped up.

I was going to kill Dante! Why in the world was he watching something we lived daily. Inspiration? "You sure? It's an old movie."

"Mmm, do you have the new Fast and the Furious? Kinda obsessed with Dom."

That was it. I officially wanted to rip off his head. Great, now I was jealous of a character who raced cars.

"We do, actually." I set the movie up to play then pulled her close to me so her head was on my shoulder and made a mental note to find out the address of the actor who played Dom Toretto.

I was sending him a bomb.

Oh, look, someone sent one already.

Halfway through the movie she nudged closer and ended up falling asleep. Not wanting to wake her, I carried her up to my room.

Seated next to her, I pushed her hair away from her face and admired her. She looked so innocent. I was afraid what being with me would do to her. I wanted to protect her from the bad and the ugly of what I did. How can I start a relationship full of secrets?

Knowing that the very secrets I kept could destroy her.

But I couldn't stay away from her even if I tried because she was the only one who had ever owned my soul.

She just had no idea.

Sometime later the front door slammed shut. Dante.

I found him in the kitchen, back toward me, pouring a drink. "Charlotte still here?" His voice was low and gruff.

"Yeah."

He took a sip of his drink turning around. "You know you need her more than she needs you, right?" His sleeves were rolled up and even in the dark I could see his shirt and arms were stained with blood.

He swirled the whiskey in his glass before knocking the rest back. He didn't have to say anything for me to know what he had done.

Torturing someone, no matter how many times we did it, never got easier. No matter the amount of alcohol we downed after every torture and kill we still heard the screams and cries for mercy of those people. When we closed our eyes, we still saw the life leaving their bodies.

We were monsters, and there was no saving our souls. It was the one thing we knew from the moment we made our first kill.

No rest for the wicked, right?

"What did you find out?" I asked.

"They're out for blood. Everything we've done to make this city better… is getting destroyed piece by piece." Bottle in hand, he took a swig. "And these… these fuckers, idiots are falling in line with whoever is behind it all. We can't trust anyone."

I ran my hands through my hair, setting them on the countertop afterwards.

"We not only have a rat, but we have the police on our asses," Dante gritted.

My head snapped up. "What do you mean the police on our ass?"

"I just got a call from our informant who got rid of the evidence from the warehouse. But Detective Frizzell has found something on our dear dead associate. Any day now, he is going to be paying you a visit."

"*Fuck!*" I snatched the bottle taking a big gulp. "Guess who's his partner… Katherine Woodward, one of Charlotte's best friends."

Usually we just paid off the cops and were done, but this… this was her family. No way I would threaten them or pay them off. I could. But how well would that go over? Where would that get me with Charlotte?

"*Merda!*" Shit. "We have to come up with something soon. Look into everyone no matter the cost." He snatched the bottle back. "Go back to Charlotte, sleep, hold her. I've got this covered."

I knew what he was doing; he was sacrificing his own soul for me. For a chance. We were family and looked out for each other—I would do the same for him.

"Hey, Dante."

He stopped, lifted his eyes to me.

"Thanks."

"Just don't fuck it up or else I'm kicking your ass for being an *idiota*!" He walked down the hall to his room.

I slapped the countertop a couple times... *Cazzo*!

Upstairs, Charlotte lay sleeping, completely oblivious to what was approaching. Letting her walk away now would be the right thing to do, but for once in my life I was being selfish.

I wanted her. Wanted her to be mine. I would move mountains, bring the stars down, burn the world for her. Anything that would make her happy.

But I would never forget what coursed through my veins— Rizzi blood.

Lying in bed with Charlotte in my arms, I thought about what she'd think about me by allowing my cousin to damn his soul just so I could be with her. It was something I couldn't allow him to do.

We had both taken an oath. An oath in blood to defend and protect this family at all costs. And no matter what happened between Charlotte and me, I knew that she wouldn't have wanted me to leave Dante alone in this.

I was a Rizzi.

A boss.

A businessman.

A cousin.

And a man falling in love, ready to defend anyone and everyone I loved.

TWENTY

Dante

I took another swig at the bottle and stared at myself in the mirror.

My light gray shirt covered in blood, my face splattered with it, the stitches on my arm were barely holding up. My knuckles were cut and already swelling.

I snorted, annoyed, remembering the events from earlier.

Blood flew as I punched him for the tenth time, his face was swelling up. "Decided to become a chemist, Alex? Why are you messing with our drugs?" I took off my brass knuckles and threw them on the table with some of my favorite tools. "See, I seem to think they are fine the way they are."

"Why the fuck do you care? I thought you wanted nothing to do with the drugs anymore." He spat blood on the floor.

We had been at this for hours. His two buddies next to him had passed out a while ago. Probably blood loss or pain. Eh, what did I care? They would all be dead soon.

"Why you assuming shit now?" I grabbed the needle-nose pliers, walked behind him grabbing a finger. "Who told you we were done with the drugs?"

A nail between the pliers, he held his head high.

"Oh, tough guy now huh?" I yanked off his fingernail, and he screamed. I pulled another. "I can do this all night, so either you get to talking—"

The guy next to him groaned.

"Or I start chopping off hands for messing with what's not yours to mess with. See fingernails grow back but limbs... well I think you know." I pulled another nail.

He yelled out and then—he started laughing.

And maybe it was the adrenaline, but that laughter was really starting to annoy me.

"You must be too busy fucking all of Boston, you don't know what is even going on. A new dynasty is coming, and you won't even see it until your cousin and you are begging for mercy." Alex laughed his swollen face off. "So, kill me because you can't stop what's coming—the Rizzis will cease to exist."

Rage boiled through me at his words. Taking the knife from my back pocket I lunged for the guy next to him just as he woke up. Jabbing the knife into him again, again, and again. Blood spattered everywhere while Alex shouted, cursing me to hell. Even as his cries became sobs and he pleaded with me to stop, I didn't. Not until I saw the life in his eyes leave his body. Until the soul no longer existed only the lifeless body.

I pulled back cleaning the blade on my jeans. "You fuck with my family and I kill yours off one by one." His nephew's lifeless body sat next to him; eyes still open.

Tears stained his face, but rage filled his eyes as he screamed, "YOU WILL PAY FOR THIS! You are nothing but a child who *doesn't know how the world works!"*

I laughed. "Wrong thing to say to this so-called child who holds your pathetic"—punch—"little"—punch—"life"—punch—"in"—punch—"his"—punch—"hands." I finished with a one-two punch to the jaw. "Start talking."

"Those who lurk in the shadows have their eyes set on the moon," was his reply.

"Pfft… fuckin' poetic." I took another swig of the bottle with a shaky hand, savoring the heat of the liquor burning down my throat. I had tortured him and the other guy for another hour before I saw that I was getting nowhere. I shot his companion in the chest and Alex between the eyes.

No amount of liquor was ever enough to wash away the memory of life leaving someone's body. The way their faces looked when they realized they were done for.

For a moment, it brought me peace but then the demon settled in. But I did it in the name family… again and again. And would continue to do it.

Another chug of whiskey.

To give Lorenzo a chance of love. To have what I never could, because who was I kidding? I was a beast, and who could ever love a piece-of-shit beast? Yeah, that Disney movie was just a fuckin' fairy tale.

The file on top of my dresser stared back at me, with her picture at the top. *Bellissima.* Crystal blue eyes that were so full of life. Unlike mine, cold and dark. She would never be able to love a beast like me because instead of protecting her from her fears I was the very demon himself.

Maybe even worse.

Tearing my clothes off and throwing them in the trash I walked into the shower. I stood under the rain shower watching the blood wash away…as if it was never there. As if the sins were gone; yeah, right. No matter the amount of water, soap—shit even bleach couldn't wash away the blood.

It was always there staining my hands.

Once the water ran cold, I wrapped a towel around my waist, grabbed the bottle, and headed into my room. My hand couldn't stop shaking. The very hand I used to kill with.

It pissed me the fuck off that after all this fuckin' time I still felt every soul I took.

I let out a scream falling to my knees. My reflection stared back at me—laughing at the man before the mirror.

Irritated, I threw the bottle across the room. It hit the wall, shattering, and raining shards of glass all over the floor.

"FUUUUCK!"

I grabbed the extra bottle of whiskey I kept in my drawer and chugged. Chugged until the liquor no longer burned. Chugged until my hand stopped shaking. Chugged until the point I was numb, too numb to feel anything at all.

Forgetting it all.

Not remembering when I passed out.

"Dante!" Antonio's voice reached through the fog and hit my brain like a knife. "Dante, Dante… wake up! We've got a problem."

With one eye open, I looked up. I had passed out face down… buck naked. "This better be important Antonio because you are staring at my ass right now, and that isn't how I imagined waking up this morning… unless you are into that shit." Fuck, what was that pounding in my head! Oh right, the two bottles of whiskey.

Whoops.

"No…" He cleared his throat. "Sorry, but there's something you need to see." He handed me his phone and turned around.

What I saw had the whiskey making a comeback and not in a good way.

"THE HELL!" I stood no longer caring that I was naked. "Enzo know yet?"

He shook his head.

"Meet me in the office. Let me try to fix it first. And call Alessio."

We couldn't do this alone anymore, and I trusted him. He was part of the one of the strongest families in Chicago and also family.

"Yes, sir," he said and took his leave.

I stood there fuming, consumed with so much anger. My hand began to shake as memories from the previous night returned. Looking down at my hands, all I saw was red.

Dripping from my hands.

Barely making it to the toilet I puked until I felt like the only thing that was left inside was my cold dark soul.

War was on its way and we were going in blind.

Time to unleash the beast.

TWENTY-ONE

Charlotte

*S*omething heavy wrapped around my waist in a tight hold.

I opened one eye then two. I was lying on a shirtless chest. Tattoos ran over and across some amazing set of muscles. Reaching over, I trailed my finger along the one over the heart; it looked like a coat of arms of some sort with writing around it that I couldn't quite read.

"Good morning."

"Good morning." Looking up, I smiled. "I wasn't expecting to wake up in your bed this morning."

"You fell asleep so instead of waking you I decided to bring you up here. Why? Disappointed?"

"No." *How is waking up next to this a disappointment?*

"Good. I like having you here." Pulling me up, he found my lips and ran his hand through my hair, giving it a gentle tug. I moved to straddle him. "Fuck, I really like it."

Well that makes two of us.

Deepening the kiss, he pulled me down, flipping us over, pulling back just a little and muttering something in Italian before his lips ascended on mine then down my neck.

Kissing and licking before moving back up to my lips. The wetness between my legs was inevitable. One leg hooked around him as I kissed him with everything in me, all while his big hands ran up and down the sides of my body pressing his weight down onto me.

His mouth swallowed the moan that I released at the feel of his arousal in between my legs.

And fuck it felt big. *Thank you, Jesus!*

A knock came from the door— we ignored it, but it came again and more persistent.

"WHAT?!" Lorenzo barked out between kisses.

"Sorry to interrupt but we are having trouble with the blueprints for the warehouse," Dante said from the other side of the door.

Lorenzo tensed. "I'll be right there." At the sound of footsteps walking away, he gazed at me with a rueful smile. "We have perfect timing, don't we?"

I giggled. "The best. It's okay. I know you're busy, plus I promised I would go shopping with Isabella today. Her company is part of the charity as well."

"It'll be nice to see her again. You don't work today?"

"No, but I work the next three days." My hand caressed his cheek, in the morning light the brown in his eyes was lighter. "At least I get a break today."

"You deserve it." Still kissing me, he pulled me up with him. "What are you doing after your shopping trip? Want to come over?"

"I was going to go to the gym, but coming over sounds better." I winked and totally realized I had been kissing Lorenzo with morning breath. "Do you have any mouthwash I can use?"

"Yeah, follow me. Oh, and… we have a gym here you could use but"—he slapped my ass hard; was it weird that I kinda liked it?—"I don't think you need it."

"Ahaha OUCH!" I followed him into a huge bathroom, where he handed me a new toothbrush from a drawer full of them. "Have overnight guests often?" I eyed him seriously and he was silent scratching the back of his neck. Was I slightly jealous? Maybe… but we did have lives before we saw each other again. I wouldn't tolerate it now, though, if we were going to…wait what the hell were we? I released a soft laugh. "I'm messing with you. You're obviously single, and… well…" I eyed him up and down.

Fuck, who wouldn't want to jump his bones, especially with that eight pack?

I literally counted them right now! *Jesus, you did a great job creating him. I'll make sure to light a candle for you as a thank you.*

My eyes made their way back up to his grinning face. Heat flared in my cheeks… Quickly, I turned back around and started brushing my teeth vigorously before I climbed him like a tree.

And then those perfect buns of steel moved in front of me as we walked down the stairs.

I prayed his jeans would rip when he bent down to grab my boots. I just wanted a small glimpse. Was that too much to ask for?

"Good Morning, Dante," I said when we walked into the kitchen for coffee and found him sitting at the table.

"Good Morning, Char." He smirked into his mug. "Nice night?"

I noticed his swollen hand and was about to ask about it when Lorenzo pulled me against him.

"Dante," Lorenzo said in a warning tone.

His cousin, it appeared, couldn't care less and just kept grinning.

Lorenzo released me, and I sat at the table while he picked up the coffee carafe and poured us both some morning brew. Tension hung thick in the air as I doctored my coffee then took a sip. Perfection! I decided it was time to ease some of the strain. "It was very… mouthwatering."

Lorenzo choked on his coffee, and I proudly sipped mine.

Dante chuckled and stood. "I like you, Charlotte. I'll meet you in the office," he said to Lorenzo before walking out.

"Mouthwatering?" Lorenzo raised a brow.

"Best pasta I've ever had." I got to my feet and put the coffee mug down on the white marble counter. "I have to go. Isabella is probably waiting for me."

Lorenzo nodded and walked me to my car.

But before I got in, he put something in my hand. "Buy anything you want."

I looked down at his Amex credit card. "What? No. It's okay, I've got it." I didn't want him to think I was with him just for interest.

"Charlotte, take it…the dress, anything you want is on me."

I leaned in and kissed him. "No, save it for the charity."

"You aren't like other girls, are you?"

I shook my head, handing him back his card. And I really wasn't. I wanted him, not his money.

"Alright. Text me when you're done, and say hello to Bella for me."

"I will." I sat and let him close my car door. With a light feeling in my head, I took off, hitting the call button on my console as I drove past the big gates.

"Wow, an overnight stay—details please." Isabella answered.

"Well, good morning to you too. Don't worry, I will. I'm on my way home right now. I just need to shower, and we can head out."

"Fine, but hurry up. The suspense is killing me."

"I'll see you soon." I hung up with a laugh and a smile.

I needed to contain myself. It was barely our second date— In a row, but still. Was it too soon? But it felt like it had been weeks, months… Being with him felt right.

But that was the problem.

It could all come crumbling down just as fast as it started.

*L*ater that afternoon, Bella and I sat at the Nordstrom's cafe grabbing a late lunch after we had spent the morning shopping for dresses, shoes, and maybe some extra stuff I didn't even need. I did not want to see my credit card statement next month. I might need to pull an extra shift or three.

"So, you're meeting up with him again tonight?" Bella asked, surprised.

"I am." I moved my food around, sighing. "Do you think I'm moving too fast? I mean I almost had sex with him this morning. Don't you think that a little too… you know?" The last thing I wanted was to seem too easy. But God dammit! It was getting harder and harder to keep my hands off him.

"Fast? Girl, have you seen him! I would have devoured him twice maybe three times by now."

For a second there I was about to throw my drink at her. For the first time ever, I was jealous.

She must have noticed the grip on my drink because she laughed. "I meant if I was you. Look, if you think you are then step back, take it slow. But if you feel like things are right and you like him, then go for it. No one is judging you. Charlotte, you are a twenty-five-year-old, independent woman if you want to have sex with someone you like GO FOR IT!" she said a little too loudly. The older couple next to us gave us a weird stare. "Sorry." Bella mouthed.

I giggled behind my hand. "Well, you just made their lunch interesting." They probably thought we were some hussies. "Okay, you have a point, and the truth is I want it! Freakin' been wanting it since Sunday…" I huffed. "Oh hell, high school."

"High school!" She let out a whistle. "Okay, so jump his damn bones already! But first finish your greens. You'll need all the energy you can get. You two are going to be like jack rabbits tonight."

The older couple looked at us again. The husband looked annoyed, but as soon as he turned around his wife gave me two thumbs up and said. "Order the kale salad, sweetie."

We lost it and laughed so hard we were holding our stomachs. We cried when she asked if I was on birth control. I answered yes.

A grin spread over her face. "Go get 'em, tiger!" And then she walked out.

Bella swore that was the kind of grandmother she wanted to be.

When we got home, I changed into some workout clothes. After all, he had offered his home gym. I wore my blush-colored leggings with the matching sports bra, my white Nikes and black fitted sweater that I'd bought earlier and just in case I packed a small overnight bag. I might not use it, but better safe than sorry because I had to work the next day.

I texted Lorenzo that I would be heading over in a few and walked into Isabella's room to say goodbye.

She was sitting on the bed, phone to her ear and looking pissed.

"Levi! No! Stop asking because I am not..." She blew out a frustrated sigh. "Fine, be angry, but you can't be stealing my ideas anymore... But...no...hey, don't!" She stared down at her phone. "ARRGH... He hung up on me. God I can't wait until Thursday once this presentation is over."

"Hey, I can stay home, and we can bake some cookies... I think we even have some tequila left. Maybe I'll tell you about Dante's muscles." I winked.

"No tequila please, muscles maybe. Is it an eight pack too?" She laughed. "Kidding... ugh I have to finish this presentation for Friday." She bumped my shoulder. "You look good! I like the whole workout vibe."

"Well, he did offer his home gym."

"Oh, yeah and where's the Stairmaster? His bed?"

"HA-HA, very funny." I walked toward the door. "It's him! Okay bye, love you!" I ran out at her laugh. "I'll say hi to Dante for you!"

"Don't you dare!" she hollered back.

I drove to Lorenzo's with butterflies in my stomach the

whole time and when I saw him walk out as I exited the car, they only intensified. Part of me told myself to calm down and take it slow, and the other part said run into his arms.

Guess which I did.

"Hey." It felt nice to be in his arms again. "You look ready to go for a run."

"Well, you did offer up your gym and I was thinking if you still had some work I would work out for a bit."

He pressed a kiss to my lips. "Actually I'm already done, need a workout partner?"

"Are you going to show me how to get those buns of steel?"

His laugh rumbled through me, shaking me to the core. "Let me just change. Head over into the gym and I'll meet you there." I followed the path he told me to take and dropped my jaw when I saw the gym. Here I thought it must be just a few weights and a treadmill; I was wrong. It was full of weights, three treadmills, a Stairmaster, sauna off the side, and a boxing ring in the middle.

No wonder Dante and Lorenzo looked like the Hemsworth Brothers.

I was just warming up on the treadmill when I saw him walk in through the floor to ceiling mirrors. Low hung gray sweats and a tight white shirt wrapped his perfect body. "I thought it was a small room with a couple weights, not full on 24 Hour Fitness," I said getting off the treadmill.

He handed me a water bottle from a fridge in the corner. "Oh, I don't do small… Ever." He winked.

I almost choked on the water but swallowed instead. Ha! Pun intended. Great, now I was thinking of his huge…

"Ready?"

"Ready." I stood in front of him, taking off my sweater and

flipping my ponytail to the side. "So, what are we doing first?"

He looked down at my sports bra and grinned. I guessed my plan was working. "You've boxed before?" He nodded over to the ring.

"I grew up with two brothers. One is in the army and the other is a cop. Please, they showed me how to defend myself and to shoot a gun." I didn't need to tell him that I asked my brothers to train me after what happened that night.

I didn't think it was worth an explanation of why I wanted to know how to kick a man's ass if he ever dared to touch me.

He blinked once, twice. "I don't know whether to be impressed or turned on right now that you know how to shoot." His lip twitched and he moved toward the ring. "Alright, show me."

We hopped into the ring, shoes off...and fuckin' turned on.

My brothers had not gone easy on me, for which I was thankful right now, because as gentle as Lorenzo could be with me, I knew that if he ever wanted to hurt me, he could snap my arm without even trying. So, when he advanced on me, I threw two jabs, surprising myself with the power I hit. And his eyes?

They just about soaked my panties.

But I wasn't about to back down. I spent the next several minutes stopping his hits, kicking where I could, and when he slapped my ass, I elbowed him in the stomach—hard. Pretty sure I knocked some air out of his lungs. I flashed him an innocent smile.

And what did he do?

He smirked, doing a small circle around me, eyeing me up and down. Stopping behind me. So, close I felt the heat radiate off him. I did my best to act unaffected...yeah, I had about ten seconds left of self-control, nine, eight, seven... It was starting to be pretty ridiculous how much power he had over me.

"One more?" He hugged me tight. "Okay, what now?" He leaned down and licked the top of my ear. I let out a whimper and felt his smile where his mouth lingered. Asshole. He licked again and I used it to my advantage. Leaning back, I pressed my butt into his groin and swirled my hips. Lorenzo tensed then released a groan.

Taking my chance, I bent forward quickly and grabbed his right ankle, pulled up…knocking him on his ass. But then I made the mistake of celebrating my victory too early, because next thing I knew my back was on the mat.

Lorenzo straddled me. "That…" His eyes were wild. "…was fuckin' hot."

"What, getting your ass kicked by a girl?" I teased.

"Yes, just don't tell Dante."

"Mmmmm, what am I getting for my secrecy?" I ran my index finger down his chest, tugging him closer to me.

But before he kissed me, he looked down between us. As if he were holding himself back, thinking if this was the right move or not.

I moved my hand to his right cheek telling him it was okay, only to have him flinch at my touch. Dropping my hand, I panicked, feeling like an idiot. My head turned to the side as I tried to move away. But he caged me in, turning my face back to him.

Only this time it stung because the light in his eyes had gone dark.

Did I read this wrong? Was it just me who felt something, wanted something?

An eternity seemed to pass. Waiting for him to say

something…anything. If I held my breath any longer, I was going to explode!

"Charlotte," he whispered, brushing my hair back. "I want you. I've wanted you for a long time now, but this between us…" He bit out a curse pulling back as he sat next to me. Crap. I knew what was coming, and I braced myself.

I sat up, eyeing the door.

I thought about running out—maybe that would be easier than hearing what he had to say. Because getting rejected by him would probably hurt more than anything. To me he wasn't just anyone. And I would rather walk out that door than be rejected… again. I made a move to stand, but he gripped my hand.

"I don't want a random hookup with you." He looked at me and spoke like he could predict the future. "I want to make you mine, worship you like you deserve, but I know the minute you know who I am… who I *really* am, you are going to walk out the front door forever. And honestly, I don't know if that's something I can endure."

I sat there processing his words.

The real him?

But like he said, I was not just anyone. Well he was the same to me and always had been. It was as if that night eight years ago had united us in a way that neither of us could explain. As if it were fate.

The same fate that brought is together now.

His head hung, unable to look my way any longer. Like it pained him to look at me because in his mind I walk.

Out that door I had been eyeing.

And maybe I should have but I wanted this, I wanted him… all of him.

"You couldn't be more wrong. When you say you want to make me yours…" I hooked one leg over his, straddling him. Taking his face in my hands. "I want to be yours just as much as I want to make you mine."

And as the words spilled out, I wondered if I could really endure whatever secrets he had.

TWENTY-TWO

Lorenzo

"What did you say?" I barely got the words out. Did I just imagine it or did she really just…?

"I want to make you mine. So, make me yours, Lorenzo, because I want nothing more than for you to be mine." The last word lingered on her lips.

Mine

My lips slammed down onto hers while her hands moved around my neck. My tongue coaxed her as I flipped us. Moving down her exposed neck, kissing the spot I'd loved this morning.

Her skin was so smooth against my tongue, and I couldn't wait to taste more.

To savor her like she was the last glass of fine wine.

And I was Italian; we knew how to savor a good bottle.

With each kiss, I lowered myself, and when I got to the top of her yoga pants, I asked. "Charlotte are you sure?"

She licked her lips. "I'll always be sure with you, Lorenzo, I promise."

"I vow to you that I will always protect you, and I'll do my very best to never hurt you." I moved up her body again and kissed her lips before moving back down.

Kissing every part of exposed skin.

Slowly sliding off her yoga pants…leaving her in only a pink thong and sports bra.

She sat up and pulled off my shirt, while my hands moved to remove her bra. Testing the weight of her breasts in my hands before pushing her back down. I sucked each nipple then nipped with my teeth, making her squirm. She whimpered when I took one in my mouth and sucked the perky pink nipple. With one last lick of each I kissed down her body, sliding her thong down and then throwing it to the side. I lifted her right leg and pressed opened-mouthed kisses on the inside of her thigh.

Charlotte moaned in approval.

I kissed all the way to her core. Running my tongue up her wet folds nearly combusting at her taste.

Como miele. Like honey.

"Lorenzo." She let out a breath. Moving her hands to the top of my head, she tugged my hair. It should have hurt, but it turned me on even more as I drank.

I was a man thirsty for more.

The more I had, the more I wanted.

"Ohhh, Lorenzo, yes…" Each moan she let out was fucking music to my ears, and even when her legs trembled on my shoulders, I didn't stop. Not until she came undone with my name on her lips. But I didn't stop drinking the sweet honey that poured out of her. I sucked her clit adding a finger, pressing her g-spot and drank as she climaxed again. As she bucked her hips, I ran my tongue up once more and pressed a kiss to each inner thigh before pulling up and admiring the perfection in front of me.

Her chest rose and fell in perfect synchrony.

Charlotte was a goddess, and she was mine.

"That was..." She tried catching her breath.

Instead, she tugged me down kissing me and started pulling my sweats down, and once off. She wrapped her arms around my waist and squeezed my ass. "God I've wanted to do that ever since I saw you in those tight jeans at the hospital." She smiled.

My heart exploded. I didn't think I would ever get over that smile.

"You could have just asked," I joked.

She smacked my chest and giggled before kissing me again, and then she tried to flip us over. I chuckled before I flipped us. She sat up bending down to kiss my chest.

Painfully, I closed my eyes as her lips touched my family crest. She didn't know what it meant, but one day she would. I just hoped I had time to tell her before she found out the ugly way.

I grabbed her hips and slowly lifted her to where I wanted her. With a cry she sank down.

Her inner walls clenched around me, adjusting to my length.

And nothing, absolutely nothing could compare to the feel of me inside her.

My heart almost gave out with every move.

Every bounce.

Every moan.

Unable to hold on any longer I rolled us once more and savored every single second of her with every thrust.

The ring could go up in flames, and I wouldn't even notice because I was making love to the one woman I always dreamed about.

The one I had been in love with back in high school.

❧

Charlotte

Stars clouded my line of vision…
Every thrust.
Every kiss.
Every lick. I couldn't get enough.

Lorenzo was making me feel things that no one else had before, but it was more than that. This wasn't just amazing sex. No, this was real. I felt it from the top of my head down to the tip of my toes as his thrust became deeper. All while his tongue tangled with mine. Wrapping my legs around his waist I brought him closer… crying out in such amazing pleasure.

He was mine, and I was his.

Locking his gaze with mine, he pounded into me. Giving me a peek into his soul. It was dark, it was beautiful, it was… everything I couldn't explain. But it was everything I wanted even with all the unknown. It was as if our souls were connecting through our eyes.

With a scream, I came undone as he pumped into me faster, sending me off the cliff right alongside him with my name on his lips. "Charlotte!"

Filling me with all of him.

It was like heaven was brought down in this very moment. The moment my savior made love to me.

With one last kiss he pulled out of me, handing me his shirt to clean myself off with. We lay together afterwards, catching our breath.

"Stay the night," he murmured into my hair as he rubbed his cheek over my head. "Because I don't think I can let you leave after this."

I laughed softly. "Getting a little possessive there?"

His lips found my neck. "With you... always."

"Mmmmm... well, I do have an extra set of clothes with me, for work tomorrow."

"Good." He pulled me closer. "Now let me feed you so you have energy later. What are you in the mood for? I'll place an order."

"Oh, I like the later part." I winked. "But I can cook something if that's okay with you."

"Fine with me, if we don't have something you need, I'll send for it." He got up and then helped me. I laughed while we got dressed. "What?"

"Oh, nothing, we just have to wipe down the mat before you guys train here."

He chuckled. "I don't think I'll be able to train without getting a hard-on." Then he slung one arm around me as we went into the kitchen to find something to cook.

And all I found was pasta, pasta, and more pasta. I tapped my chin. "How does pasta sound?"

"Ha-ha, we love pasta. We are Italian, after all." His cellphone rang, and he swiped the screen. "Antonio," he answered. Apparently, what was said on the other end was not good because pinched the bridge of his nose releasing a breath.

"Alright, keep me updated." He hung up. "Work is aging me ten years at a time. I need to answer some emails."

I studied his face then grinned. "Don't worry, you don't look a day past forty."

He made a face.

"Totally kidding...thirty-seven tops." I laughed, and he slapped my ass. "Go, I got dinner covered."

"You sure? I can order something instead."

I got on my tiptoes and gave him a kiss. "Go, I'll let you know when it's ready."

"Okay, call me if you need anything. Make yourself at home."

He left, and after opening every cabinet and drawer I finally had the pasta boiling and made a creamy sauce with sun dried tomatoes. Once the pasta was ready, I added some chicken and threw everything together, making extra in case Dante joined us.

Hell, I even made dessert.

Which surprised me. Who was I? I barely cooked for myself, yet here I was making a full-on dinner like Martha Stewart.

When everything was ready, I went in search of Lorenzo. But when I approached the office, I heard different voices.

"So we agree?"

"Yeah, we do whatever it takes to eliminate them."

What the fuck?

I was about to knock when a tall, beautiful man opened the door. Erasing my mind from what I just heard. Yes, he was that beautiful. It was as if David Beckham and Charlie Hunnam had a baby and somehow made it even more beautiful. Angellike.

Tall—like giant tall with ocean blue eyes, light brown hair, strong jaw line, and tattoos that peeked from his rolled up sleeves black sweater that hugged his bulging muscles beautifully. Even his side neck tattoo looked like a work of art.

I couldn't look away. Pretty sure my mouth hung open and was about to yell "unicorns really do exist."

What did I come here for again?

Oh, dinner. "H-hi, is Lorenzo in there?"

"You must be Charlotte." He held out his tattooed hand. I shook it then he released me and opened the door wide so I could walk in. But he was like a siren; I couldn't look away. .

Until Lorenzo cleared his throat and my cheeks heated up. "Stop flirting with my girl, Alessio." He was sitting behind his desk, looking every inch of the CEO boss he was even if he was still in workout clothes. Lorenzo stared Alessio down while Dante chuckled. Alessio just shrugged as if saying *not my fault.*

I rolled my eyes. "If you guys are done, dinner is ready. Just give me five minutes to set the table."

"No need, Char. I'll take this *stronzo* and set the table." Dante stood and pointed to the door, following Alessio out.

Lorenzo crooked his finger toward me lifting a brow. Yeah, as handsome as Alessio was, he had nothing on my man.

With a huge grin on my face I sat side saddle on his lap.

"Whatever you cooked smells amazing, but dessert looks even better." He kissed the spot on my neck that was guaranteed to have my panties melting off.

A lick and I don't think we would make it to dinner. "Mmmm I actually made some dessert."

"Well, looks like I'm having double today."

TWENTY-THREE

Lorenzo

I t had been years since the dinner table here was filled with laughter.

The four of us sat around the dinner table, eating the delicious pasta Charlotte had made –she wasn't Italian, but damn, I would believe otherwise. Her creamy pasta sauce had a similar taste to one my grandmother used to make when I was growing up. I could also see the look on my cousin's and Alessio's faces that showed their enjoyment of the meal.

Charlotte was no longer that shy girl I remembered from high school. She cracked jokes with my cousin, talked to Alessio like they had been friends for years and was not shy about sharing funny stories about her and her friends that had us all laughing until our stomachs hurt.

And with everything going on it was a nice distraction; having Charlotte there made it so much better. She brought light into a house I once saw as haunted...the house my mother died in.

"Oh, I almost forgot I have dessert in the oven!" She jumped from her seat and ran into the kitchen.

I followed quickly.

"She might be my dream girl." Alessio's eyes settled on Charlotte as she bent over the open oven.

I was ready to gouge his eyes out. "Mine!" I growled, sounding like a rabid dog ready to piss on her and mark my territory.

"Don't worry, Enzo. If he forgets, I'll take him out back and chop off his favorite body part, right buddy?" Dante padded his back.

"If you want to see my dick just ask." Alessio winked.

Dante flipped him off, which had Alessio howling with laughter.

We had been friends for years, so this was normal behavior. He came from a powerful family in Chicago... Agosti family. His older brother Marcello was their boss, and it was also the family that Dante's mother came from.

"Alright, I hope you guys like apple crisp." Charlotte set the white baking dish on the table.

"Is that what smells so good?" Dante was about to sneak a taste but Charlotte smacked his hand. Alessio and I both tried holding back our laugh at his reaction but without success. Nobody had ever said no to him, much less smacked him... well aside from his mother.

"I still need to grab the ice cream and bowls—no touching." We all held our hands up. "You touch and no dessert." She pointed at Dante and he shook his head quickly as he if were actually afraid. When she came back we served us each a bowl with vanilla ice cream on top.

Dante literally moaned on his first bite, which had us all turning in his direction.

"Should we give you two a moment?" I lifted my brow.

"*Vaffanculo.*" Fuck you. He turned to Charlotte. "Char, this is amazing."

"Thanks. Isabella gave me the recipe."

He choked on his spoonful at the sound of her name.

"Delicious, right?" She smiled innocently.

He hit his chest a couple times, Alessio smacked his back so hard he choked on the wine he was tipping back. "Wrong pipe." He barely got out. "Yes, it is. Make sure to thank her for it, I mean… um providing a"—cough—"good recipe." The spoon in his hand nearly bent from his grip.

"Don't worry I'll let her know *you* enjoyed her desert." Emphasis on *you* was not lost. Squeezing her leg, I gave her a look that said I know what you're doing. Her response? A wink.

After dinner, Alessio offered to clean up while Charlotte and I grabbed her stuff from the car. "Mmmm, that looks to me like you had plans on spending the night."

"Yeah, well your seduction went according to my plan, so…" She shrugged.

"Your plan?"

She yelped at the ass slap I gave her. "Good thing I like being seduced by you, *Charlotte*." I whispered in her ear as we walked in my room.

"Mmm, I'm glad you approve. Hey question, why do you call me my full name and not Char like everyone?"

"Because you have a beautiful name, and it should be said as many times as possible."

"Well, then, I will always call you Lorenzo."

"Good, because I love the way it rolls off your tongue." I leaned in behind her and whispered in her ear as my hand traveled between her legs. "Especially when my head is right here and you're screaming it out." I rubbed her through her leggings and groaned when I felt how ready she was for me. I bent her over my bed and took her from behind, until my name was the only word on her lips. When it was all over except the cuddling, I left her in my room getting ready for bed while I went downstairs.

Fucking happy that she was sleeping in my bed again.

"Aww, there's that skip again," Dante teased, interrupting my thoughts as I walked into the office.

I flipped him off. "Any word?"

He shook his head.

Earlier today, we had received news that the police had gone into the office of our dead associate, searching for answers. Someone had tipped them off, stating he stored drugs in the warehouse.

"It makes no sense how drugs were found when everything had been cleared out already." I pinched the bridge of my nose. "There's a code to get in where we have them."

The evidence the police had collected had been removed from the chain of custody, reported "lost," but that didn't mean that the two detectives on the case hadn't seen something already.

"Only answer is that someone went in after because the first time the detectives went to check the place out it was unlocked."

"And you've cleared everyone?"

"Antonio, Alessio, and I have checked everyone out. All clean." He ran his hand down his face. "Enzo, I have a bad feeling, after last night…what Alex said." He paused, a frown creasing his forehead. "I don't even know who to trust anymore."

"*Merda*!" Shit. "How long before police come asking for answers?"

Dante released a breath. "Tomorrow, but as far as they are concerned, he just worked for us. No personal ties. I personally cleaned that office before they got there. Just make sure to be at the office downtown all day, better they go there than come here."

I knew what he was saying. Charlotte's brother and best friend investigating me wasn't really the way I wanted to start my relationship off.

Dante stood and I saw the dark circles under his eyes. Last night must have been a long night. "Hey, there's more apple crisp in the fridge if you want it."

"Hmph." He rubbed his bottom lip with his thumb. "Never thought something so simple would…" He scoffed. "*Non importa.*" Never mind.

I knew what he felt and sometimes words weren't enough because as much as men such as us try to explain the darkness we carry inside, it can't be done.

There were no real words for them.

All we can do is claw our way back to ourselves.

There was just one problem.

The person we'd once been got further and further away as we clawed our way back.

That was why we held onto memories of who we used to be; because they were the only tie of who we once were or wanted to be. All we wanted was one person to be the one to bring us back from the cold, dark empty space.

Someone brave enough, strong enough to be the anchor that pulled us back or dove into the deep end and pulled us out.

Selfishly, I prayed that person was Charlotte because I had given her my heart. Losing her would be like taking a bullet right to it even if I knew she would be leaving a monster behind.

I walked into my room where she lay fast asleep. The moonlight from the window peeked through giving me a perfect view of her. On her side, one hand on my pillow and her hair cascading down her back. I laid beside admiring her long lashes, cute little nose, and kissed the small birthmark on her right cheek.

She stirred a bit when I pulled her toward me. "Goodnight, Lorenzo," she sleepily whispered.

"Goodnight, *amore*." Love. I kissed her forehead. "*Stai con me per sempre.*" Stay with me forever. I wrapped her in my arms and fell asleep to her light snoring… Yes, her snores lulled me to sleep.

I should just call Dateline and apply myself, given how obsessed I was with her. But I tried to appreciate all I could of her because I didn't know how much longer I had with her.

In the morning, I joined her in the shower and claimed her against the tile, giving her everything I had once again because I would always give her my all.

She had me completely, even if she didn't know it.

And because I was obsessed with her and scared of the future, I took her again before she left for work.

Tasting and memorizing because I was honestly terrified about what would happen after today's meeting.

TWENTY-FOUR

Katherine

"All I'm saying is, don't jump to conclusions." I had been trying to calm Julian down after he found out who we were going to question.

He wanted to go pay Lorenzo a visit last night, but I had stopped him since we didn't have enough evidence. And the little bit we had managed was now lost in the evidence locker. Shit, even with no evidence, I couldn't stop him. But I understood. It was his little sister. Colton and Julian were her only family.

"I'm not letting Char date someone who is bad news no matter how much she likes him." He pressed down on the gas, speeding down the highway. "I'll protect her from herself before I let anything happen to her!"

And so would I, and the evidence we had found potentially led back to Lorenzo, but gone, did no good. And what we did have wasn't enough. I always knew his family was powerful especially after that night in high school, one I would never bring up.

Especially not to her brothers.

We pulled up to the building downtown and I practically ran after Julian.

"Look I get it, okay? Just let me do the talking. The way you look right now, it's like you already found him guilty."

"What if he is?" he snapped. "Fuck, I should have seen something the day I met him."

And what could I say to that?

Lorenzo and Dante pulled out guns in order to save us back in high school, and at the time I didn't think anything of it. But now?

Now I wasn't a naive seventeen-year-old. I was a detective who knew having a gun at that age was not normal unless... nope I didn't want to think about it.

"Holy crap!" We stepped off the elevators to the Rizzi Energy floor, and I was shocked. "Are they hiring?" This was a dream office, with the open space concept with glass wall meeting rooms and offices. Couches and tables took up the space around and a patio with a green wall was off to the side with a view of downtown. It even had a full coffee bar... like Starbucks! "Where do I apply?"

Julian just glared my way.

"Hi, can I help you with anything?" The receptionist behind the desk stood.

"We're here to speak with Mr. Rizzi." Julian pulled his badge out.

"Okay, one second." One phone call later, and we were walking into his back office. It was the only one of two offices that had wooden walls from floor to ceiling and polished oak doors. Lorenzo sat behind a giant mahogany desk with a wall of windows behind him.

"Detectives." He stood and shook our hands. "Please have a seat."

"I think after last time you can call me Julian," said my partner. "And I hear you went to high school with Katy. First name basis?"

I knew what he was doing: act like their friend and they talk.

"Alright, well then call me Lorenzo." We sat and I could feel the tension radiating off Julian.

I cleared my throat. "Lorenzo, this is merely a formality. We just have a couple questions about Cino Marci. He worked for your construction company and was found shot to death a couple days ago."

"Yes, he worked for me. He managed some of our construction sites. It was hard to hear the way he died." He sounded upset.

"Would you happen to know anyone who would want to hurt him?" I looked for any signs of him lying; sweat, shaking of the leg, or movement of any kind.

"No, I don't. He was always very good at his job and treated everyone with respect." He didn't even flinch.

"Did you know that he leased a warehouse where drugs were found along with evidence of blood? We are running it through the system now to see if we have any matches on the DNA." Julian was lying, we had nothing. He just wanted a reaction.

"I knew he leased some property" Lorenzo nodded. "He rented to companies for storage space."

"Did you ever rent out the space for your…" Julian looked around the office. "businesses? He was in with some shady businesspeople." He asked in a tone that had me ready to kick him under the table. He needed to stop.

He was letting his personal feelings into the case, and I knew all too well what could happen. I almost lost my job last year, and I wasn't going to let the same thing happen to him.

"If you're asking if I ever did business with him… yes, I did. He worked for me. But no, I had no idea about his illegal dealings."

"So, if we look into your books, we won't find anything?" I asked.

He turned to me. "No, but if you like I can send them over so you can go through them."

"No need. We'll pay you a visit if we have any more questions." Julian stood, and I followed.

Lorenzo got up and stepped around his desk.

Then Julian stuck his hand out to shake Lorenzo's. "I hope we don't, though, for my sister's sake." He shot Lorenzo a stern glare.

Lorenzo leveled his gaze on Julian and held it. "I would never hurt your sister."

Great, a pissing match! God help me.

Someone lift a leg and pee on my friend already, why don't you?

"I sure as fuck hope you don't because the minute you do, I'm coming for you." With that Julian walked out leaving Lorenzo clenching his jaw.

"Sorry about that. Her brothers are very protective of her, especially now that Colton is away." A pang hit my heart. I missed him. He had yet to call.

And I had a bad feeling.

But I kept telling myself everything was okay.

"Charlotte told me about Colton. I'm sure he'll call soon." He said it like he actually cared.

"Thanks." We walked over to the door. "Oh, and if you hurt her, I'm planting the drugs we found and arresting your ass."

He froze.

A smile slid over my face. "Just kidding, but really... don't hurt her."

He chuckled. "I won't."

I walked back to the elevators where Julian waited with a murderous expression on his face. Once inside the elevators, he said the very thing I knew he was feeling. "There's something we aren't seeing."

Shit!

I had the same thought, and we were usually never wrong, but for Char's sake I hoped it was nothing.

I didn't want to be the one to break her heart.

Because the Rizzi name was attached to the warehouses and drugs; we just had no way to prove it.

TWENTY-FIVE

Charlotte

Finally, it was Friday and I was heading home. I had spent the last few nights with Lorenzo, and it had been amazing. The sex? Well I was getting turned on just thinking about it.

He was gentle but rough. The kind of rough I didn't know I liked but when given had my body humming and sore in the best possible way. But it wasn't all about sex.

There was a connection.

It had only been a couple days, but it felt like weeks.

Yet it scared me and felt so right all at the same time.

I told Lorenzo I wanted to come home and get ready with Isabella for the charity event. I missed her. She'd been busy with her presentation, and I was really excited to see how it went.

"Hey, I brought some dinner. I hope you're hungry." I made my way into the living room. "So how—"

Bella glanced up at me with red, puffy eyes.

Dropping the bags on the coffee table I rushed to her side. "Bella, what happened?"

Between sobs she barely got out, "He stole my entire presentation! I was the laughing stock of the company!"

"What! That son of a bitch!" I murmured as she laid on my shoulder.

"And since he went before me, it looked like I stole *HIS* ideas. When I comfronted him about it, he simply said he deserved the promotion and I should be happy for him. I broke it off right after."

"Happy for him?" I almost screeched. "Who does he think he is? If it weren't for you, he would have gotten fired a long time ago." Bella had done a lot of his work just to make sure he didn't get fired.

"I know! How could I have been so stupid all this time?"

"Bella, you aren't stupid." I pulled her up and wiped her tears with my sleeves. "You were just looking for that one person to make you feel wanted and deserved. The one who would hold you tight when you were upset, who would dance with you even if there was no music playing, and the one who could heal any injury with a kiss but most of all could make you smile more than he could make you cry." I wiped another tear. "Isabella Montgomery, you deserve a man who will spend every day of his life, showing you why he is deserving of your love, smiles, laughs and your soul."

"When did you turn into such a love expert?" She lifted a brow. "I think Lorenzo is seriously doing some wonders on you."

"Nooo, I've always been this knowledgeable."

"Sure." She hugged me. "I don't know what I would do without you."

"You'll never find out. Now, why don't we wallow our way through some sushi and ice cream?"

"Dragon roll?" She grabbed one of the plates. "So, for tomorrow you want to leave around noon for our hair and nail appointment?"

"Yeah, sounds good. Hey, I know before all of this you were going with Levi, but why don't you ride with us?"

"I would but I have to leave at five p.m., I offered to deliver some last-minute vacation raffle gift. I need to make up for looking like a failure today. So I'll see you there."

I gave her a look of sympathy but didn't say anything knowing full well it wouldn't help. "Okay, but fair warning, if I see Levi tomorrow, I might trip him and I hope he rips his pants in front of your bosses."

She let out a laugh. "Let's hope he is wearing his pink polka dot boxers."

"Oh God, I still can't believe he has those."

The rest of the night we watched Gilmore Girls and finished our dinner and I held her while she cried, because not only had she broken things off with Levi but her job was hanging on by a thread.

I had to give her some melatonin and tea for her to be able to get some sleep. By the time I looked at my phone, I had two messages from Lorenzo.

Me: Hey, sorry, I was with Isabella all night. She had a rough day.

Lorenzo: Don't worry, amore. I was busy with work all afternoon. Everything okay?

Me: Long story. I'll tell you later.

Lorenzo: Okay, get some sleep. I'll call you tomorrow morning. Sleep tight, amore.

I smiled and put my phone down, ready to crash. I was spent and tomorrow was going to be a long one as well. At least I would be with him tomorrow, spending a magical night together.

Lorenzo

I put my phone in my pocket after texting Char. I missed her, but I knew she wanted to get ready with Isabella tomorrow. Which was good because we were going over security for the event tomorrow with Dante.

"Okay, so we have the parking down, some of our men will be there in attendance and then we will check everyone who comes in," Dante explained.

"You sure we have everything covered?"

We had received an encrypted message at the office that afternoon: *"It will soon end, beg for mercy."* It might be nothing, but we could never be too sure... or too careful.

"If anyone tries anything, we will be on their asses long before."

I ran my hand over my jaw. "Okay, this event needs to go out without a hit." And I meant literally. I was not in the mood to shoot people tomorrow, especially since I was going to be with Charlotte.

"Trust us. Antonio and I are on it. Now, I have some news on the fun little visit you received the other day." Dante smirked.

Stronzo! Asshole! It was anything but.

"Keep that smirk up and see what happens to your morning coffee tomorrow."

"*Non lo faresti*" You wouldn't! "You know I need it."

"I thought you'd be happy after yesterday's morning coffee wanted to stay until dinner."

Dante grunted. "I need to switch to Starbucks." His little barista'd had to be thrown over one of our men's shoulders and carried out while she begged to stay. One look at our house and her eyes turned into dollar signs while planning a way to trap Dante. It wasn't the first time. Women just wanted us for our money and power. Thankfully, Charlotte was nothing like that.

"What's the word?" I asked him knowing our informants called in.

"Julian didn't believe you. He is doing some digging, but our guys are on it. You're squeaky clean. They have no proof that you did anything."

"They should take a look at my soul," I muttered. It was blacker than black, and my hands? Stained for life.

"We got this, Enzo. Don't worry, I'll let you know if anything changes." He stayed quiet for a couple seconds. Then, "We might need to hire another tech person. Ours can't do it alone, but we need someone we can trust."

"Not now. Get our men to help."

"Alright, so I think that's it. Remember, the car will be here by 5:30. It's best we ride together."

I nodded.

"Don't worry, everything is going to be fine," he said, patting my back before leaving.

I sure hoped he was right, because I sure wasn't feeling so confident.

TWENTY-SIX

Charlotte

By the time six p.m. rolled around, I felt like I had gone through an extreme makeover. Nails were painted, my hair was teased, pulled, put into a low bun with two strands of semi-curled hair to frame my face, and sprayed down with enough hair spray to create a hole in the ozone layer. My eyeshadow was a subtle bold to highlight green eyes, a nude lip to bring it all together and more setting spray than I needed.

If someone splashed water on me, I wouldn't even crack.

I was going to have fun taking it all off later.

My dress was black mid length black with thin straps, an asymmetrical neckline and a front split up my thigh. I was adjusting my nude strap heels when I heard the doorbell ring.

My mouth dropped open when I opened the door and was met with Lorenzo.

The black-on-black suit had obviously been made especially for him. The fabric hugged those muscular arms and legs I loved so much. The top buttons on his shirt were undone showing his tattoo. His hair was combed over to the side showing off his fresh cut.

Taking a step forward, he kissed me as one hand squeezed my ass. "I'm ready to lock you in your room for the rest of the night."

"Same could be said about you." Heat was already spreading. I never understood how just a few words from him had me ready. "But we would miss the event. Think about the kids."

"Mmmm…" he growled. "Let's go before I pop a stiff one and can't walk the rest of the night."

I laughed as we made our way down to the car. My jaw dropped once more when Dante stepped out of the black SUV. Damn, Rizzi men knew how to clean up!

He wore a tight-fitted black suit, white dress shirt, and black slip-on dress shoes. The matte black watch made his finger tattoos stand out, and his hair was combed back but tousled.

He whistled. "Are you trying to give my cousin a heart attack?"

"Hahaha, and you." I eyed him up and down.

Lorenzo cleared his throat.

I shifted my attention to his intensely glittering eyes. "Don't worry you are still my favorite Rizzi."

"Thanks for the reassurance." He tugged me against his chest making my heart flutter. I would never get tired of this.

"Okay, love birds, get in. We don't want to be late," Dante said, opening the back door.

Going in first I encountered Antonio, looking all CIA in his tux. "Hi, Antonio."

"Damn, Char you can bring any man to his knees dressed like that." Antonio winked,

A rumble emerged from Lorenzo's throat.

Dante chuckled. "Don't worry, Enzo, we know she's yours."

There went my heart again. I was Lorenzo's. Looking over at him and noticed that same smirk that told me, we were thinking the same thing.

Antonio drove off, and Lorenzo asked, "Hey, so is everything alright with Isabella?"

"She will be. It was a hard day at work, and she broke up with her boyfriend, not that I can say I liked the guy. I want to castrate the asshole."

"Remind me never to piss you off." Lorenzo chuckled at the same time Dante muttered something.

"What's that?" I asked.

"Ummm... no." He coughed. "I thought I forgot something but all good."

I gave Lorenzo a questioning glance, but he just shrugged it off.

A few minutes later, we arrived at the venue and pulled into the underground parking lot. Antonio parked by the elevators, and as we were getting off I could hear voices arguing. We all turn in the direction of the echoes trying to find where it was coming from.

"What's your problem?" asked an irritated male voice.

"You stole my presentation, Levi! That's my problem!" Bella was pissed and not hiding it. "Get *off* me!"

"Like you could ever win that promotion. What do you bring to the table besides your ass?" said the asshole who had brought nothing.

We round the corner and discover that Levi had her backed up against her car, trying to make a move on her.

"Oh, hell no!" I advanced, as the memories from

homecoming came flooding back. I saw red and wanted to hang Levi by his balls, but Dante stopped me with a hand on my arm and then stomped over in her direction.

They kept arguing so loud they didn't even notice us arrive. Bella kept pushing Levi away, but he just backs her up more.

"Get away from me!" Her voice is becoming high-pitched and a bit desperate.

"I think she has made it very clear she doesn't want you near her," Dante barks out as he approaches.

Isabella head snapped in his direction

Levi rolled his eyes. "This is a private matter, buddy. Now run along before I have security kick you out." Levi pushed off Bella.

Dante released a soft laugh. "I'd like to see you try. It's my fuckin' event…" He stopped in front of Levi and jabbed a finger in his shoulder. *"Buddy!"* He lowered his voice. "Now let her go."

Levi scoffed and stared down his nose at Dante. "Yeah, right. Fuck off and leave my girlfriend and I alone."

Before Bella had the chance to speak, Dante was in Levi's face. "From what I've heard, you're a dick and you two are no longer together."

"*I'll* decide when it's over." Levi grabbed Isabella and jerked her hard toward him just as we approach. His glare landed on me. "Ahh, Char, of course. They with you?"

"Let her go, Levi! You're a piece of shit that never deserved her." I was ready to claw at his face, but Lorenzo held me back as Dante stepped even closer to Levi. The guy seriously annoyed me, and I hoped Dante punched him. "Let her go asshole!" I repeated.

Levi tugged Isabella again, but she was able to shove him and pull away. She stumbled to stand beside me.

"You okay?" I asked.

She just gave me a shaky nod.

"You know what? Keep her. She'll repay with a good blow job and—" His words were lost to a grunt as Dante punched him.

Levi went down so hard his face hit the pavement. "Get near her again or speak bad about her"—he kicked him in the ribs—"and you will fuckin' deal with me. You hear me?"

"You will be hearing from my lawyer!" Levi cried out.

"Call him—I'm Dante Rizzi."

Levi's eyes went wide as he clearly realized he'd just fucked up.

"Antonio get this *pezzo de merda* out of here," Lorenzo said, and when Antonio grabbed Levi by the collar, Dante turned to Isabella. "Are you okay? Did he hurt you?"

"N-no I'm fine. Might need a drink or two though," she answered, her gaze flickering across the parking lot as Antonio dragged Levi away.

"Well, let's get you one." Dante held out his arm and after a moment of hesitation, Bella accepted it.

Lorenzo pushed the button on the elevator before us and the doors slid open with a whisper.

I even caught Dante staring at Bella as she walked in. How could he not? She looked *hot* in her emerald green satin sheen dress with a slit all the way up her thigh. It hugged her in all the right places. We followed them into the elevator, and Lorenzo pulled me into his arms as Dante drew Isabella to the rear of the car. "You think that—"

Lorenzo silenced me with a finger on my lips. "No matchmaking tonight."

I pouted. "You're no fun."

"Oh, I can show you fun." Leaning forward, he delivered a lick to my ear.

I released a moan while his hand traveled up my exposed leg. "Later, I'm going to rip that slit up higher," he murmured just as the elevator doors opened to the event.

Taking my hand, he guided me into the hall and I was in awe.

The event was held at the Longwood State Room, perched atop 60 State Street, a skyscraper that had a skyline view of Boston's city lights. Soft dim lighting casted a beautiful glow along the gold chairs and black table cloths. On the second level there were different photo booth stations, white couches, a second bar, and areas that displayed the prizes for tonight.

By the time we made it to our table, Dante and Isabella already had two drinks each in hand. "Well, I see you guys didn't waste any time."

"Nope!" Isabella knocked back her Champagne like it was Irish whiskey. "My boss is staring me down right now but he can fuck off for all I care. Oh, and this…" She lifted the other flute and gulped it down. "…was yours."

I gave a soft laugh. "Well, thanks for keeping it secure." I figured she was going to wake up hung over the next day, but she was laughing along with Dante, so it was worth it after the last couple of days she had.

In truth, we all deserved a night full of drinks and fun with no worries.

TWENTY-SEVEN

Lorenzo

"May I have this dance, Miss. Frizzell?" I held out my hand to Charlotte.

The raffles had just ended and we ended up raising 2.5 million dollars. Not to mention my personal donation in Charlotte's name, which brought the total up to 3.5 million. The smile on her face when she saw her name on the donation check was everything.

She turned her shining gaze on me, and her lips tipped up into another smile. "Why, I would love to, Mr. Rizzi."

We walked over to the dance floor, where I spun her and brought her close to me.

Holding her close to my chest as we swayed from side to side while *The Way You Look Tonight* played. Spinning her, I thought about how forever would look with her.

Marriage, kids, growing old together.

Her smile against my chest was enough to make my heart burst.

I'd hold her all night just to keep this moment forever burned in my memory. Her green eyes sparkled as she lifted her eyes to me. Taking a mental picture, I kissed her softly, soaking up the moment.

"Who's ready to get this party started!" Dante's voice came over the speakers.

Charlotte giggled against my lips as club-like music started playing.

I groaned. "I'm going to kill him."

She released another of her laughs. "No you won't. Look around." She nodded behind me and sure enough all of the guests seemed to be running toward the dance floor. "Come on, Rizzi, show me your moves."

"Yeah, cousin… show us your moves!" Dante said as he and Bella approached, each with yet another drink in hand. They hadn't set the drinks down since arriving.

"Enzooooo… drop it like it's hot!" A tipsy Bella yelled as she and Dante started dancing, still clutching their drinks. A little too close, I might add. Halfway through her spin, she tripped forward. Dante caught her but almost slipped when he grazed her breast. Bella tripped again, the drinks almost fell. Another groan slipped past Dante's lips when her butt touched his groin while he was saving the drinks. "Woo! Drinks are fine!" They finally stood up straight, cheered and knocked back their drinks then started grinding on each other.

Charlotte put her hand on her mouth and stifled a laugh.

"Something funny?" I asked, tugging her toward me.

She removed her hand and let out the laugh. "No! Now dance, mister!" She swayed doing a little spin, pressing into my groin. I was going to have a heart attack after seeing her move like that in that dress. "Show me what's in store for later," she whispered in my ear then backed up and circled her hips.

Cue heart attack!

With a groan I grabbed her hips and held them against me. Dancing the night away and enjoying every single minute of it, the four of us laughed, swayed, spun, jumped to every song that played. It was hard to think of a time where Dante and I just enjoyed the night.

When all family business was stored for another day.

We had been forced to grow up sooner than expected. I don't regret it, but sometimes it was nice to have a night where we could forget about it all.

After a few songs, Charlotte and I took a break to grab a drink, but when we got back to the table there was no sign of Dante or Bella anywhere. "Did you see where they went?" Charlotte asked.

"No idea," I responded when my phone dinged.

> Dante: Bella was tired. Took the SUV with one of the guards. Antonio already arranged another car for you guys.
>
> Lorenzo: Careful. I'll see you later.

I looked up and caught sight of Antonio, he gave me a quick nod telling me what I read was correct.

"Was that Dante?" Charlotte asked.

"Yeah, he said Isabella was tired and he took her home. "

She snorted in her drink, giggling. "In that case, I'm exhausted."

We laughed, enjoyed a dance, and shortly after that Antonio gave me the signal that our car had arrived.

"I had a great time tonight," she said, once we were in the

back of another SUV, and placed her head on my shoulder.

"So did I." With a kiss on her forehead, I sighed and then lay my head back against the seat.

And for a few minutes everything was fine… until the hairs on the back of my neck stood.

Something was wrong.

I could sense trouble before it even happened and one look at Antonio through the rearview mirror confirmed it. He hopped off the highway making a right turn then another.

We were being followed.

Cazzo!

By the looks of Antonio's driving, he couldn't lose them and was heading toward our office underground parking. Somewhere we could fully control the cameras.

Figlio di puttana! Son of bitch.

This was the last thing I'd expected tonight.

Charlotte was about to meet the man I never thought she would see, nor did I want her to see. The man who stood tall next to his demons in the name of family because he swore to protect them until his dying breath.

"Charlotte… baby…" I shook her knowing we didn't have much time as we were four minutes from the office.

She turned to me with sleepy eyes. "Are we here already?" She looked around. "Wait, why are we still downtown?" Her head snapped toward Antonio who was calling up for backup adding in the word kill. "What's going on… did he just—"

"I don't have much time to explain. I need you to listen to me very carefully." I reached under the seat and pulled out a gun. "You know how to shoot, right?"

"Y-yes, but…why?"

I handed the gun to her and pulled out my own, making

sure it was fully loaded as we pulled into our office underground garage. "Lorenzo?" Two cars pull in behind us amid screeching tires. "Who is—"

"Stay inside the car." I grabbed her face, gun in hand. "Get down and if anyone but me or Antonio opens the door, shoot."

"What? But I-I…" She looked back as guys got out of the cars, guns out. Her eyes watered and she started to tremble. "What's happening?!"

"Get down, baby, no one will hurt you. I swear it!" I spoke fast, already on the move to the door. "Shoot if someone gets near you, okay?"

Tears streamed down her face.

"Promise me!"

More tears streamed down, and I paused.

Holding her face close to me, I insisted, "I need you to promise me that you will protect yourself. *Charlotte*… Promise me!"

Trembling, she nodded. I leaned in and pressed a kiss to her lips before pushing her down to the car floor.

Antonio was already out, taking cover behind his door, gun at the ready. I hopped out of the car, gun raised.

After tonight we would never be the same.

She was about to see the monster within, and I wouldn't blame her for running the other way.

But I would rather she see the monster before I ever let something happen to her.

Three, no four men, approached with such anger. With no remorse, I shot one of them in the leg, showing them who the fuck was in charge. They wanted to play? Well, I was about to unleash the fuckin' monster.

"Who are you?" I snarled. "I'd start talking before I blow your friends' kneecaps."

TWENTY-EIGHT

Charlotte

I laid low in the car, clutching the gun to my stomach as more tears streamed down my face when a gunshot rang out.

I tightened my grip on the gun.

I couldn't see what was going on, didn't know what to do. *Should I call Julian? He could help.*

No! Lorenzo could get arrested. But what if he needed help? But what if he didn't?

FUCK!

What the hell was going on?

Is this what Lorenzo meant when he said I didn't know the real him? When he was scared to let me in?

What was he a part of?

I felt as if part of me already knew what his world looked like and I had just been turning a blind eye.

And if I was... did I want to be a part of it?

Could I?

Carefully, I crawled onto the seat, still staying low as I peeked through the back window, desperate to see what was happening. Lorenzo was lifting his gun as two other guys shot his way, but he shot back, killing one with a shot to the chest that would never be survivable. And then Antonio was pushing him out of the way.

At full speed, a car pulled in, sliding between Lorenzo and Antonio and the strangers, shielding them both from the shooters.

I threw myself against the car floor as more guns fired outside the window... many ricocheting off the SUV. I covered my head with my arms, the gun still in my right hand. Tears poured and I prayed for Lorenzo.

The noise got louder and closer.

At one point I thought I heard a semi-automatic. "Please God, please let Lorenzo be safe." The back window was broken, and glass rained over me. The shots got louder. I tried not to scream... to keep myself unknown. But it felt as if any moment now one of the bullets would hit me. So, when the bullets started hitting the seat, I screamed burying my head tighter against the floor, rolling into a little ball.

"Please God if something happens to me, let my brothers know I love them."

Then it stopped.

My ears rang in the abrupt silence.

Slowly, I raised my head but froze when I heard someone by the door, the handle being jiggled. I tried not to panic and remembered everything my brothers had taught me when it came to using a gun.

Taking a deep breath, wiping away the tears I aimed at the door, ready to shoot just like I promised.

And when the door opened, I fired off a shot.

BANG!

The guy flew back.

Only the shot hadn't come from my gun.

"CHARLOTTE!!" Lorenzo appeared two seconds later.

Jumping into his arms, I burst into tears.

"It's okay I got you. You're safe now," he said, checking me for any injuries.

I could barely speak. "I-I… What the hell is going on!"

"Later, right now we have to get out of here." He pulled me from the car.

Broken glass crunched beneath my feet as I looked around. My eyes widened in horror as I saw all the bodies that laid on the ground with their blood pooled around them. One of them was still gasping for air.

My nurse instincts kicked in and I moved to help him, but Lorenzo pulled me back. "Charlotte no!"

"What do you mean NO! I'm a nurse. I help people!" I shoved him away and took a step forward.

He gripped my arm and turned me back to face him. "I know, but he needs to die," he gritted out.

I stared at him like he was crazy. I didn't recognize the man before me. He looked like Lorenzo, but he didn't sound like him, didn't act like him. Then he no longer even looked like the man I was falling for, his face contorting into something unrecognizable when he lifted his gun and shot at the man's chest.

Like it was nothing.

Shaking, I turned to the man on the floor whose eyes were still open, lifeless.

I lost all sense of control—angry and terrified my hand flew across Lorenzo's face. His cheek turning red immediately.

And he took it like he deserved it.

"Why, Lorenzo…why?" Sobbing, I pounded at his chest. Then I was screaming, clawing. "Why did you kill him!" I shrieked. "Who the fuck are you?"

He stood with no discernable expression on his face, just watching my tears fall, and that pissed me off even more. I didn't know what flowed through me, I raised my hand again, but he gripped my wrist.

"Enough!" he barked out, chest heaving with eyes cold and dark. With no remorse whatsoever. My legs gave out at the sight, but he caught me before I hit the ground.

In the car he held me in his lap while I cried for what I just witnessed. For the guy I couldn't save. For feeling something for someone who had tried to kill me. For ignoring all the signs, I had seen. But especially for being conflicted in my feelings.

I wanted mercy on the enemy.

I wanted revenge.

What was right and wrong anymore?

My whole life, I wanted only to help others and when I became a nurse it was so rewarding and watching Lorenzo do the complete opposite tonight broke my heart. Deep down I knew, though, and yet I had chosen to ignore it.

By ignoring that part of him, I had fallen for him.

Was it love?

But how could I love someone who was a killer?

Or was I mistaking my lust for love?

When we pulled up to the house, Lorenzo carried me all the way to his bedroom where he sat on his bed with me still in his arms.

"*Amore...*" He wiped away my tears. "I am so fuckin' sorry. I never wanted you to ever be a part of this... Ever."

I couldn't move, speak... could hardly breathe. Nothing.

And yet in his arms, I felt—

Safe.

In the arms of a murderer.

I pulled back and grabbed his face connecting his eyes with mine. "Who are you, really?"

"Boss of the Rizzi Family," he said without skipping a beat.

"Boss?"

"Mafia Boss."

I reeled. My lungs stopped working. My heart hammered against my ribs.

Lorenzo was mafia.

At my silence, he let out a breath. "You honestly can say you didn't see it?"

I had seen it, I just chose to ignore all the signs. The private hospital wing, the guards, the guns all those years ago, tonight. I wanted to slap myself for being so naive.

Unable to be his, I stood and walked to the other side of the room. It all felt like a lie. Everything between us didn't feel real anymore. He had lied. Then again, how could it be a lie when he might have just been protecting me?

"Can I ask you something?"

He nodded.

"Why do you kill people?"

"Because they deserve it." He stood.

"When do they deserve it?"

"When they fuck with family, go against me, put those I care about in danger." He hesitated. "Threaten someone who is innocent in all this."

Against the family? What did he mean by that? My world was coming undone. Was this like in the movies where they...

"Do you deal with drug and sex trafficking?" I took a step back almost bumping into the wall, not wanting to know the response but I had to know.

My mind was running rampant.

"Drugs, yes. Sex trafficking, never. That's not what my family does. I would never hurt women and children. And for you to think that I would..." He scoffed. He had me there, because I knew he wouldn't, but it was nice to have his confirmation. "Anything else you want to know?"

"Were you ever going to tell me?"

"No," he said without even thinking.

And that hurt more than anything. Was he planning on hiding it from me forever?

As if he read my mind he said. "The less you know the better." He took one step forward and I took one back. "And for this reason, Charlotte! I knew the moment everything came to light you would be running the other way. Which you should. You have no idea what I have done or what I'm capable of doing. Once you see the monster, you'd be running out the front door leaving me forever and I don't blame you. Maybe I should have shown you who I really was before starting this with you. But I am a selfish motherfucker who couldn't let you go once he had you."

Hearing those words broke my heart because to me he was anything but a monster. Where he saw darkness, I saw light.

Even after tonight—after I saw him kill.

"You aren't a monster, Lorenzo," I whispered.

"Really! Because you sure as hell look like you're standing in front of one right now!" He threw his arms out as if to show me what I was looking at. Him. "I am everything that everyone warns their daughters to stay away from. The one under your bed, in your closet, in your nightmares… I am the very monster who has blood on his hands… all in the name of family. And I do it with a fuckin' smile on my face because I know I am protecting those I love. I should have stayed away but I couldn't. I fucking couldn't! Like I said…selfish bastard. You are my light. The person who brings me back from it all because with every soul I send to hell, a part of me dies. But it's unfair of me to damn your soul in order to keep even a sliver of mine. You deserve better than that, not…" He ran his hands through his hair, pulling on it. Hurting himself.

It pained me to see the struggle within him.

"Not the monster that puts your life in danger. So, if you want to leave, I'll let you go even if it fuckin' destroys me, because you deserve better than what's standing in front of you right now." He took a step forward, and I flinched, almost slapping myself for it.

It wasn't that I was scared. I was confused! He had scoffed at me.

"And the very one you fear right now!"

I stood there, refusing to move backward again, watching him clench and unclench his hands. Even in the dark I could see the pain.

He was struggling… as was I.

And even after everything, I still wanted to lay in his arms.

To just exist with him even if it was only for tonight.

To become one, even with the blood that stained his very hands.

To let it stain my body how it did his hands… to share any pain he carried.

To share it all.

Slowly I moved one foot in front of the other until I reached him. So close I was breathing in his whiskey scent that he released with every breath, drinking in his dark brown eyes and feeling the heat radiate off his body.

He stood there watching—waiting for my next move.

Rising on my tiptoes, I went for his ear. "You are anything but a monster to me, Lorenzo." I licked from his ear down to his jaw and up to his lips. "Far from it." I licked his bottom lip.

"Charlotte…"

I attacked his lips not wanting to hear his words. I needed him—all of him.

"Charlotte, wait…" He pulled back.

"Please," I begged.

"In the morning—"

"Forget about everything. Except for us in this moment. I need you, Lorenzo, the way you need me." It was all I wanted, all I needed. Even if the battle in me continued… because I knew he would never hurt me.

I kissed him with fury, and soon he reciprocated, walking me backward until my back hit the wall with a thump. Then he turned me around and pressed my body forward as his hand pulled the zipper of my dress down ever so painfully slow. Pressing open-mouthed wet kisses down my exposed neck and shoulder as the sound of the zipper taunted me.

It felt like the longest zipper in the world as heat pooled between my legs.

The dress was dropped around my feet as he spun me back around, leaving me in only a lace bra and thong before dropping to his knees. He brought my left leg up and propped it over his shoulder, slowly inching up my leg. His hand rubbed against my nearly soaked laced thong, making me quiver.

His touch was gentle, but knee-breaking.

One finger hooked on the lace he moved it over and swiped his tongue. Then let the cold air hit.

I threw my head back, hitting my head hard on the wall. Did I care? Hell no! I wanted MORE!

"*Miele,*" Lorenzo growled out. "My favorite flavor."

He pressed a few kisses on my propped thigh before he went back and swiped, sucked, tugged, and licked, my pussy again and again. Until I could barely stand. Playing with my clit while I begged for more. Barely standing on one leg, while the other was on his shoulder.

And as if it wasn't hard enough to stand up straight he added a finger, thrusting it in and out of me. I pushed back with my hands in his hair gripping to dear life and cried out.

"Lorenzo." I drew out his name like a sweet melody.

My craving for him was like my need for air. I craved his heart, his soul... even the darkest parts of him. I now understood his eyes the first time we joined our bodies together. The unexplainable was this part of him.

Daring to look down, my eyes connected with his, while his mouth continued to work me. Eyes dark and still raw from our argument showed a sliver of opening from his soul. My hand pushed back his hair and his eyes closed at my touch, diving in deeper to my pussy.

"Ahhh..." My knees started to go weak at the combination of his tongue and fingers. Bringing me over the edge only to pull out his fingers and keep going. Squeezing my ass in a bruising manner. Pressing me forward into his face as his tongue circled my opening.

Drinking everything that fell from me.

My breathing was erratic and just when I thought I couldn't anymore Lorenzo ran his tongue up my body as he stood and molded his mouth with mine. Giving me a taste of what he called his favorite flavor.

Unable to wait any longer for his bare body to touch mine, I ripped his shirt open—buttons went flying, the shirt came off—never once removing my mouth from his. With a squeeze of my ass he lifted me up and I wrapped my legs around his waist, feeling his hard abs underneath my wet core.

He walked over to the bed where he dropped me but not before unhooking my bra and sending it flying. At the edge of the bed, he stood, reaching for his belt while I watched hungrily, wanting the process to go faster.

Impatient for him to be in me, filling me.

Pushing myself onto my knees I pulled the belt off, unbuttoned his pants and pulled down. Licking my lips when I finally released him from his black briefs.

I couldn't take him in my mouth any faster…tasting him, savoring him as he held one hand on the back of my head. Pushing me down deeper and I fucking loved it. Moaning when I heard him in full pleasure, I sucked harder, swirling my tongue and taking him all the in.

"*Cazzo, amore!*" he roared and pushed me onto my back then leaned over me. "You're everything." He kissed me with a deep passion I never wanted to end.

My thin lace thong was ripped off, and with one fluid motion he thrust into me so hard and deep, stars appeared in my line of vision.

Lorenzo felt he was a monster, but he was so much more to me.

It wasn't lust, it wasn't a childhood crush, it was real.

I was in love with Lorenzo.

And because I loved him, my heart was torn between that love and seeking the right in what he did.

Would my love outweigh everything I ever believed in? Was I ready for his world? Most importantly was it ready for me?

TWENTY-NINE

Lorenzo

I was her fuckin' prisoner.

Fuckin' starving for her taste.

Her touch.

Her love.

When it came to her, I lost all sense of sanity.

Willing to kill anyone who got between us.

Charlotte moaned and screamed with every thrust I gave, each one deeper than the last and harder than I had before. Filling her. Giving her what she asked for but selfishly taking my need for her as well.

I was near the brink of the edge with her, feeling like it wasn't enough. I craved her like a man craved water in the Sahara Desert. I craved her entire being, her soul, her heart... Her love.

Pushing her legs open wider with one hand I massaged

her clit with my thumb. Taking the cries, she let out as a sweet melody. Until a loud crack hit the house.

Thunder rumbled, and it began to rain, heavy drops pelting the windows in a punishing downpour. It was like the heavens knew this was the end, and with each boom of thunder I felt her slipping away. Charlotte felt it and held in her tears as she dug her nails into my skin. She once told me thunderstorms terrified her, but in this moment, it wasn't the storm that scared her.

It was me.

"It will never be enough," I said thrusting in and out of her. I wanted her to remember me, remember us, remember this moment.

"Never," she moaned out as I sped up. "Lorenzo I'm... Oh fuck! No. Please." Her voice cracked.

We were both about to find release and I knew why she didn't want it to end. We knew what would happen after. "Let go, *amore*, let go," I said leaning in. Tears ran down her cheeks, and I kissed each one that fell. "Everything will be okay," I whispered.

She shook her head.

"Charlotte—" I kissed her, holding back my own emotions. It hurt me to see her spill tears for a monster that was unworthy of her. Slowing down my movements I tucked one arm under her and pulled her closer to me. "It's just you and me, baby, right now, in this moment. Just you and me." I held her face with my other hand catching the last tear.

"Just you and me." She clenched around me and finally let go. I caught her scream in my mouth, while I spilled everything I had into her. Holding her there for a few minutes before I pulled out and cradled her in my arms.

She was my everything.

My world.

My beginning and my end—and this felt like the end.

Because I knew her, and she was battling between my fucked-up world and her humanity.

So, I gave her everything in me plus more. All my love, my passion, my desire and my willingness to protect her. Showing her that she was mine and only mine even if this was the end for us.

Mine.

And I was hers.

I felt it in my bones that this was the end as I wrapped her tighter in my arms and a small tear landed on my family crest. It burned like acid.

A reminder of the cost this life brings. The cost of choosing family over love.

But why did I have to choose? Why couldn't we have both? I wanted to be selfish and lock her in the room for her never to leave.

I wanted to beg her to stay as she held on tight to me. But I couldn't bring myself to say anything because she needed to make the choice herself. Just like I once had. So I wiped her tears away, kissed her and held her in my arms until she fell asleep. Hoping that while she slept my demons didn't get to her and haunt her the way they did me.

Praying the light in her still shined.

I thought about my mom in that moment and the danger she was put in because of the man she had chosen to love. She had known the risk and even then chose to stay by his side up until the day she was killed while saving my life. My father never forgave himself for her death. One drunken night he confessed that he should have let her go. It didn't matter how much he loved her, how much his soul craved her, or the peace she'd brought him when she was in his arms. Her death was his fault for not letting her go sooner. He could have prevented her death even if it meant not having me.

Tonight was one of the first times, I felt like I fully understood his pain; letting her go would be far better than having her death on my hands. This was not her world.

I knew that she wondered if she could see herself in it.

I swiped away some of her hair from her face, tempted to wake her and make her mine once more. Instead, I kissed the top of her forehead and whispered, "*Ti amerò per sempre.*" I will love you forever.

With her in my arms I imagined a world where I was a normal man who fell in love with a beautiful girl. Living a life where I didn't have blood on my hands. But that wasn't a reality that could ever exist.

I was bound to this life and forever will be.

And I could never give it up.

In the morning when I woke she was gone leaving only a note behind.

I need some time. —Charlotte

I heard her voice in those four words, making it burn even more knowing it was the right thing.

In the shower I remembered her. How I had made her mine against the tile.

With a scream I punched that tile over and over again until it cracked. Until my knuckles were split and until blood ran down my hand.

The fuckin' irony.

Never would I ever be free of it.

One last punch. I welcomed the physical pain, replacing the pain of my shattered heart.

THIRTY

Charlotte

I couldn't stay in his arms any longer.

I was suffocating in my own body.

I felt safe.

And like I was on fire.

Last night's thunderstorm hit like a stab to the heart.

I could barely breathe. Let alone think. I needed to get out of that house for a moment and process everything.

And I couldn't do that wrapped in his arms.

So, I did the very thing I knew would break his heart-but did he know it hurt me even more. I was in love with him. I had asked him to make me his. I promised him I would always be his and I always would be, but I needed time.

Even if what I desperately craved was to be in his arms as he told me everything would be okay.

So, I wrote him a note and ran out, all the way down the driveway, and when Antonio yelled for me to stop, I froze then turned toward him. Tears still tracked down my face, I was wearing last night's clothes, with messy hair, and shoes in hand. So maybe he felt sorry for me, because he opened the gate, letting me go in to my awaiting uber. And I couldn't have been more thankful.

I need to be alone, a drink and… fuck! I didn't even know what I needed.

The world Lorenzo came from scared me. What would my life become if I stayed with him? I wanted him, but it was a lot to take in.

I was human and I was allowed to have fears.

I walked into the apartment and headed toward Bella's room. I needed advice.

My footsteps faltered. Wait, could I tell her the Rizzi family was mafia?

Dammit! I could always lie and say we had an argument and…

I stopped dead in my tracks when I saw Dante sneaking out of her room, quietly closing the door behind him. "Dante?"

"*Merda,*" He cleared his throat. "I, uh, mean good morning Char." He turned to me, tilting his head. "Everything okay?"

"Yeah." I looked away, crossing my arms. "So you and…"

"Yup." He coughed. "I thought you would be with Enzo this morning."

"No I…um…" My voice cracked and a small tear escaped.

His phone pinged, and he cursed under his breath when he glanced at the message.

"You know…" I nodded and he bit out another harsh curse, taking steps forward. "For what's it's worth, Charlotte, I know why he hid it, but believe me when I tell you it was safer to keep you in the dark."

"Why?"

"It's dangerous to know too much, and our enemies would use you to hurt us. It was the only way to keep you safe."

Apparently not so much after what happened last night.

"What am I supposed to do now?" Maybe this was a question for the wrong person.

"That's completely up to you." He looked back at Bella's door. "What I do know is you are going to need a friend right now… talk to her." He turned back and for a second just a small second, I saw something in him that I had seen in Lorenzo last night. But then he straightened up and was back to his normal expression.

Emotionless. So he, too, was a killer. But he didn't scare me.

Neither of them did.

"But what about you two?" I indicated Bella's bedroom door with my chin.

Dante stood to my side facing the front door. "Life isn't a fairytale. A beauty doesn't deserve a beast. No matter the amount of stories you read." Expression unreadable, he never took his eyes off the door. "We are all killers, Char, but compared to me, Enzo is a saint. He would burn the world for you. So, whatever you saw… just know…it was to keep you safe." With that, he walked out, leaving me more confused than ever.

When I walked into Bella's room, I felt as if my heart had been ripped out of my chest because she looked sated, content, almost glowing. So telling her the truth of things was worse. And as I had destroyed the magical night she'd clearly had with the truth, it became all the more real.

"I slept with a gangster?" Bella repeated for the third time.

She sat up, resting on the bed frame as I lay next to her staring at the spinning fan above.

"And I fell in love with one."

"You almost died last night?"

I nodded.

"Aren't we a complete mess."

I sighed. "You know what's the worst part?"

"What?" She asked, brushing my hair with her fingers.

"When he saw himself as a monster I never once believed he was, even when I saw him kill…" My voice began to crack. "Even with the blood stains. I knew it was wrong, but my heart still felt at home with him. I wanted to kill anyone who hurt him but save them at the same time because who are we to decide who lives and who dies? But for a moment… I wanted to have that power. I wanted to pull the trigger if it meant I protected him."

I hated feeling this way because I knew it was wrong. But then again what was really right in this world? Sometimes what we see as right is the exact opposite.

"Char…" She lay beside me, taking my hand. "Love is not always simple. It causes us to climb the mountain of doubt, swim the ocean of fear, and ride the roller coaster uncertainty." She squeezed my hand. "In the end it's only you who can choose what is best for you."

"But will loving Lorenzo change everything I believe in?"

"I don't think so because in the end you know who you are. And the Charlotte I know would never betray her morals— you will always be you, Char. You just can't help who you fall in love with."

I turned and smiled at her. "Thanks Bella, I don't know what I would do without you."

"And me without you." We hugged. "I'll never judge you if you choose him." Her words meant so much because I knew others would.

After a few moments of silence, I turned to her. "Soooo... Dante, huh?"

"Oh no, no, no. Don't even get me started." She jumped from the bed "I still can't believe it myself and even more so now!"

"Mmmhmm... what did you say—can't help who you fall for?" I sat up.

Her jaw dropped and then a pillow hit my face. "First of all, that was for you! Second of all it was just one too many drinks, and third..." She blushed.

"The sex was amazing?" I wiggled my eyebrows.

"CHARLOTTE!" She covered her crimson face, mumbling behind her hands. "Best I've ever had."

I clapped. "That's a ten for Dante Rizzi, ladies and gentlemen!"

Another pillow was thrown. "Damn the Rizzi men and their magical dicks!"

"Magical and huge!"

Bella turned even more red. I laughed so hard my cheeks burned, and soon after she was crying from how hard she was laughing.

It felt nice to laugh after a night full of crying.

And to help release some more stress, we hit the gym, inviting Katy and Ava along. After a quick discussion, we decided to keep the Rizzi secret to ourselves. I just invented something about taking some time after a big fight I didn't want to discuss. Although Bella did let it spill that she had slept with Dante after a couple glasses of wine.

For a while working out with my friends distracted me, but later that night in bed I held my phone in my palm, pulling up a picture I had taken of Lorenzo in the office working one day after I'd stopped by after work. I had walked in as he concentrated so intently on the file in front him, he didn't even notice me. I snapped a shot, and when he heard the click of the camera, he'd looked up and smiled. In seconds he was on his feet, walking toward me as I kept snapping pictures until he reached me. He had taken the phone from me and snapped a picture of us as he kissed me and another of us smiling at each other.

I fell in love just as quickly as it ended. Tears stung my eyes, and all I wanted was to run into his arms.

I didn't want it to be over.

Pulling up my messages I debated on whether to text him. But what would I say after leaving earlier? I'd wanted time, but at this point taking time made no sense. I loved him, so why couldn't I just go to him?

I typed a message then deleted it, typed another and also deleted that. Message after message, I typed then wiped out, about ten times over. Finally deciding on something simple and clicking send.

Me: I miss you.

The bubbles next to Lorenzo's name popped up and I waited, watching it like a hawk. Only to have them disappear. I waited for them to pop up again, but no more came.

It was like a second stab to the heart.

I'd let myself feel and hope for the possibility of us, only to realize that maybe we weren't meant to be. That maybe I really didn't belong in his world and he was letting me go.

Maybe it was a sign that a love between us could never exist.

The next day, I hoped Lorenzo would call or that I would find the strength to call him, but every time I tried or thought about it, I set the phone down. It was a game of tug of war in my head… in my heart.

With zero response, I doubted that he still wanted me after I showed my weakness.

The next couple of days passed in a blur of work, gym, home. Bella did her best to distract me since she had quit her job and was home every day. But even with her efforts, I always found myself thinking about him, wondering if he thought about me.

At night I lay awake imagining how my life would be in his world, and the more I thought about it, the more I saw myself in it. It didn't scare me. What scared me was the fact that I could see myself fitting into it so easily.

So willingly.

So *wanting* to integrate myself into it.

And night after night I lay in his gray high school hoodie thinking, wondering about it all.

On top of everything, my brother's lack of communication was worrying me. It was normal when he was on tour to go days without calling, but Katy couldn't shake the feeling of something bad happening. I told her if it did, we would have gotten news or worse we would have had two soldiers knocking on my door. Which I prayed would never happened.

Julian and I decided that a movie night might get her mind off things for a bit. And to be honest, it was a welcome distraction for me as well.

"Okay, no chick flicks," Julian protested, taking the popcorn from me.

"Please… you cried watching The Notebook. You love them." I laughed.

Katy snorted. "I think he did that in order to get laid."

"It worked." Julian winked.

The apartment door swung open, and Ava and Bella walked in with the pizzas.

"Julian complaining about chick flicks again?" Ava asked.

"I thought he got laid because he cried during the Notebook," Bella added.

We all started laughing and messing with him when my phone rang. My heart skipped a beat at the thought it would be Lorenzo.

It wasn't.

I stopped laughing at the sight of the number on the caller ID.

My heart dropped. Panic seized and I felt the blood from my face drained.

Bile rose in my throat as I stared at the screen.

I knew. I could feel it in my bones. And I just fucking knew.

Julian looked over and froze. His face mirrored what I could only imagine mine looked like. Everyone went silent at our reactions. With a shaky hand I tapped the green button.

"He-ello?" I answered.

"Hello, ma'am, my name is Colonel Derek Hastings," said a man's voice. "I'm looking for the family of Sergeant Colton Frizzel. I'm his commanding officer."

"Yes, this is his sister." My voice shook.

Colonel Hastings began talking, but the words all seemed to bleed into one another, not making a lot of sense. As the meaning of what he was saying crept into my consciousness, the phone fell from my hands and I cried out. Tears ran and Katy started crying in her hands. Ava held her as Bella ran to my side.

Julian quickly picked up the phone and walked into the kitchen.

"Char, what happened to Colton?" Katy asked between sobs.

I opened my mouth, but the words caught in my throat. I closed my mouth and painfully swallowed down the bile that had risen. Paralyzed, I stared ahead at the military picture of my brother on the wall.

My brother.

"Charlotte!" Katy yelled.

"H-he, um…they were out patrolling and… got caught in the line of fire and…and—"

"But how is he?"

"I d-don't kn-know. I couldn't…I—" Colton, my older brother who always made me smile when I felt down was injured, and I imagined the worst.

I had thought about him a couple days ago when I cried myself to sleep one night. Imagining him there telling me everything would be okay like he had when I was little.

Julian walked back into the living room, and Katy ran to his side, begging for answers.

"He suffered some injuries saving others who were part of his unit," said Julian. "They were able to get him help and stabilized him then flew him to the nearest military hospital. He wasn't able to call because of his injuries and Colonel Hastings wasn't allowed to until all of the survivors were debriefed."

"But he is alright?" I asked.

"So far, yes. He's being transported back home now. and I asked if he could be taken to your hospital."

"Yes, I can be there for everything. When does he arrive?"

"In a couple hours." Julian turned to Katy. "Colonel Hastings gave me a message from Colton for you."

"Wh-what?" She wiped her tears.

"He loves you and can't wait to see you."

Katy burst into sobs again as Julian held her.

My brother had fallen in love with Katy during the worst time in his life. When he thought all hope was lost and had nearly taken his life, but she saved him. In a way they both helped each other because at the time she was still dealing with the death of her father.

Without even knowing what was happening, they fell in love as they helped each other in a way none of us were ever able to.

Hearing that Katy was always in Colton's mind and heart brought me happiness that they had found each other.

If Katy and Colton were able to find each other during the darkest moments in their lives, would Lorenzo and I be able to find a way to be together?

THIRTY-ONE

Lorenzo

"How the hell is this all you fuckin' have for me so far?" I dropped the bloody knife on the table.

"Boss, we're looking, but whoever is behind this is good. Roberto is doing some digging into everyone in the family and all the company associates," Antonio answered, handing me a cloth as Dante walked into the back house. We had converted it into an interrogation room after all our warehouses had been made possible crime scenes.

He whistled low. "Still not talking?"

We all turned to the guy currently tied up to the metal chair in only boxer shorts. His face was bloody and bruised, and he dripped with blood from the cuts I had inflicted all over his body. I made enough cuts to know he would suffer from blood loss not die and if ,he started to pass out, I just injected him with adrenaline.

Antonio had brought him in because he was about to blabber all about our underground fights to the cops. It had been my fifth torture of the week, and it was only Wednesday. If you ever wondered if the mafia got down time? We don't. At least this was a good stress reliever.

"No." I picked up the hammer walking over to the guy while Dante and Antonio stood back. "And you aren't going to, huh?" I leveled with him. His eyes were nearly swollen shut.

He spat, leaving his bloody spit on my face.

Swiping two fingers down my cheek I laughed. "Real mature."

His response was a chuckling shrug, which looked ridiculous considering he was missing teeth. Yeah, I had pulled them. Good teeth, by the way; his dentist would be proud.

Laughing with him, I glanced over at Dante and Antonio, who were both grinning like idiots. They knew what was coming. I pulled the guy's hand and spread it on the table. He panicked and tried pulling back but I held it firm and lifted the hammer—smashing the top of his hand. Breaking bone.

"Still think it's a good idea to stay silent, motherfucker?" I swung again and then wiped the rest of my face while waiting for him to stop screaming.

Adrenaline must have kicked in, because he started laughing again. "You say you're a boss, but you've been so busy chasing tail, you haven't even noticed, have you?" He grinned as blood oozed from the side of his mouth and ran down his chin.

"Notice what?" I asked curiously.

He looked up. "Hmm, you really are blind, aren't you... *Capo?*" Boss. I was just about to punch him when a phone rang.

"Enzo, you got a call." Antonio held out my phone.

"What?"

"I think I found someone you might want to look at." Roberto voice came through sounding exhausted. "I'm at the downtown office."

"We'll be right there." I hung up and turned back to Dante.

The idiot in the chair laughed. "Enjoy the last days of the Rizzi name—soon you will be begging for your pathetic lives."

Dante pulled his gun, eyes black. "Want me to take care of it?"

"No." I swung the hammer one, two, three times, cracking his skull open. His blood splattering on the back wall and my face. "Roberto is waiting for us. Antonio, take care of this. I don't want any mistakes!" I walked out of the room, needing to change.

Dante followed behind. "You know one bullet would have been enough, right?"

"Yeah, well…I needed to release some stress." I said taking the stairs two at a time.

It had been nearly two weeks since I'd seen Charlotte. The last thing she had sent me was a text message that I couldn't even respond to. I wanted to let her go, wanted her to live a normal life, but every day I struggled with that decision. I fucking missed her as well and wanted her in my arms.

Letting Charlotte walk out of my life was the best and hardest thing I'd ever had to do next to burying my mother. The other day my father had come for a visit and noticed something was off.

"Ah I know that look. Who is she, figlio?" Son. My father stood in the frame of my office door. I had a bottle of wine open on my desk. One of Charlotte's favorites.

I forced a smile. "What?"

Chuckling, he made his way in. "Ah Enzo, you are my son. Blood of my blood... I know when something is wrong, and by the look on your face, I can only assume it's a woman." He poured himself a glass. "Chi è lei?" Who is she?

"Hmph...it's no longer important."

"Are you sure?" He swirled the red liquid around in his glass. "A man only drinks alone in the dark when he is heartbroken."

I was silent, just moving my glass around, taking sips. The taste reminded me of the way the sweet cherry tasted on her lips after she had a glass.

"Il suo vino preferito?" he asked into his glass. Her favorite wine?

I nodded, and we sat in silence a few more moments. I felt the burn of his eyes watching me, waiting for either one of us to speak. My whole life I'd wanted to be a boss like him, strong, ruthless, and well respected. But now... I was letting him down.

"Your mother used to say that you were an exact replica of me." He smiled, lowering his glass. "You may have my good looks, my need to protect others, and my character, but you have her heart. You love just how she loved, with her entire soul. And her eyes, while they scared the shit out of me when she was angry—God, nothing got past her." He chuckled. "She impaled my foot with her high heel one day at church for forgetting to say 'Amen.'"

I laughed, remembering. My father was the baddest mafia boss around, but when it came to my mother, she was the boss in his life. She was a woman to be reckoned with.

"You have her eyes, Enzo, not mine. You carry that fire in you. I know this life takes a toll on your soul, but you know that your mother gave you her two best qualities."

"You ever regret loving her?"

He sighed. "I did, once. Losing her was like losing part of me.

She was my world, the love of my life, the mother of my son...she owned my soul. She was my reason for living. I would have done anything for her. Even died a thousand deaths just for her to live and watch you grow. But life doesn't always do what we ask for." He released a breath. *"It's true, what they say, that it's better to have loved and lost than to never have loved at all. I tried letting your mother go many times, but she was resilient... she knew the dangers of this life. Yet she chose to stay, and for that I am grateful. The years I had with her were some of the best years of my life, and she gave me you. My greatest accomplishment."* He looked at me in a way he had never done before. *"I am proud of you Lorenzo; you are a better man than I was or ever will be. So no, I don't regret loving her because without her I wouldn't have you and it wasn't your fault she is dead either Enzo. So, whoever she is— don't ever regret it. Life gives you that one love, hold on to it, son. Fight for it, protect it, worship it, kill for it, and love it until your last breath."*

My father rarely showed compassion, so this moment was a rare one I didn't know how to react to.

"Thanks, Papà," I croaked out.

He stood, walked over, and gave my shoulder a squeeze. When I looked into his eyes, they were full of emotion. "Ti amo, figlio." I love you, son.

"Ti voglio bene anche io, Papà." I love you too, Dad.

He smiled, swirling his wine once more before lifting it toward me. "It was your mother's favorite as well." And with that, he walked away leaving me in my dark office, only illuminated by the moonlight. Alone with my thoughts of Charlotte and my mother.

"*Che cosa,* Dante?" What. On our drive to the office, he couldn't stop side glancing me.

"*Niente.*" Nothing.

He gave me a really sharp look. "You okay?"

"Stop asking and just do what I asked of you." I had told him to keep tabs on her to make sure she was safe. It was better this way.

We were approaching one of his favorite coffee joints. Sighing, he pulled into the parking lot.

"What are you doing?"

"Grabbing a coffee. I don't know about you, but I can't speak to Roberto without caffeine. The man literally puts me to sleep with all his explanations and go arounds."

"Fine, but just coffee, no special order."

Dante put a hand to his chest, acting hurt. "You think so little of me." And then he flipped me off.

I returned the flip-off because I knew him.

And point proven, I almost stabbed him when he flirted with the barista. Literally. My switch blade pointed at his ribs. Did that stop him? No, no it didn't. The girl almost fainted when he winked at her.

I was looking over some emails on my phone while we waited for our drinks when I heard Dante curse. Looking up my gaze collided with Bella and her sister.

"Enzo, Dante." Bella plastered a fake smile while Ava stared Dante down like she was ready to castrate him. Well, I guess she knew about their wild night. And good luck because if looks could stab he would be bleeding on the floor right now.

"Bella, Ava… How are you?" Dante acted unaffected. But the vein on his forehead was about to burst if he kept clenching his jaw.

"Good," Bella answered, tucking a piece of hair behind her ear. I swear Dante inwardly groaned at the sight of her exposed neck—he clenched his jaw tighter.

"Ava, it's nice to see you again. How have you been?" I asked, drawing the attention away from the frustrated pair.

"Good. You?" she responded with another murderous look. Well, I guess she wasn't my biggest fan either.

"Good, good." I coughed and looked around. Bella gave me a sympathetic look. "How is she?" I shouldn't have asked but it came out before I could stop myself.

Ava sighed. "She's doing good, considering—"

Bella elbowed her. "I'm sorry, Enzo, it's not really up to us to say."

"Is she okay?" I asked and Bella nodded just as our drinks were called.

Dante passed them around, brushing Bella's fingers as he handed her the latte. She bit her lip, he stared, and all of sudden there was way too much sexual tension in the air.

Ava felt it and rolled her eyes. "We have to get going." She practically dragged her sister away while Dante flipped me off while taking a sip of his coffee watching Bella walk away.

But just as they were out the door Bella pulled out her phone. "Hey we were just… What!" She yelled. "Wait, Char… I can't… calm down…shit!" I tensed at the mention of her name and at the thought of something being wrong.

Bella struggled to pay attention as Ava mouthed, "What?"

"Okay, okay, we'll be right there." Bella disconnected the call. "Ava, order the Uber!"

Before they were out the door, I grabbed Bella's, arm which had Dante growling behind me. I didn't give a shit. "Bella, what's going on? Is Charlotte okay?" She looked at me as if she didn't know if she should tell me. I lowered my voice. "*Bella,* is she okay?"

"It's her brother." Ava blurted.

"Julian?"

"No, Colton...he is in the hospital and by the sound of her voice—"

"We'll drive you!" I said instantly.

While Dante drove toward the hospital, Bella told me how Colton had been transferred from a military facility a couple days ago and upon arrival he'd suffered minor complications. They had put him into a medically induced coma, and something had just happened, but Charlotte had been too hysterical to explain over the phone.

When we arrived at the ICU waiting room Julian was holding a crying Katy. "Lorenzo, Dante, what are you guys doing here?" she asked when she saw us.

"We were at the same coffee shop when Char called," Bella explained while Julian shot daggers my way. "What happened? I thought he was recovering."

"He was... but he just suffered a heart arrhythmia right now," Julian said through clenched teeth, looking like he hadn't slept in days. Add the pain in his face to the mix? He looked older. From what I knew the Frizzell siblings were closer than a couple of peas in a pod.

"Where's Charlotte?" I asked.

Julian stared me down for a second then sighed. He obviously wasn't in the physical or mental shape to argue, and neither was I. I didn't care if he didn't want me near her. I would find her. "After it happened she walked away. She went that way." He nodded his head toward one of the corridors leading away from the unit.

Without another word I went in search of her, looking down each hall that intersected, in the stairways, supply closets and asked nurses if they had seen her.

My heart raced knowing that she needed me.

Cazzo!

How could I have left her alone to deal with this?

I should have texted her back, told her I missed her too. I should have texted and told her I would give her the space she needed while letting her know I was still there if she needed me.

I wanted to comfort her and tell her everything was going to be okay.

To hold her while she cried.

To take her pain away.

Fuck, how could I have let her go?

I loved her and I had let her go.

My father's words pounded in my head.

Fight for it, protect it, worship it, kill for it, and love it until your last breath.

Every hallway seemed to look the same... getting longer as I ran down them calling out for her.

Frustrated, I ran my hands through my hair.

"Where are you, *amore*?"

THIRTY-TWO

Charlotte

My head was spinning.

I wanted to yell.

Scream to the heavens.

My protector, my superhero, goofy, caring, honorable, loving big brother who was more of a father to me than my own was currently lying in a hospital bed in a coma.

Suffering a heart arrhythmia that was all too frequently fatal, and all we could do was, "Wait and see." Doctors' words.

I wished I wasn't a nurse in that moment. Maybe then I would be able to have some hope. Maybe then I could pray for a miracle.

I knew after all the trauma his body had endured his chances were slim. A painful awareness that I kept to myself when asked by Julian and Katy.

I had to get away from them. I hated lying to their faces

that were so filled with hope, because in a way I still wanted to hold out hope.

Locked in one of the supply closets of the floor I worked on I tried breathing through the pain in my chest. It was always empty here. A place I could be alone to think. Resting my forehead on one of the racks I closed my eyes. Calling up a special memory of my brother.

"Colton?" I whispered peeking through his door. It was the night before he was to leave for basic training, and a thunderstorm was raging outside. I was thirteen and still scared of them.

"Yeah, Char?" He sat up, looking at me, clearly knowing why I was there. "Come here." He pulled back the cover motioning for me to come under.

I jumped in and laid my head on his shoulder. "Do you think things will be different now?"

"Different how?"

"Well, you won't be home anymore, you're leaving me...who am I going to go to when there's a storm?"

"Pray lightning doesn't strike you."

I smacked his arm and he laughed.

"Kidding. Charlotte, you know I'll always be here, no matter where I am. The moment you need me, I will be here, plus you got Julian."

A knock sounded at the door. "I knew you would be in here," Julian said as he sandwiched me in between them. To others it might be weird to be in bed like this, but for us it was normal. The love we barely received from our parents, we made it up between us. Sometimes I swore my brothers acted more like a father than my own. Together we stared up at the glow in the dark stars Colton had on his ceiling for years. "So, you're really leaving tomorrow."

"Yup." Colton sighed.

This was the first time one of us would be separated from the others for so long. I didn't want Colton to leave but I knew it was his only way out, the only way he could escape our father's wrath toward him.

Julian held up his hand covering a star. Colton did the same, I held up mine, covering in the middle one and uniting all three hands.

"To the stars and beyond," Julian said, a phrase we had since I could remember.

"To the stars and beyond," I echoed.

Colton moved his hand, hugging both of ours. "Along with the stars we shine and burn for eternity."

Was it cheesy? Yes, it was. But it was something my brothers made up when I was four years old in a situation very much like this—during a storm where I cried and they each took turns comforting me. Our father was angry they had "played into my fear" but Colton told him off, and he was only eight. He was whipped and grounded for a month afterwards, but he couldn't have cared less. Plus, Julian and I always sneaked him in chocolates that he wasn't allowed to eat.

We smiled at each other just as thunder cracked and made the house shake…I jumped holding both their hands tight. They laughed. Angry at my embarrassment, I kicked one and whacked the other. "Not funny!"

"Good luck, Julian." Colton joked.

"You sure you can't take her with you?" Julian followed.

"Heeyyy!"

"Oh, come on, Char. If you left, who would I have to punk on?" Julian said.

I pouted until thunder boomed again and I scooted toward Colton.

He chuckled, hugging me with one arm. "If he messes with you, I'll kick his ass."

Now Julian acted hurt while I snickered. "Like I said, always there for you." I smiled up at him and hugged him tighter.

He was always my hero.

My chest ached as the tears burned in the back of my eyes.

I hadn't cried since the night he arrived to my hospital, so broken and battered. I wanted to stay strong for everyone. But it wasn't easy to be positive when all you wanted to do was roll up into a little ball and scream at God.

"Why!" I shook the racks. "He doesn't deserve this!" I hit the cold metal over and over until my hand went numb. Even then I continued.

I looked heavenward, angry. "This is bullshit!" With a grunt I threw back the rack.

Screaming, I threw supplies across the room.

My hope was fading, and I was angry! Furious because I couldn't do anything. Mad at the world. Livid with God. I grabbed a big box and flung it over my head cursing, allowing my tears to fall. Making a mess of everything—just like my life.

"What did he ever do to deserve this?" I shrieked to God, throwing anything I could get my hands on.

I had barely slept or eaten in days. Bella had to force me to eat a protein bar yesterday when I almost fainted after leaving a message for my parents for the twentieth time. They had yet to call back. It was like they forgot we existed or they didn't care what happened to their son. Julian tried to comfort me, but he was in just as much pain. And Katy was just as bad or worse.

So, I left Julian to comfort Katy.

And I tried to be strong on my own, but I couldn't anymore. The pain squeezed at my chest and I could feel every part of me breaking. I screamed, throwing one more box before I slid down the wall surrounded by the mess. Burying my face in between my legs. I wanted to call Lorenzo. To share my pain with him but he wanted nothing to do with me.

Not one call.

Not one message.

Alone.

I was alone dealing with my own pain as the last bit of hope was slipping from my fingers. I just wanted to be held for a second.

But the one person who I wanted had let me go without even a second thought.

Then again, that had been my fault. If I had just been stronger, realized that my love for him outweighed all the bad.

I wanted nothing more than to reverse time and never leave his side.

The tears cascaded, and I imagined myself in his arms. In his warm embrace while he told me he loved me and told me everything would be okay.

I craved the safeness he provided.

The strength he gave me.

His scent enveloping me.

"Charlotte?"

Snapping my head up I froze. "Lorenzo?" He stood by the door looking around the room at the disaster I had caused and in three strides he was there lifting me up in his arms. Giving me the comfort I desperately required.

"I should have been here sooner."

"H-how did you know?" I asked in between sobs touching

him, seeing if he was real or it was my imagination. But his warmth in my hands was all the confirmation I needed. And everything I craved was there, holding me.

"I ran into Bella at the coffee shop. I was with her when you called."

I hugged him tighter, and once I calmed down, we went to a private waiting room where I told him everything.

He was silent for a heavy moment after I finished. Then, "But there is still hope?" he asked.

"We need a miracle."

"Believe in the miracle, Charlotte."

"My heart wants to, but my head believes otherwise." My voice cracked. "How can your heart believe in something when you're torn between seeing reality and a longing for a fairytale?"

"Are you talking about your brother?" he asked softly. "Or us?"

I wanted to scream *"us!"* For days I'd wished he were with me after I received the news about my brother. I wanted nothing more than to be in Lorenzo's arms, but he had chosen to ignore me.

Had he not run into Bella, would he have come for me?

Pulling away from him, I stood. "Lorenzo... I—I just can't right now."

Standing, he turned me back toward him. "I know it's all too much right now, but Charlotte... It was a mistake letting you walk away, for not texting you back, for not driving to your house the moment you left, for not telling you about—my life sooner." He placed a finger under my chin and nudged my head up until I met his gaze. "I regret the things I didn't do, but I'm here for you now, tomorrow, next week, next month, next year. Always. When you're ready I'll tell you everything you want to know."

My eyes burned with tears as his eyes focused on mine.

"I love you, Charlotte."

A knot the size of a golf ball formed in the back of my throat, rendering me speechless. Did I just hear him correctly?

"I love you," he repeated. "Always will. My feelings are real. Like I said, I'll always be here for you. Never once doubt I won't rescue you but just know that a monster will be the one coming to your rescue, not prince charming. I am a killer and that's never going to change just like my love for you it's forever." He leaned in so close his breath whispered across my lips. "I will *fight* for you."

I opened my mouth to speak but was interrupted by a knock on the door. I pulled back. "Hey, the doctor came by and wants to talk to you and Julian."

Bella shot me a *sorry* look.

"Th-thanks I'll be right there." I turned back to Lorenzo. "I have to—"

"It's okay, go. Just remember what I said." He kissed my forehead and walked out.

My mind raced a million miles a minute.

He loved me.

And I loved him? I did. But what about everything else? How was I supposed to get past everything? Turn a blind eye?

It was all too much. My head hurt from all the thoughts running through my mind, and the closer I got to my brother's room the more it felt as if my brain would explode.

"What do you mean take him off the ventilator?" Julian yelled as I walked into the cold hospital room.

Instantly, I recognized Dr. Mika as the head resident on

my brother's case. She heaved a sigh and stepped away from the bedside.

"What's going on?" I could tell Julian was pissed, and the doctor looked uncomfortable. "Do you want to wake him up already, after what just happened?"

The doctor offered a tentative smile. "At this moment, I believe it's the best option. The coma might not be the best thing for him now."

"He had a critical heart arrhythmia today," I pointed out.

"I know, and we think it might be the medication we are using while he is in the coma that caused it. That's why I believe waking him up is the best thing." She glanced at Colton then returned her focus to me. "We will monitor him closely as we ease him out of it."

It was a risk, but I knew it was one of the only options. "Okay."

Julian shook his head. "Wait, Char, you think this is a good idea?"

I grabbed Colton's hand. "It's the only option we have, Julian. Trust me, or more important, trust his doctors. If they knew another way, they would be doing that right now."

Julian ran his hands through his hair, his breaths coming quick and harsh as he seemed to consider. Finally, he nodded his agreement.

After going over everything, we went to Katy to let her know, and while she was scared, she agreed since there was nothing else to do.

"I know it's not ideal, but I wouldn't have agreed to it if I didn't trust the doctors," I said.

Katy nodded.

"Hey, why don't you go get some rest? It's going to be a

while. I promise to keep you updated."

"Yeah, Katy get some rest. I don't think Colton will like those bags under your eyes. You look like hell," Julian said seriously.

"Julian!" Ava, Bella, and I said in unison.

Katy punched his shoulder. "This is why you're single. But you're right, asshole."

"Just keeping it real, partner." She punched him again as he laughed for the first time in days which earned him another punch.

"Alright, Mike Tyson let's get you home." Ava pulled her away.

After they left, Julian and I went back up to Colton's room, where they were getting things ready. Grabbing Colton's hand, I started to pray. I finished my prayer then began mentally talking to Colton. *Wake up, please, wakeup. I needed my brother now more than ever.*

Julian came up next to me, laying his hand on my shoulder.

We looked up and out the window into the night sky.

"To the stars and beyond, forever?" Julian asked.

Teary-eyed I said Colton's line. "Along with the stars we shine and burn for eternity."

THIRTY-THREE

Lorenzo

"I can handle this if you want." Dante suggested as we rode the elevator up to our office. Roberto was still there waiting for us. He had called us again to say he just found something else.

"She'll call if she needs me." At least I hoped so. I knew my words today gave her a lot to think about, but I was being honest—I would always be there for her though probably not always how she expected me to be. My life would always be mafia, and my love for her wouldn't change who I was.

I was born into this life. Bred to be boss. Sworn in blood to protect family. I couldn't go back on my oath—ever. Nor did I want to.

This was my life.

We walked into one of the conference rooms Roberto had been using for the past few weeks. It had a personal code to get in, making sure anything we stored in there was safe.

"*Ragazzi.*" Boys. Roberto sat, cigarette in hand, a wisp of smoke coiling from the end. The expression on his face made the hairs on the back of my neck stand up. Dante glanced my way, mirroring my own reaction.

"What did you find?" I asked.

He slid over a folder. "At first it looks like nothing... But then you get to this part." Roberto pointed. "It's—"

"What the fuck?!" Dante pushed off his chair so fast it flew back.

"What the fuck is this shit?" I looked at page after page, not believing what I was seeing.

"I went over it a hundred times myself." He ran his hands through his hair. "Everything right in front of us."

My cousin let out a string of pithy curses.

Rage burned the edge of my fingers. Standing, I flipped the table. "I have a fuckin' rat to kill!" I walked out, taking the keys from my cousin.

I pressed down on the accelerator, hitting sixty...seventy... eighty...pressing down harder, testing the limit on the M8. Bypassing car after car on the highway.

Through tunnel vision I drove.

Dante cocked his gun back. "How the fuck did I miss this!"

"It wasn't just you!" I took a sharp right turn burning tires. "Do you have his location?"

"I got that *figlio di puttana.*" Son of a bitch.

"*Cazzo!*" I slammed my hand against the steering wheel wondering how this was fuckin' possible.

Five years!

For five years he had worked with us, proving his loyalty, earning my respect. I had treated him like a brother only for him to go out and betray me. Five fucking years! "Open the fuckin' gate!"

Dante pressed some buttons on his phone and seconds later I made a hard left turn speeding down the long driveway. Slamming on the brakes when we got to the front door. We jumped out of the car and took the steps two at a time guns in hand. Our men around stared but knew better than to ask questions unless they were ordered to.

"ANTONIO!" I made a beeline for the offline, kicking open the door. "ANTONIO!"

Empty.

Only his phone sat on my desk.

"SHIT!" Dante pulled out his phone. "Alessio...we got a problem... Location on Antonio... I'll explain later... thanks I'll see you soon."

Going through his phone I noticed all calls were from Dante or me. Messages all erased, emails nonexistent, pictures zero. Everything was too clean.

We were accustomed to keeping our shit clean but this, knowing he was the rat we were looking for, looked a little too clean.

Right under our noses and I fucking missed it!

"Have Alessio look into this." I tossed the phone to Dante.

He inspected it. "Mother fucker knew we were coming. How?"

"That's exactly what I want to find out." I rubbed my hand down my face, walking out to the living room. "MANNY!"

Dante stood tall beside me, folding his arms as Manny walked over.

"Yes sir." He stood at attention.

"You see where Antonio went?"

He looked around, confused. "No sir, he hasn't stepped out today. He let us know a few hours ago he would be in the office."

"So, you guys never saw him leave?" Dante asked.

"We've been here all day, haven't seen him since."

Irritation crawled through me, leaving me even edgier. "What do I pay you guys for? You are supposed to be aware who is in and out of this house, Manny!" I pulled my Glock from its holster. Could I not trust my men anymore?

"Boss, we—"

I didn't give him a chance to finish. I fired my gun into his foot. "I don't need your excuses!" I barked out. "Clean yourself up and make sure you and the others do your fuckin' job. I want extra men here at all times."

"Yes, sir." He limped away, leaving blood on my wood floors.

I turned toward the bar and poured myself a shot of whiskey, gulping it down in one swallow. I was unable to feel the burn of the liquid because of the rage that flowed through my veins.

Our world was based on trust and loyalty. Neither came easily. So, when trust was given it was because you trusted that person with your life. And on rare occasions that person became part of your family. Antonio had been that person ever since he came to us. His grandfather and father had worked for us. Both of them loyal till the end. When they died, we took him in like one of our own. He bled Rizzi blood even before my family crest marked his arm. His grandfather and father must be rolling in their graves right now after seeing what he'd done.

This was unforgivable. He didn't deserve a quick death. He deserved to suffer for ever thinking he had the power to betray us and going back on his loyalty, his promise.

I would skin that fucking tattoo off.

Then I would kill him like the fucking rat he was. I didn't care who I had to kill in order to find him, because whoever was with him was against us. It was them or us, and I would make damn sure it would be us, the Rizzis who were left standing.

"Ready for the blood bath?" Dante poured himself a drink.

I knocked back my drink, Dante poured me another. "Time to unleash the monster and the beast."

We clinked out glasses together. "For family."

Our answer every time blood was spilled.

THIRTY-FOUR

Charlotte

Hours upon hours had passed.

Each one feeling longer than the last, waiting for Colton to wake up on his own. The clock on the wall ticked in mockery as the minutes, seconds, hours passed.

It was a waiting game that felt like the longest game in history. I begged God to allow the game to be over and award me a win.

My prize? My brother waking up.

I felt useless sitting in that chair next to him. Counting his breaths per minute, checking his pulse every few minutes, watching his oxygen levels and heart rate.

Going over every single scenario as to why he was taking forever to wake up. Remembering everything I learned and waking up in between naps in a panic thinking I had missed something, just to realize I hadn't.

At one point, Julian had to pull me away from the chair for a breath of fresh air, just so I would stop checking Colton's pulse every five minutes. I barely lasted ten minutes before I was running back.

Katy had come to check in on Colton but got called in to work. She and Julian had taken a couple of days off work but it was a big case they were working on, and someone needed to be actively working on it. She thought it was best for her to go in, and we promised to call her with any changes.

That had been hours ago.

We sat in that cold hospital room waiting for Colton to wake up blanketed by an awkward silence. Ever since Lorenzo had stopped by, my brother had been acting weird. I knew something bothered him when he saw Lorenzo, which was weird because when they had briefly met before, he seemed fine.

My phone dinged, looking down I smiled at the encouraging message from Bella.

"By the smile on your face, I can only assume it's your precious boyfriend." Julian's tone surprised me.

"Excuse me? That—"

"Do you really know him Char, know exactly what type of person he is? Because I do, and he's not someone I want for my little sister."

What the hell? "What are you talking about?"

"Let me guess, he didn't tell you that Katy and I interrogated him a couple of weeks ago?" I froze. "Yeah, that's what I thought. One of his workers was murdered, and the guy was tied to some shady shit."

A chill ran down my spine, as I remembered the night Lorenzo killed all those people to protect me. I knew what he was capable of, but I felt the need to defend him. "What does that have to do with Lorenzo? Doesn't mean he is involved with whatever the guy was involved in or his murder."

"Oh, come on, Charlotte, don't be so blind. He's wrong for you, and I won't stand by and let you get involved with someone like him."

"You won't *let* me? And someone like who, Julian? A man who loves me, cares for me, and protects me from—" I shut my mouth before I told him about that night. My brother was already suspicious of Lorenzo, and telling him about that wouldn't go over well. If I knew anything about my brother, it was that he was a damn good detective, and if he had suspicions about someone, they were likely true.

Julian stood, catching my last words. "Protect you from what?"

My brother had a way of reading people; it's what made him one of the best detectives in the city. He would stop at nothing in making sure his little sister was protected.

But I couldn't have him digging into Lorenzo's life, because sooner or later he would find out who his family was and that couldn't happen. Ever. I had to find a way to stop Julian.

I inhaled a breath and spoke in an authoritative tone. "Stay out of my love life. Don't you think you might be digging into his life because he is dating me?" I wanted to make him believe he was getting his work and personal life mixed.

"No! Listen to me, Char." Finger pointed he raised his voice. "He isn't good for you, and you will stop seeing him!"

I jumped to my feet, pissed he wanted to discuss this now. "You can't tell me who I can and cannot date, Julian! I am not a child. I don't say anything about you whoring all over town, do I?"

"That's different and if Colton was awake, he would agree with me." He challenged me, knowing how much I respected our brother and that I would do anything he asked me, especially now.

I opened my mouth to respond to his comment when a voice croaked out.

"No, that's... up to... me," Colton rasped, trying to pull himself up.

"COLTON!" we said in unison, and I threw my arms around his neck bursting into tears, pulling back checking if he was really awake then hugging him. "Thank God you're okay."

"Wa...ter." I poured the water from the pitcher into a cup with a straw and held it up to his lips. Slowly he sipped then sipped again. I set the cup down. It wouldn't be good for him to take too much at once.

"Had us holding our breaths there for a second brother." Julian squeezed his shoulder.

Colton chuckled with a cough. "Oh, come on I don't think I was that bad."

"That bad?" I moved to smack his arm but halted at the last second and just laid my hand on his wrist and squeezing instead.

"Ouch," he said, his eyes glittering as he feigned exaggerated pain. "Careful. Laying in a hospital bed, you know." He looked between us. "So, what's all this bickering about Charlotte's new boyfriend?"

Julian opened his mouth, and I shot him a *not now* look. He plastered a fake smile instead. "Hey, why I don't call Katy? She didn't want to leave but the station needed her to go in." He pulled out his phone and slid his finger across the screen.

"Hey, guess who... hello... hello?" He looked down at his phone. "I heard a gasp and a scream. So, I'm guessing she will be here soon and with *her* driving skills." Julian gave a low whistle. "I'm guessing... fifteen minutes tops?"

Colton's lips curled up at the mention of Katy's name. It was obvious how in love he was with her; she was everything to him.

"More like ten... you know she's going to use the sirens." I laughed, remembering the time she was late for a dinner. She'd used the siren and then flashed her badge at the host so as to not lose their reservation.

Dr. Mika choose that moment to look in on Colton. She checked his machine readouts and listened to his heart, examined his wound dressings, then deemed herself satisfied with his progress.

And, not even kidding, less than eight minutes later Katy ran into the room, out of breath, hair mussed. She came to a dead stop when she saw Colton sitting up.

"Detective Woodward," Colton said, eyes full of love

Katy's voice cracked. "Sergeant Frizzell." She ran, throwing herself at him. Face covered in tears, hiccupping and attacking him with kisses all over his face. We looked at them smiling, happy they were finally together.

Wincing Colton, he held her, nudging his head in her hair as if he were memorizing the way she smelled. "I just needed a little rest."

"Rest?! Don't ever scare me like that again!" She hugged him tighter. "If something happened to you I-I—" She couldn't finish her sentence because she started crying and muttered a curse to him about leaving her alone. He laughed it off and kissed the top of her head. "Never again, Colton, you got that?"

Pulling back, he held her face, kissing her softly on the lips, glancing over at us then back at her. I gasped…because without him saying a word I knew. I squeezed Julian's arm while he smirked.

"Marry me?"

Katy hiccupped. "Wh-what?"

"Every day I was away, your angelic face was the one that kept me sane. It's what brought me peace the moment I thought I wasn't coming home. Your voice was the one I heard when I was injured, *you*… telling me to stay alive. To come home to you." He cleared his throat. "I had this big way of asking you planned, but I can't wait any longer." Colton let go of her teary face and grabbed her hands. "Katherine Woodward, marry me because without you my life isn't complete. You not only own my heart, but my soul and I want to spend the rest of my life with you and all eternity as well."

There was a tense pause in the room as we waited for her to answer. I literally held my breath. Julian had his arm around my shoulder so tight I was for sure going to bruise. And Colton?

Well, he looked like he was going to go back into the coma.

"Yes!" Katy all but yelled.

I released my breath. She was really one for dramatics. I raced over to them hugging them, crying. Feeling something in my heart I had never felt toward them.

Jealousy.

Jealous of what they had. The love they shared without any complications, without worry of what their world would become if they loved each other, what their family would say once they knew.

No concern about the obstacles they would face.

My decision had been made long before Julian shared his thoughts on Lorenzo and nothing or anyone was going to change my mind.

I was going to lay claim to the monster.

I was in love with Lorenzo Rizzi, and it was time he knew.

THIRTY-FIVE

Charlotte

Five days since I last spoke to Lorenzo, four days since my brother woke up, two days since he had been sent home from the hospital, one day since Julian told him about Lorenzo, and twelve hours since I had last heard their warnings to stay away.

And I had stayed away.

Until now.

I was over for dinner at their place and it looked like it was going to be a dinner and a scolding kinda night.

How nice!

I stuffed my mouth with chow mein while they yelled. No literally! They were both talking over each other—I had silenced them fifteen minutes ago.

"Charlotte Juliet Frizzell!" Colton used my full name. Great. "Are you listening? You can't be involved with someone who Julian has some serious accusations on."

"But you don't—"

"But nothing, Charlotte, we're your older brothers. We want what's best for you!" Julian cut me off like I was a child. "And we will protect you before you end up getting hurt."

And I knew they would.

Ever since our parents had so graciously left me alone and gone away one day, my brothers had taken the responsibility of caring for me. Always overprotective, making sure no one would hurt me the way our parents had.

I rolled my eyes, stabbing my kung pao chicken. It was hard getting them to understand my reasons for wanting to stay with Lorenzo. Yes, he might be a mafia boss, but that didn't make him a horrible person.

Right?

Great, now they had me doubting myself.

I looked up at both of them, tuning them out as they continued going back and forth on my love life, each thinking they knew what was best for me. Sweet, but that didn't give them a right to dictate my life.

At one point I heard one of them say, "We prohibit you from seeing Lorenzo."

What the…

Irritated, I stood so fast my chair hit the wall. "ENOUGH!"

They both looked surprised, and to be quite honest so was I, but there was no backing down now.

Colton raised his eyebrow.

"I am a grown woman! You can't tell me who I can and cannot see. If I want to fall in love, make mistakes, and have sex, I will."

Julian coughed.

Colton choked.

I snorted. Clearly, in their eyes I was still a virgin. Ah, if only they knew. "And. Lots. Of. It!" I added. "Because I sure as hell don't tell you who to whore around with or who to marry!" I pointed to each of them in turn.

They both spoke at the same time.

"Don't say sex anymore." Colton's face went sour.

"Stop saying you have sex." Julian closed his eyes.

"Oh my God, I can't with you two!" And before they both said anything else, I walked out of there with my head held high and a destination in mind!

But first I needed to stop by the apartment to change and... I sniffed my breath...get rid of the kung pao chicken breath.

Yeah scrubs and Chinese food breath didn't exactly scream sexy.

After I brushed my teeth, I went through a quick outfit change that Bella picked out in five minutes while yelling, "Finally! Get 'em tiger, be happy. I love you, and please be careful."

Then I was on my way. She had put me in tight black ripped jeans, a low plunge black bodysuit, black leather jacket and handed me a red lipstick. I had to admit I looked hot! And I confirmed it by the cat call and the slap on the ass she gave me on my way out. Was she worried I was going to be with a mafia boss? Most probably yes, but she also knew he wouldn't hurt me.

I had risked losing my element of surprise by texting Dante asking where Lorenzo was, hoping he wouldn't be with him. By luck he wasn't.

So here I was getting off the office elevators with butterflies in my stomach. It was late, so the floor was dark and empty. Except for the light in his office.

Just as I was about to knock, Lorenzo's voice sounded from behind the door.

"Bring him alive when you find him, I'll deal with him. No one tries to double cross my family and gets away with it." He sounded beyond angry. "I am going to skin the *figlio de puttana* myself!"

A chill ran down my spine at his words.

"Understood, boss," someone responded, then footsteps came toward the closed door and before I could move out of the way it swung open.

And there I stood like an idiot staring at the huge man in front of me.

"Um, miss—"

"I—I um..." Why weren't the words coming out? And what did they feed this man when he was little? Muscle milk? He was a giant full of muscles that I was sure could break me using just one finger. I just stared; mouth open unable to speak.

I came here with a purpose, with courage and now...now I stood here like a lost puppy.

"Aaron, what's going on?" Lorenzo's voice came from behind the giant.

"S-sorry I—" I half walked and half ran toward the elevators trying to pry them open with my mind.

What the hell was wrong with me? I knew what his life would bring, so why was I running the other way?

I was about to turn around when a hand grasped my arm, tugging me back.

"Charlotte." Lorenzo's voice rumbled against me.

I turned into his embrace and retreated a step.

Dark circles framed the bottoms of his eyes, his hair was

a mess, and a little stubble grew along his chiseled jaw. His chocolate brown eyes connected with mine.

I wanted to scream his name and tell him I loved him, but instead I stood there, two feet apart, incapable of allowing my words to be released into the world.

Knowing that once they were out there… there was no going back.

The elevator doors opened. "Leave," he said to the big man, without taking his eyes off me. After the man got on the elevator and the doors closed, Lorenzo asked, "Why are you here?" His words were gruff.

My mouth worked, but no sound came out.

Taking a step forward he gripped tighter onto my arm.

My heart beat so fast I would have sworn he could hear it.

A step closer—I could smell the whiskey on his breath. His spicy cologne wafted around me. And the closer he got, the more his eyes revealed.

I wondered if mine revealed the same.

Love.

Lust.

Fear.

Or was the fear just in my eyes?

"Charlotte." My name came out in barely a whisper, as if it hurt to say. His eyes looking deep into my soul "Is everything—"

I couldn't anymore.

I knew what I felt and what I wanted—no matter how uncertain the future was.

Moving forward, I pressed my lips to his.

Electricity coursed through my body at the touch, jolting me awake from the nightmare I had been living without him.

I had forgotten what one kiss from him did to my soul.

He pressed hard before jerking away.

I wasn't going to hold back anymore. I was jumping in both feet into a world I didn't know—full of bloodshed. But one I was fully committed to because of my love for him.

"I don't want a prince on a horse, I want a monster with a gun and blood on his hands ready to kill for me."

His eyes studied me.

Seeing of those words really came from me.

"What are you saying Charlotte?"

I took a step forward.

A step into this life.

"I love you."

There was no coming back now and there was no way in hell I wanted to.

THIRTY-SIX

Lorenzo

Three words.

Three words, and I was attacking her mouth, pulling her into my embrace. Standing on her tiptoes she wrapped her arms around my neck.

"I am never letting you go again... ever. You're mine," I said against her red pouty lips.

She sucked on my bottom lip. "Yours. Always." She let go with a pop.

"I fuckin' love you, *amore.*" With a groan I picked her up. Her legs wrapped around my waist already unbuttoning my shirt. I walked us back to my office, kicking the door behind me closed.

I sat her on the edge of my desk, kissing down her neck, removing her leather jacket in the process and kissed her lower until I got down to her perky boobs that were spilling out of the shirt. Then licked my way back up.

My thumb ran across her lips. "Red...*il mio colore preferito*." My favorite color. She bit down, and it had me spinning, wanting to get more of her... to taste her once again.

She ran her hand down my opened shirt, stopping at the belt. Working in a frantic fury until she finally unbuttoned my slacks. Snaking her hand in and pumping me. Almost making combust then and there.

Her touch was my undoing.

I pressed opened-mouthed kisses to her neck and down her shoulder, where I sank my teeth in and she moaned, throwing her head back. While her hand still worked me—hard.

This was anything but a soft and gentle reunion. No, this was raw need for one another. It had been days, weeks, way too long without her touch. Pure yearning for each other's love.

I tugged off my shirt and then unbuttoned her jeans. She lifted, just enough for me to rip them off, shoes and all. Leaving her in only her sexy bodysuit.

Dropping to my knees I shoved her legs open wide, kissing and nipping my way up to her core. With a yank, I unhooked the bodysuit, and she gripped the edge of the desk when my tongue lashed out.

Never would I get tired of her taste. The way my tongue danced around or the way her back arched at my touch.

Too long deprived of her taste I drank as though I had become dehydrated.

Sucking her sweet juices.

Rehydrating my body, mind, and soul.

She panted, pulled my hair, whimpering at every lick, suck, and kiss I gave her. "Oh, my God!" She fell back when I blew against her wetness and added a finger. "Lorenzo I'm... I'm coming." Her legs shook, and I sucked harder, curving my finger. Making her explode all over my tongue.

And I drank.

Every.

Single.

Fucking.

Drop.

Standing, I pulled her up, kissing those soft red lips of hers.

Giving her a taste of her own pure sweet honey perfection.

"You're fuckin' perfect, *amore*." I pulled off her body suit and she pushed my pants down.

She wrapped her dainty hand around my length, spreading the wetness down with her thumb. Smirking, she held my gaze as she brought it up and licked it.

An animalistic growl erupted from my lungs at the sight.

"Make me yours." Her voice was like hearing the angels.

"My fuckin' pleasure." I flipped and bent her over my desk, and with a slap to her ass, I thrusted into her hard and deep. She cried out as she clenched around me while I held her hips in place for a few seconds.

Memorizing the feeling of her walls around me.

Pulling out just enough I started thrusting in and out of her, hard and fast. She pushed back making it even deeper. We took our ecstasy to a whole other level. And when I felt her getting close, I flipped her back over.

I chuckled at her protests, but I wanted to look at her as she came apart in my arms. Picking her up I carried her across the room and laid her down on the leather couch by the large floor-to-ceiling windows. Without hesitating any longer, I dove into her again.

The soft moonlight touched her face, and I still couldn't believe she was here.

For a moment it felt like a dream… until her hand pressed my chest.

With tears in her eyes she looked into my soul. "I don't care who you are… I love every part of you, Lorenzo Rizzi, always and forever."

My heart broke and repaired within a matter of seconds. She was taking a risk in loving me and accepting all of me.

Mafia boss.

Killer.

Man and monster.

At the end of the day, I was only human and just wanted someone to love me for me. No matter what I did in life.

Slowly I brought my lips to hers, coaxing them apart, my tongue tangling with hers.

With each slow deep thrust I spoke with the same conviction she had. "You own all of me, Charlotte. I don't deserve you. Yet you chose to love me, monster and all. I love you more than life itself, and I will die before ever letting anything happen to you."

She moaned, arching her back.

"*Sempre e per sempre amore mio.*" Always and forever my love.

A tear escaped from her big green eyes. "You're mine and I am yours forever."

That's all it took for both of us to go spiraling off the edge, screaming each other's names. Letting the world know who we belonged to.

Each other… Always.

She was here now, and I was going to protect her until my last dying breath.

No matter the cost.

"Can I ask you something?" She laid on my chest after some time.

I knew what she was going to ask me, I knew she'd heard what I told Aaron. I saw it in her face when I had chased after her. It was the reason she had run. Would she have left if I hadn't stopped her? Would she have told me how she really felt about me?

"Is it about what you heard?"

She nodded, gazing up, propping her chin on her hand.

"Hmph, you wouldn't have ran away if you hadn't." I tugged a strand of hair behind her ear "Would you have come back to me if I didn't go after you?"

The pause was three seconds long, but it felt like three hours.

"I won't lie to you and say it didn't shock me to hear you say what you said. My first instinct was to run. This world—your world… is new to me. I know everything you do is in the name of family, but understand I grew up with a different view of the world." She sighed. "I fought with my brothers because they don't think very highly of you…but I do. Aside from being a mafia boss, you are the man I love, and I know that you wouldn't hurt anyone who doesn't deserve it."

"I wouldn't, but you have to understand that there will be times I have to do things we may not agree on because I'm looking out for everyone to ensure their safety."

She sighed, and I waited for the other shoe to drop. "Just promise me one thing."

"What?"

"No more secrets. No matter how bad, I want to know."

"Charlotte, I can't—"

"Lorenzo, I just fought my brothers… knowing very well what I was walking into. I need you to be honest with me."

I ran my hand down my face, sighing. It was dangerous for her to know too much, and… it was dangerous for her to know too little.

"I'll make you a deal."

She lifted an eyebrow.

"No secrets, but if something is absolutely too dangerous for you to know, you have to accept the fact that it's better to know less then to know all of it and be in danger."

"Will you tell me once the danger has passed?"

"Depends on the reward for telling you."

She laughed.

I nearly whimpered. I had missed the sound of her laughter.

"I'll think about it."

I slapped her ass.

"Ouch! I said I'll think about it," she said in a sassy tone, smacking me back.

Missing her lips, I kissed her again. "Hungry?" I asked her.

She started running her nail down my abs. "Oh baby always."

"Okay." I winked. "But let's take this back to my place and grab some food on the way because don't think for one second I'm letting you go after you just came back to me." Kissing her, I squeezed her ass. "We have to make up for lost time."

She giggled some more before we got up, got dressed, and made our way downstairs.

"So, your brothers don't like me?" I asked curiously. I couldn't blame them because if I had a little sister, I would have locked her up from all men.

The closest thing I had to a sister was my cousin Gina, Dante's little sister, who lived in Chicago. The last guy she started seeing was her bodyguard and when Dante found out he flew out and shot him in the arm that was touching her when he caught them together.

A bit much? Hell no! They were seeing each other in secret, and what Dante did was a favor because others would have killed the guy.

Charlotte bit her lip nervously.

"What's wrong?"

"Well… you know how my brother Julian is a detective? They—" She sucked in a breath. "They're investigating you, and I think he might have told Colton about it." She couldn't look at me as we rode the elevator. "What's going to happen when they find out who you really are? They're going to force me away from you and lock you up."

I placed my thumb under her chin and tilted it up. "No one is taking you away from me, not even your brothers. As for the investigation… I already knew. I'm handling it; they won't find out anything."

She snapped her head back, shocked to find out I already knew about her brother asking around about me. Which was cute, but a man like me always had a few cops on our side.

I was running a multi-million-dollar corporation, legal and illegal. I had to make sure they were secure, and if that meant I had cops, FBI agents, and politicians on payroll to keep them running; I'd cut checks left and right.

"How did you…" She shook her hands in front of her. "You know what? I don't want to know. I just hope my brothers one day come around and like you."

"I'm a simple businessman, what's not to like?" I opened the passenger side of my car.

"HA! Yeah, simple is the word I would use."

Chuckling, I closed the door.

I'd had a shitty past couple of weeks, and suddenly it was all clear.

It was all because of her, the one person who had always brought light into my dark world. The moonlight on a dark night.

She was an angel amongst the darkness of my world. One she had chosen to be in because she loved me. And I loved her more than life itself.

This time I was never letting her go, because I needed her like I needed my next breath, and I would do anything to keep her safe.

From ever suffering the same fate as my mother.

So, when she asked me again about my conversation from earlier, I told her everything I could, because I had promised her. Still, she knew I still kept most of it from her but understood my reasons.

Understood that it was to keep her safe.

That night, I held her in my arms for the first time in what felt like ages with my heart bursting with love and a fucking smile on my face knowing she would be there in the morning.

Next to the monster for whom she had proclaimed her love.

THIRTY-SEVEN

Charlotte

"He is going to come around. Trust me." Katy poured some wine in her glass.

We were in the kitchen of my brother's place, celebrating his return home and their engagement with a few friends and family. My brothers and I were still at odds.

Especially after Colton had been at my apartment waiting for me after the night Lorenzo and I had gotten back together. The moment he saw me he knew. He'd walked out without a word and ever since then both my brothers had been distant with me. It was killing me. That had been over a week ago.

There was never an argument we couldn't resolve until this.

They might not understand my reasons for wanting to be with Lorenzo, but it didn't matter because I knew what kind of person he was. He wasn't one of those men you saw in the movies. The ones that killed because they were having an off day, treated women like shit and took advantage of the poor.

"I know. It's just that—" I sipped my wine and shrugged. It was hard to put my thoughts into words.

"It pains them as well, you know," she added, lifting her glass to her lips. "But they just want what is best for you. You have to admit, Lorenzo has his fair share of secrets."

"Wait." I sat up straight and stared at her. "You agree with them?"

She sighed. "Char, back in high school when he and Dante saved you from that guy, they did it with guns." She whispered the last part. "It wasn't normal. His family is into something and don't tell me they're not because I can back it up."

I remained silent. I couldn't lie to her, and I hated that I was lying by omission. The only person who knew Lorenzo's secret was Bella.

"Exactly my point. I didn't say anything to Julian." She let out a breath closing her eyes. "I won't ever say anything to him because not only do I believe you deserve happiness but because of what you told me and what I have found out through a little digging. He helps so many people. So, whatever he is doing is doing more good than harm." She squeezed my hand. "I'll do everything in my power to get Julian to drop the case, but he is my superior and if Lorenzo gets caught doing something illegal there is nothing I can do, Char. I am putting my job and relationship on the line as it is, so please be careful."

She was risking so much for my happiness, and I couldn't be more thankful. "Thanks Katy."

"Just please promise me you will call me the moment you're in danger, and if he hurts you, I'll chop his balls off."

I laughed.

She didn't. "Not kidding." Then she caved and laughed.

"What are my two favorite girls laughing about?" Colton asked as he walked in and draped his arm around Katy.

"How you cried yesterday during another Nicholas Sparks movie," Katy teased, and I pressed my lips together to keep from laughing.

"Ah no, I touched my eye after we ate spicy food… my eye was burning!" Colton defended.

"Sure, honey. Hey Char, bring some more wine when you come out, please." She kissed Colton's cheek and then made a face over his shoulder that said talk to her or else. And with that she walked out of the room.

Leaving my brother and me standing in awkward silence.

Dammit, Katy.

Colton scratched the back of his neck, avoiding eye contact. Rolling my eyes, I reached in the fridge for a beer. Closing the refrigerator door, I held out the longneck bottle to him.

"Thanks." He twisted off the cap, took a long drink and cleared his throat before we both tried to speak at the same time. He lightly chuckled. "Hey, I'm sorry for acting like a…" Cough. "I just want to protect you."

"I get it, but please trust me when I say he is a good guy. You only know what Julian thinks he has found."

"Okay, so let me meet him so I can make my own conclusions about him."

Shit, not what I thought his answer was going to be.

I wasn't very good at hiding my emotions, because my brother scoffed. "What? Don't want me to meet him? So, I guess Julian is right about him."

"No." I cleared my throat. What was I supposed to say? *Sure let's go have dinner and oh those guys in suits you see all over the place, yeah they are there just in case someone tries to kill us. Not the first time by the way. So red or white wine?* "I'll let him know, and we can double date." Maybe having Katy there would be easier.

"Make that a double date plus one. I'm coming too." Julian stood by the threshold. "A couple drinks maybe we'll get him to talk."

"Julian!" I snapped.

"I'm with Char on this one," Colton agreed, holding up a hand as if to ward Julian off. "If we meet him it's going to be as her brothers. Not as the law."

Julian popped open a beer. "You guys are no fun, but fine I can play nice. By the way, are we good? Because Katy is seriously one step away from causing major damage to my shoulder." He rolled it back a couple times. "She slaps or punches me every time she asks me if I'm talking to you again and doesn't like my response." He made a face.

"Fuck, tell me about it. She has been holding off—" Colton shut his mouth real quick.

I grinned. "Holding off what, Colton?"

Julian patted his back. "How long since the soldiers have gone into battle, Sergeant."

"Too damn long." He chugged his beer. "Purple shorts." He shook his head then downed the rest of his beer. "Char, please tell her we all made up. I'll do anything. You want a new phone, clothes, a hundred boxes of Oreos? Anything please, just get your brother laid by his fiancée."

"A hundred boxes?" I laughed. "Just be nice to my boyfriend or—oh, you know I think there is a Victoria's Secret sale. Maybe Katy wants—"

"I'll be nice!" Colton nearly whimpered.

"You better, or…" I moved to grab the wine bottle. "…

Katy is getting silk booty shorts as an engagement present."
I walked out of the kitchen leaving Julian chuckling while
Colton groaned.

Yeah, I'd just blackmailed my brother into playing nice,
but at this point it was the only way I had the upper hand. If
I had to beg Katy to keep withholding sex from Colton and
causing bodily injury to Julian's shoulder I'd be on my knees.

*Let's just hope from here until we have dinner nothing happens
that will put Lorenzo in the line of fire.*

Literally and figuratively.

With the recent betrayal of Antonio things had been on edge.
No one could be trusted.

Associates were tested, some were tortured in order
to know who they were loyal to. So many people from the
company were fired because they had worked under Antonio.
They needed people they could trust. So obviously, when they
started interviewing people for employment, I scored Isabella
an interview… she got the job of course. Not just because of
me but because she was good at what she did.

Rizzi Energy was moving into the tech world and Bella
was just the person they needed to get started. She thought
it might be awkward with Dante there but I convinced her it
would be fine. It was her dream job there was no way I could
let her pass this up plus Dante didn't really visit the office. He
mostly dealt with family business.

"Hey, Char…" Ava came up to me as I was serving wine.
"Do you know if Colt has any more ginger ale?"

"Ummm… I think so. No wine tonight?" I held up the
bottle of rose, and her face went sour.

"Not tonight. Bella and I had lunch at this new Indian
restaurant today, and I think the food was bad—"

"You think?" Bella came up behind her, looking a little green. "I knew we should've just had sushi."

"It was an hour wait and…" Ava's stomach grumbled and she winced.

Bella's laugh was cut short when she grimaced and clutched her stomach.

"Ohhh… let me see if I can find you guys some ginger ale to settle your stomachs." I turned toward the kitchen and walked past my brothers, who were laughing with a group of friends. Colton caught my eyes and gave me a small smile before going back to talking to his friends.

An invisible but very heavy weight lifted off my shoulders.

I just hoped it would last.

Searching through the fridge, I located some cold ginger ale and set two bottles on the counter. Taking advantage of being alone for a few minutes, I slipped my phone from my pocket and sent a quick message to Lorenzo, letting him know about the dinner with my brothers. Hopefully, he would agree.

Dante and Lorenzo had been out all day, following up on a lead of a group that was loyal to Antonio.

I knew what would happen once they found him, but if they weren't stopped the ramifications would be far greater. Kill or be killed, right?

My breath caught. Who was I turning into?

Was it wrong to justify someone's death just because I knew it would protect Lorenzo and his family?

Then again, I would kill for my family no questions asked.

THIRTY-EIGHT

Lorenzo

"*Merda!*" Shit. Sitting in the back of the SUV, I ran my hand down my face as I read the message from Charlotte.

"What? We leave someone alive? Want me to go back?" Dante asked with a smile on his face.

I studied him with a critical eye. "The fact that there is a smile on your face is a bit concerning."

Roberto had given us a possible location for Antonio's group of followers. It was at a restaurant in the outskirts of downtown Boston. When we arrived, the assholes were having a full-on party with enough booze for a hundred people, two girls per man, and our drugs laid out on the table. Our drugs! They had been stolen days prior. Even after we had changed everything about our shipping methods, routes, and dealers.

Meaning we still had someone loyal to Antonio in our midst.

We tortured them for answers, killed them, and then paid the owner of the restaurant a hefty amount to keep his mouth shut.

My clothes were covered in blood. Dante had splatters of blood on his face, arms…well all over. Apparently today he had some stress to relieve. Sliced off a guy's bottom lip because he thought his lip ring shined too much.

"Ehh…" Dante shrugged. "So, what is it? Char back at the house and you don't want to scare her? You know the girl is used to seeing blood. The other day she showed up with flecks of blood on her scrubs—took me a second to remember she works in a hospital. Chucked her water bottle at me when I asked who she killed. Laughed after, though." He laid his head back on his head rest. "We bonded over our blood stains and Oreos after."

From the front seat, Alessio chuckled. "Bloody stories and Oreos is how she relaxes now."

Cursing, I hid my smile behind my hand. It was honestly a little scary how fast she was getting used to all of it. Especially the last couple of days when we came home injured. She always had the first aid kit ready to go and didn't so much as flinch at our bloody clothes.

"She wants me to have dinner with her brothers," I said.

Dante whistled.

"I know." My problem wasn't that I didn't want to meet her brothers, it was a question of whether we could get along or not.

Overprotective brothers were nothing new to me but if they thought I was going to cower down just so they would like me, they had another thing coming.

I loved Charlotte, and they had to understand that, no matter who I was.

And if Julian's feelings were an indication of how Colton felt about me before even knowing met me then I'd assume we wouldn't be making it to dessert.

Scratch that—we'd be lucky if we made it to the main course.

"So, you gonna go through with it?" Dante asked.

"I have to meet them sooner or later."

"Well at least you met one already, maybe the other one won't hate you as much."

"Thanks for the vote of encouragement, *stronzo.*" Asshole.

He patted my shoulder. "It's what I'm here for. Hey Alessio, you hungry? Your turn to buy."

"It's been my turn the last five times," Alessio deadpanned.

"How could you possibly be hungry, you ate a burger on the way here." I asked my cousin.

"Yeah, and I just tortured and killed four *ratti.*" Rats. He shrugged. "I burned it off." His phone dinged, and a smirk grew on his face when he read the message. "On second thought head home, looks like I have a better offer."

Alessio looked back. I knew what he was thinking. Dante had paraded girls around for the last few weeks, fucking any girl who was willing to get Isabella off his mind. But it never worked, because he would drown himself in any bottle he could find afterwards.

After the charity event, a smile had been plastered on his face for two days before all hell broke loose. Then he started picking fights with anyone who didn't move out of his sights fast enough. It had gotten so bad Alessio was two seconds away from shooting his ass yesterday, had I not intervened.

Then again, there were days I wanted to shoot him myself just to get him under control. And seeing Isabella at the hospital had only made it worse.

If we thought my cousin was blood thirsty before, he was on a whole other level now.

He had dropped the veil that had masked the anger. A feeling I knew all too well.

He was wrong to do so, but I couldn't be the one to tell him that. He needed to see it for himself, understand that we were capable of love even with the many sins we carried. Like the ones that stained my very hands.

Just as predicted, Dante went straight for the bar and grabbed the bottle of whiskey the moment we got home, pouring Alessio and him a hefty amount while I went upstairs to wash the blood off me.

I threw my clothes in the trash, making a mental note to burn them later, then stood in the shower watching the blood go down the drain until it was as if it were never there. As if it had never touched me. The blood might have washed away, but the sin still stained my hands.

Who was I, thinking I was God in choosing who lived and who died while my reflection showed the opposite? While the demon stood beside me, taking another sliver of my soul and saying "good job, son."

After throwing on a pair of gray sweatpants, I grabbed my phone, needing to hear her voice. The only thing that brought me calm in a time of war.

"Hey," she greeted warmly, bringing the sense of peace I was looking for. "I was just about to call you. Can I come over?"

"You know you don't have to ask that, right?" I chuckled softly as I flopped back on the bed like a teenager. "Wait, I thought you were staying home with Bella tonight."

"Ava and her got food poisoning from a new restaurant they went to, soooo…"

"I might sound like a bitch, but thank God, because I wanted you in my arms tonight."

Her laugh washed over me like a soothing balm. "Send them some wine, and they'll forgive you."

A rustling, crackling sound had me pulling the phone from my ear for a second. When I brought it back up, she was breathing heavy. What the hell?

"Look out your window."

Pulling the curtain back, there she was—staring up, smiling. Looking every bit as angelic as ever. I wasn't even near her and my body was already reacting to her.

My vision switched over to slow motion as she came up the outside stairs, taking my breath away with every step she took. Hips swaying left to right. Her wavy brown hair bounced around her face, ready for me to tangle my hands in it.

Three steps away, and the scent of her sweet coconut lotion swept over me.

I licked my lips, ready to taste her velvety skin. I was obsessed, in love, intoxicated with all things Charlotte.

The woman who loved me, demons and all.

When she reached me, she didn't have to ask, she knew. Laying her hand on my bare chest she looked at me with those shiny big green eyes. She whispered, "Let me replace the memory with a new one."

And she did. Kissing away all that I carried around—falling into the darkness with me but brightening it up with the light that she was.

Later, tangled in the sheet, her head rested on my chest while I ran my hand down her slender back.

"Lorenzo?"

"Yeah."

"About dinner… Do you think it's a good idea? I mean with everything going on and Julian still investigating you—"

"Everything will be fine. Just don't order dinner because I don't think we'll make it that far."

She turned, one eyebrow raised as she met my eyes.

"Kidding." I picked up her chin. "I love you, and regardless of what your brothers say I am never letting go."

Her eyes watered. "It's always been the three of us. I don't want to lose them."

"And you won't. I promise."

Her lip quivered, and it broke my heart because she was torn between loving me and staying true to her brothers.

"They want to know who I am? Well I'll show them."

"WHAT?!" She sat up. "No, you can't! You know what would—"

"I am prepared to deal with them for you. I will do anything for you except let you go again. I can't live without you."

"But—"

"But nothing, Charlotte. Set up the dinner. You're off Friday, right?"

She nodded.

"Okay, we have three days, three days where it's just you and me."

"Then all hell breaks loose."

"It's a good thing hell and I are friends."

And wasn't that the truth.

THIRTY-NINE

Charlotte

A cold breeze brushed my face, and music blasted through my headphones and into my head, trying to stop the debate going on in my mind.

Lorenzo.

My brothers.

The mafia.

Family.

Picking up my pace, I ran past a couple holding hands, all smiles. I felt like punching them. Punching up the volume, I ran as fast as my legs could go—until they burned.

Even then I kept running.

Ever since Lorenzo said he would come clean about who he really was, I hadn't been able to stop stressing about what would happen once the bomb dropped. He didn't need to but he chose to—for me. It wouldn't go over well, but one thing was for sure; he wasn't going to jail even if I had to blackmail my brothers. I loved them, but I could not allow that to happen and that scared me. So, I did what I always did when I was stressed—I ran.

Especially today. I had gotten up early and had been running for the past hour. Were my legs going to be sore later? Probably. But dinner was tonight. I needed a distraction.

And by the looks of it, I was literally trying to run off my problems.

Ha! I wished it were that easy.

Just in case things went bad, Lorenzo had reserved the entire restaurant for tonight. It was the last thing we should be doing with everything going on. I suggested we postpone but he wouldn't have it. Said, the sooner the better.

A ringing erupted in my ears, stopping my music. I looked down at my Apple watch. It was Isabella. The food poisoning had hit her hard. And Ava was barely starting to feel better, herself.

I clicked the green button. "Hey, how are you feeling?"

"I have my head in the toilet—literally!" She gagged. "Never eating Indian food again. It's my first day, and I can't keep anything down. I have no idea what to do. I don't want to call out on my first day." She was supposed to start working at Lorenzo's company.

"Lorenzo knows you're sick. I'm sure he'll understand."

"I never thought I'd say this but—please have sex with him so I can get the day off."

I giggled then winced when I heard her gag again. "Ooo… Stay home. I'll call Lorenzo for you and on my way home I'll get you some medicine. Eat some ice chips for now."

"Thanks, Char you're—" Gags. "I gotta go. I owe you!"

She ended the call but not before I heard her puke.

Walking back to my car, I texted Lorenzo. When I left this morning, he'd said he had back-to-back meetings and would call me when he was done, and since he hadn't called I assumed he was still in one.

> Me: Hey, sorry I know you're in a meeting, but Bella is still very sick. I told her you would understand if she missed her first day, and if not, I would convince you.
>
> Lorenzo: Mmmm what kind of convincing?
>
> Me: Like the one last night.
>
> Lorenzo: Fuck Charlotte! Getting hard just thinking about it. About to ditch this two-hour meeting.
>
> Me: So we have a deal?
>
> Lorenzo: I was always going to say yes, but I'll take the payment anyways.
>
> Me: Cash in later tonight.
>
> Lorenzo: Oh, I will.
>
> Lorenzo: Tell Bella to take the time she needs and I will call you when I'm done. Ti amo amore mio.
>
> Me: I love you more, always.

I exited out of my messages with Lorenzo and sent Bella one. She responded with a ton of heart emojis and that she was going to take a nap. So, I drove to Target to pick up some medicine, and since she was napping I might have gone down every aisle adding things to my cart I probably didn't need—I swear Target hypnotized customers upon entering. Nobody I knew could walk out of there without spending at least fifty dollars.

After deciding not to grab another throw pillow, I stood in line. About that time, my neck began itching and tingling, like someone was drilling a stare through me. Slowly, keeping it casual, I looked around but saw nothing. I got the feeling of being watched again on my way to my car, but once more nothing stood out.

It's probably just your anxiety about dinner, Char. I needed a Xanax—maybe some wine too. Oh, wouldn't that go over well at dinner? Drunk and drugged. Well at least then I wouldn't be such a nervous wreck.

For now, I blasted my music and sang completely off key to Starboy by the The Weeknd on my drive home to relax my nerves. I had just come to a four-way stop when an alert pinged on my phone. It was Colton confirming for tonight and I made a mental note to respond to him once I got home. Then I tapped on the gas, pulling forward.

But an SUV blew the stop and almost collided with me. Thankfully, I pressed the brakes in time, swerving my car to the side. It almost hit my back passenger side.

What the fuck? Who was this idiot? If there was one thing I couldn't stand it was reckless drivers.

It took me a moment to get my composure back, looking toward the idiot who needed some driving lessons when I heard the screech of tires.

My head snapped to my left where another black SUV appeared.

Full speed.

In my direction, with no sense of stopping.

And then time stood still and everything slowed down.

Frozen in terror, I sat there gripping the steering wheel.

With no way out.

I just watched.

Everything in slow motion.

How it connected with my car. How glass flew all around me and how my body slowly fell into darkness.

I heard Lorenzo voice in those moments. His voice silencing out the noise from the outside. Calming the pain that invaded my body.

"I love you until eternity, Charlotte."

And then...

Complete and total darkness.

FORTY

Lorenzo

"**N**ext time you feel like torturing me, just shoot, stab—shit tie me up and throw me in the pool. See how long I can hold my breath instead of"—Dante threw his knife at the conference table—"this bull." He hated our quarterly review meetings.

To be honest so did I. Losing my tie, I stared through the large conference room windows overlooking the city. We still had one more meeting to go, and I was just about ready to stab my eyes. "I need a fuckin' drink."

He cursed. "No time. We've got visitors." Dante stood adjusting his jacket.

I turned, spotting Julian and Katy at the front desk.
Merda!
"Only one reason they would be here."
"The restaurant. *Fuck.*" They made their way toward us but

were stopped by our receptionist. "Call our contacts on the force and Alessio. I want to know what the fuck they found." We walked out of the conference room.

"Detective Frizzell, Detective Woodward." Dante greeted.

Julian looked from him to me, holding his gaze, clearly trying to intimidate me. Keep trying, brother-in-law. We were both matched for height, but in muscle I still had some bulk on him. I would have liked to see him try and take me down. Tension radiated between us.

Katy cleared her throat. "Sorry for the intrusion, Lorenzo, but we have a couple questions for you. Then we'll be out of your hair." She smiled and looked over at Dante. "Nice to see you again, Dante." She gave him a look of, *I know you slept with Bella.*

I suppressed a smirk. Those girls sure stuck together.

"Well…" Dante coughed. "I'll leave you guys to it." He turned on his heel and headed for his office.

"Follow me." I led Julian and Katy back to my office in silence. The strain between us thickened by the second, and by the time we sat, it was so tangible anyone who walked in here would probably choke.

It didn't help that every time I looked down at my desk, I remembered Charlotte's naked ass, legs trembling and my name falling off her lips. My dick jumped at the memory. Right in front of her brother. Who was giving me the death stare.

"So, you had a couple questions?" I asked in a cool manner.

"We do." Julian's tone was aggressive. "Six bodies were found in the marshes in the southeast side of the city."

On the inside, I turned into the Hulk, huge and filled with rage. But on the outside? Complete and total control. "And that concerns me why?" It wasn't possible. We always cleaned up once we were finished with an operation. Every location we used was thoroughly wiped down for fingerprints, the bodies burned in a crematorium with an owner we paid for the after-hours work, though he was carefully *not* connected with the Rizzis, and what little remained after that disposed of in landfills in another state, not in Boston saltwater marshes. Our cleanup crew consisted of loyal men, and—I just discovered the rat that was working with Antonio. I offered a bland stare as I mentally checked off our disposal measures.

"Two of them worked on your construction crew for Rizzi Construction," Katy interjected, giving me a look and before I could figure it out, she looked away from me..

"Rizzi Construction employs many people in the city, and I—"

"This is the second time we visited you on account of murders that are connected with your family, what do you have to say about that?" Julian said angrily.

I balled my fist. "I think you mean family *business*, not my family."

"No, I mean your family," he countered.

"Julian!" Katy raised her voice.

He was really pushing my buttons. Hard. But if anyone talked about my family, and I didn't care who it was…I would defend them. *I'm sorry, Charlotte.* Setting my elbows on my desk, I stared him down. "What about my family?" I was about ready to lunge across the surface between us.

He stood, setting his hands on the desk, looming over me. The same desk I had fucked his sister on. I gave him credit, anyone else would have shit their pants at the look he was giving off. But me? Never.

"You know exactly what I'm talking about," he said with a growl in his voice.

As a boss no one disrespected me like that. I wanted to shoot him, but he was Charlotte's brother.

"Your *family*… " He said it as if he had dirt in his mouth.

I was going to kill him! I pushed off my chair, making Katy jump to her feet. "My family is not your concern!" I barked.

"It is my concern if my baby sister is dating you!" he roared, pointing a finger at me as he stood to his full height.

"Julian, this isn't about Charlotte," Katy tried intervening. But it was no use, there was no going back to playing nice.

"Are you investigating me because there is actual evidence or because I'm in love with your sister?" I walked around the desk.

Julian got in front of me. "Listen up, you idiot—"

"Idiot? The Fuck?!" At this point, we were nose to nose. "Who the fuck do you think you are, talking to me like that?" We both start yelling over each other while Katy tried pushing us apart. We were each seconds away from throwing a punch. Only reason I hadn't swung was because Katy was in the middle and I refused to hurt her.

"I'm Char's older brother, that's who I am, fucker!" He tried to move Katy but she was resilient.

"I don't care who you are, I won't let you disrespect me in my own goddamn office!"

"Both of you calm down!" Katy had one hand on Julian's arm and the other on my chest.

"NO!" We both shouted at the same time and pushed her back, both of us lifting fists, ready to throw it down in my office.

The sound of my door hitting the wall so hard it shook had us turning in its direction.

Dante stood at the threshold, eyes dark, breathing heavy, phone in hand.

Nothing.

Absolutely nothing could have prepared me for what came out of his mouth a second later. "They took her!"

My legs almost gave out as my world came crashing down around me... *They took her.*

They took her...

Panic surged throughout my body as those three words, eleven letters. hit me like a bullet to the heart.

"Took who?" Julian asked, looking between my cousin and me.

I didn't think. I just acted.

All I saw was red as my rage built.

I walked around my desk and pulled out my gun from the top drawer then started barking out orders at Dante, who was already opening a hidden safe and pulling out a black bag. Not giving a flying fuck that two detectives are in the room.

"What the fuck!" Julian bellows out and levels his gun on me. Katy had her gun out and aimed at Dante, which he ignored as he just walked by her. "Put the gun—"

"It's Charlotte!"

They froze at my words.

"They took her! I don't have time for your fuckin' bullshit right now! I need to find her!"

"What do you mean they took her? Who? Where the fuck is she?" I could hear the worry in Julian's voice but he doesn't lower his gun. "Who the fuck are you?"

"Oh my God, I knew it," Katy whispered, lowering her gun, looking between us. I open the bag removing knives, more guns, and assorted useful equipment. "You really are—"

"Mafia." Dante deadpanned, strapping on a holster.

"Son a bitch!" Julian ran a hand through his hair.

He opened his mouth, but I cut him off. "Are you coming with me to find your sister or not? If you aren't then get the fuck out of my way because I will shoot anyone who gets in my way and I don't give a rat's ass who it is!" I tucked a gun in the back of my pants. And then I grabbed a holster and strapped it on with another gun and three throwing knives.

Another curse. "I'm calling Colton. He'll want to be there." Julian glanced over at Katy, who is already strapping a gun to her thigh. "I guess I don't need to ask if you're in."

"She is my best friend. Of course I'm coming!" she snapped just as Alessio walked in, guns strapped to his chest.

Well, this was getting to be an eventful day at the office. Good thing all the employees had signed NDAs.

"They sent a message." Alessio tossed a phone my way.

I caught it mid-air, setting it down on the desk then hitting play.

The video started off with some rattling and a cement floor, and then Charlotte came into focus. I clenched my jaw, holding in the bile that started to rise. Katy gasped, and Julian balled hands into fists at the image before us.

She was tied to a chair, scratches and bruises covered her body, her hair was disheveled, and silver tape stretched across her mouth. Antonio came into the frame and grabbed her by the hair, yanking her head back as he got eye level with her. I want a cut of his hand off for hurting her!

When he rips off the tape, she doesn't move, doesn't flinch. He tries intimating her, getting closer to her face... motherfucker was going to kiss her! But once he was inches away, she spat. A glob of spit landed just above his top lip and quickly slid along his lips. Laughing, he wiped it off and licked his hand.

Then a voice spoke from off camera. "Oooh, feisty…"

Antonio struck her across the face, so hard he nearly knocked the chair over. "What's she worth to you, Lorenzo?" The voice spoke as Antonio tugged her head back hard and the camera zoomed in. "Your life for hers?"

Julian gripped the desk so hard his knuckles turned white.

Shooting Antonio would be too merciful. I tightened my grasp on my gun.

"You have an hour before I kill her," the familiar voice says.

"NO LORENZO!" yelled Charlotte. "They'll—"

Antonio back handed her twice, then a knife flashed in his hand as he slammed the point into her arm. Her scream pierced the room just as the screen went black.

That scream replayed over and over in my head as my rage built and fury surged through me. It was my fault she was there.

All because she loved me.

I needed to find her and kill everyone who fucking hurt her.

My mother's face on the day she died invaded the forefront of my mind. Fate was repeating itself, and I had no one else to blame but myself. But this time I was not letting someone die for me.

"This is all your fault, motherfucker!" Julian charged at me.

Dante and Alessio lifted their guns, but I held up a hand, signaling for them to stand down, then I pushed Julian back.

"You think I don't know that?" I shouted in his face. "That I'm not aware it's because of me she's sitting in that chair getting tortured—fighting for her life? It *is* my fault. I know. But we are wasting time here arguing. Right now, I need you to put your hate aside so we can get her back. Once I know she is safe you and I can handle our shit over a few punches. But right now all I care about is Charlotte!" I shoved my phone at his chest. "Now if you're with me, call your brother, I imagine he will want to know where to meet us. If not, get the fuck out of my way."

About fifteen minutes later, we pulled up across the warehouse once investigated by Katy and Julian. We stayed hidden so they wouldn't see us coming, though I knew the attempt was futile. It had been intentional on their part that I recognized where the video had been shot, so they would be expecting us. Minutes later, a shiny black pickup pulled in next to us. Colton hopped out wearing a high-end bulletproof vest, a gun strapped to his side and an AR-15 in hand. "I'll deal with you after my sister is safe," he barked out, pointing at my chest as he shot me a death glare.

Why in the hell did he look so familiar? His forearm tattoo...

And then a brief memory fired up... almost a year ago I'd met him at a local bar. He was drunk, talking about a girl he loved and how he couldn't damn her with his secrets.

Just as he opened his mouth to say something, Katy approached him and gave him a quick kiss.

Whoa!

I guessed she was the girl.

Fate for you.

Maybe in a weird turn of events Charlotte and I were always meant to meet.

"Okay, so I counted ten outside, probably more on the

inside," said Dante as we looked toward the warehouse. "Alessio, Enzo, and I will enter first, and then—"

"The hell I'm staying back. If you don't happen to remember, that's my baby sister they're holding hostage." Colton snapped.

Julian stared me down as if wondering why I didn't just walk in there and make the trade. As if that would settle everything.

"We all go in—together," Katy announced, looking at Colton as he brought her in and kissed the top of her head. They understood what they were walking into—direct line of fire where anything could happen. I couldn't have been more jealous at that moment.

I glanced over at Dante and Alessio, and both give me a nodded response.

"Alright together," I agreed.

Julian turns to me. "After this is over, I'm locking you up." He flicks off his gun's safety. "Ready?"

I suppressed a smirk. *Like you ever could.* "Ready."

Guns raised, we made our way to the warehouse.

Ready to unleash hell for the woman I loved.

FORTY-ONE

Lorenzo

Gun fire erupted all around us, covering every angle as we neared the warehouse.

"Enzo go!" Dante got some shots off behind me as Julian and I reached the door.

I waited a beat before swinging it open and rushing inside the dark room. Without needing to look, I was aware of Julian, Colton, Katy, Alessio, and Dante storming in after me.

A light flashed on in the center of the room, highlighting the two rats I had once called family. Antonio and the other voice on the recording, Roberto.

I could have shot them then and there, but I didn't because I needed answers... and I wanted to kill them with my bare hands.

"I see you brought Boston's finest." Roberto cocked his head to the side while Antonio stood to his right. "Pleased to finally meet you, Detectives."

"A fuckin' pleasure." Julian responded, gun leveled.

"*Pezzo di merda.*" Piece of shit. "We trusted you!" Dante took a step forward, but I stopped him before he killed anyone. First, I needed to find Charlotte.

"Tsk. Tsk." Roberto shook his head. "Oh Dante, Dante, impulsive like your father. It's the reason you're no boss. And you, Lorenzo…" He put his finger on his chin.

"What the fuck do you want, Roberto? Where's Charlotte?"

"Thirty years I helped build this empire, for what… for you two to come in and destroy everything I built! The connections I brought, the richer I made the family, the people I killed all in the name of Rizzi—all for what? To be thrown off to the side so you two *children* could take over and ruin everything!"

"Ruin? We made it better!" I snapped. "Your ways had the FBI breathing down our necks!"

"No, you destroyed it! But don't worry. I'm here to once again restore it to its glory. Rizzi will no longer reign over Boston." His icy gaze slid to the man standing next to Dante. "Oh, Alessio…sorry you have to be a part of this. I really do like the Agosti family. But don't worry. I'll let your brother know you were brave till the very end."

Men appeared and flanked Antonio and Roberto as he lifted his gun. "Let the cleanse of the Rizzi bloodline begin with you two."

As Roberto pulled the trigger, I dropped and rolled, coming up and firing off several shots. Someone pushed me as a shot whizzed past my head, and a glance to my right revealed Dante had shoved me out of harm's way but was now clutching his right arm as crimson seeped into his shirt. He seriously needed to stop trying to take bullets for me.

"Dante, *che cazzo*!" What the fuck? I dove for cover and

300

landed on the ground behind some crates as my little army fired off rounds in the direction of the enemy and then took cover by me. Alessio and Colton each took a side, covering our backs as we looked for a way to advance.

Katy was reloading her gun when two men popped up behind her. "KATHERINE!" Colton yelled. Dante pushed her behind him, shooting one while I lunged for the other, knife in hand. I stabbed him three times before he even had a chance to shoot.

"Thanks!" Katy gasped, out of breath. Colton nodded our way in thanks while he checked her. Nodding back, I turned, my gaze darting around the warehouse.

I sensed her—but it was dark and between the back and forth shooting I couldn't get a clear view.

Come on, baby, give me a sign.

I stood and shot the man covering Antonio. I stomped over with Dante and Alessio on either side of me. "Come on, Antonio, too pussy to face me after you betrayed me?" I shot at the floor. "I treated you like a brother, and this is how you repay me!"

Antonio stepped out from behind the brick and shot my way. He missed, but I got a shot off and nicked his lower leg. He fell forward onto one knee. Throwing my gun aside, I lunged for him, letting my fist connect with his face. Then I roared, "I." Punch. "Trusted." Punch. "You."

Fighting back, he clipped my chin. "I was tired of being your errand boy, and then you put a bitch before the family!" He pulled a knife from an ankle sheath, and we struggled over control of it. "You knew I deserved Captain and you couldn't even give me that. No, I was just your errand bitch!" He pushed against my hands trying to stab me.

I pushed back.

"I was going to give it to you, *cagna!*" Bitch. "But you went out and fuckin' betrayed the family, so now—"

He clocked me in the left temple and turned the knife on me.

"Your father must be rolling over in his grave after seeing what you did!" I shoved against his hands as he got close to my chest.

"Fuck you!" He screamed as both of us shoved against each other's strength.

A faint scream erupted in the midst of it all.

"I hear her!" Katy yelled from somewhere. "Char! Char!"

Adrenaline hit me like a two by four in that moment. The sooner I killed this fucker, the sooner I'd have her in my arms. I started turning the knife slowly. Antonio fought against it, but I was stronger as well as being fueled by fury. "You should have chosen better," I spat, shoving the knife into his chest. Blood welled, and I pulled the knife out then sliced his face in the same spot he'd struck Charlotte. Blood splattering everywhere I stabbed him again and again in his neck. Where I once had seen family, I now saw a betrayer who got too greedy.

A foe.

As he lay bleeding on the ground, I pulled his sleeve up and skinned my family crest off his forearm in one swipe. He wasn't about to die with my family name attached. He didn't deserve the honor. I stood watching the last little bit of his soul leave his body.

"*Brucia all'inferno figlio di puttana!*" Burn in hell, motherfucker. I spat on his body just as a bullet whizzed by my ear.

As I raised my gun to shoot, another shot rang out, and a guy in front of me went down.

I spun around to see Julian.

"I did it for my sister, not for you." He lowered his gun.

I nodded in thanks as gunfire grew louder. "We need to find her now!"

I located and grabbed the gun I'd thrown earlier then slid my other gun from the back of my waistband.

With bloody hands I raised both guns and fired three rounds in front of me.

"COME ON!!! You wanted me? I am RIGHT FUCKIN' HERE!" I roared out into the dark warehouse as the rest shot off rounds.

Her screams came from the far left. "LOOK OUT!!"

BANG! BANG!

Searing pain radiated from my left arm and the warm blood seeped through my shirt as I fired another round, intensifying my anger. My blood burned with the need to kill, curse, and damn anyone who hurt her.

"Get to her now!" I yelled behind me as I ran ahead.

Shooting whoever the fuck got in my way. My arm dripped blood and the agony spread, but the pain was nothing compared to the rage that was running rampant through my veins.

War had arrived, and I was heading into battle headfirst to defend what was...

MINE.

Finally coming into contact with her, my fury and horror spread. I took cover the best way I could, dragging the chair with Charlotte on it with me.

Dried blood caked her once pink lips, bruises marred the face and body I had spent hours worshipping, and a knife was sticking out of her delicate arm. Her green eyes were barely visible from the tears that ran down her face. "*Amore,* I'm sorry. I'm going to get you out, okay?" I worked on freeing her as shots were being fired around us. I shielded her with my body and once she was untied I took her in my arms, covered her with my body as we ran behind the crates.

"Stay down!" I warned her, hoping she could hear and understand.

Through the tears, she just nodded, holding her arm.

Loading my gun, I peeked out then shot more rounds as bullets flew by our heads.

"Thought you were a smart man, Rizzi. Come on." Roberto laughed.

The sound made my blood boil even more.

"And I thought you were loyal, you fuckin' *rat*!" I shouted, firing off two shots his way.

"HAHAHA tell me…what would you do for the one you love?" he yelled.

"NOOOOO!!" Charlotte screamed and tried to move.

CAZZO!

I ran and jumped in front of Julian firing four rounds… BANG! BANG! BANG! BANG!

My body hit the ground with a jolting thud, and I gasped for air.

Another shot rang out.

"SHIT!" Julian dropped to his knees, holding his shoulder.

"Enzo!" That was Dante. Then I saw him, Alessio next to him.

"Awwww… isn't this cute?" Roberto's voice taunted, as I felt blood come up.

This was it.

Born into a life surrounded by blood, now I was dying surrounded by it.

Everything around me slowly faded. Voices grew distant.

They say when you're about to die you get one last memory. I saw her beautiful face. The way her smile brightened a room. How her green eyes sparkled in the light and how her long waves framed her face.

My angel, my love, my world.

"S-save…" Between gasps blood spewed from my mouth. "Get her ou-ut…tell h-her I-I lo-love her."

Lying there, gasping my last breaths of life I remembered my mother.

The day she died,

Her last words.

Never thinking that one day I would be repeating them.

"Finche non ci incontreremo de nuovo amore mio." Until we meet again my love.

"Let the cleansing begin." I heard Roberto's voice and I hoped he burned in hell one day.

BANG.

A last shot was fired before my body fell into the darkness.

My demons were welcoming me home with open arms.

Per Sangue Rizzi vivir y Per Sangue Rizzi Morira

FORTY-TWO

Charlotte

There are moments in life you never forget.
And this was one of them.

The love of my life lay on the ground, bleeding, fighting for his life.

I couldn't breathe. The emotional pain was stronger than any trauma my body had endured.

He had saved my brother's life—who was currently on the ground next to him.

Alessio and Dante ran to Lorenzo's side the moment he dropped to the ground and Roberto had his guns trained on them.

And there in front of me lay a gun on the ground, next to a dead body.

I didn't know what I had done until Roberto's body hit the ground.

The heavy gun slipped through my fingers, hitting the ground with a loud clunk.

I'd killed him.

I had killed Roberto.

The enemy.

The man who shot the love of my life.

Shot my brother.

And kidnapped me.

I shot him point blank. Right between the eyes.

The hands I used to save lives had just killed someone for the first time.

I stood there glued to the ground.

"Charlotte!" Colton's hands were on my face, getting me to react. "Hey, hey look at me… Char… Charlotte!" His voice sounded distant.

My hands started to shake.

Pulling me for a hug, his voice cracked. "It's okay you're safe now."

"Enzo, wake the fuck up!" Dante's voice snapped me out of daze. "ENZO!"

Pushing Colton away from me, I ran toward Lorenzo's body and dropped to my knees beside Julian.

"Lorenzo!" I pulled the knife from my arm, and blood began spurting from the wound. Ignoring it, I started chest compressions. Not even caring about the pain or the blood flowing down my arm. "Stay with me! Don't leave me!" Tears ran down my cheeks. "We need to get him to the hospital!" Turning to Dante I yelled, "NOW!"

Sirens sounded in the distance. Dante gazed at Katy, who stared down at Julian, who looked at my brother then at me.

Cursing, Julian stood. "We'll deal with this, but go—now!"

Alessio and Dante picked up Lorenzo.

"Charlotte, go." Julian shouted as he helped me up.

"Thank you, I love you!" I rushed out right behind Alessio and Dante as I heard my brother call in the scene with the words "officer down" while we hauled ass to the car.

Alessio drove while Dante shouted orders into the phone, and I held Lorenzo in the back. His pulse was weakening.

"Drive faster!" I yelled, and Alessio pressed down on the gas, jerking the car forward.

My hand wouldn't stop shaking; they were covered in Lorenzo's blood while his near lifeless body lay on me.

"I killed someone," I croaked. Who had I become?

A killer?

Or a person who had defended those she loved—Family.

Dante glanced over his shoulder. "Char, I'm—"

"I would do it again!" I snapped my head up, letting my eyes connect with Dante's. Knowing that nothing was the same now. "Nobody fucks with family."

No one could stop me from entering this life, and I would kill anyone who dared fuck with them.

"No one fucks with family," he echoed and looked to Alessio who looked at me through the rearview mirror... repeating the same.

A staff full of nurses and doctors awaited us once we pulled up to the private entrance of the hospital. I opened the car door before we even came to a full stop. Then I jumped out, giving orders to the doctors who were looking at me like I was crazy. "What the fuck are you waiting for!" I screamed, my voice cracking from the knots strangling my throat. Barely keeping it together, I motioned for them to hurry and save him.

Could they not see he was bleeding out?

I was starting to lose my goddamn mind as they just stood there staring as if I were speaking in another language.

Dante pointed his gun. "Do as she says, or I'm putting a bullet in you," he roared.

In a sudden flurry of movement, they all scrambled to get him out the car and onto the gurney.

Tina, my friend at the hospital, paled at the sight of me. I knew I was covered in blood and bruises marked my skin. But I had a feeling that wasn't what caused her reaction, but instead the fact that Dante stood to my right and Alessio to my left, guns out as we made our way in.

"I'm in charge right now, and I am putting Charlotte in charge of this place so do as she says or get your hand chopped off, " Dante said to no one in particular.

"Yes sir," Dr. Davis responded and started pushing the gurney toward the OR.

I pushed past Tina and ran alongside Lorenzo, gripping his hand.

Begging him to stay alive.

When we made it to the doors of the OR, Dante dragged me away. I was barely able to lean down and press a kiss to Lorenzo's lips. "Don't leave me please," I whispered before they took him in.

The doors swung closed.

And it felt as if they were shutting forever. Like that was the last time I would see him, touch him, feel him.

I opened my mouth to scream, but the noise didn't come. In my mind, I was screaming into the abyss, where the walls were caving in and the air thinned out making it harder to breathe.

Dante held me as I cried while a nurse tried to tend to my wounds. I fought everyone away not wanting to be attended.

"Code blue to OR two," came a female voice from the intercom speaker overhead. "Code blue to OR two."

Medical personnel in scrubs and lab coats raced toward the doors.

"Nooo!" Kicking and pushing Dante, I tried to follow them, but he held me in a death grip.

His own eyes red, full of emotion, he held me on to me.

Alessio stood to the side, frozen in place, gun still in hand, while doctors and nurses ran toward the operating room pushing carts with equipment and blood bags.

Screaming, I begged to be let go.

I begged until I was on my knees.

Because there wasn't a world I wanted to live in without Lorenzo by my side.

Dante fell to the floor beside me and gripped tighter as I clawed at him.

"Please, Dante, please...let me die with him! Please!" Voice hoarse, I pleaded as the air no longer reached my lungs. With a gasp, I screamed out his name one last time.

Darkness clouded my once clear vision, and I shut my eyes allowing myself to fall.

To fall into the darkness that was once a light.

If this was Lorenzo calling me to him then so be it, because a life without part of my soul was one I didn't want.

I wanted him.

My savior.

My monster.

My everything.

FORTY-THREE

Lorenzo

Blanketed in a sea of darkness, my body felt cold but warm.

A figure in front of me smiled, brightening up the emptiness.

It was just how I remembered. Radiant as always and dressed in her favorite white pantsuit.

Even after all this time.

I reached forward wanting to get closer to her, to feel her. To hold her in my arms and let her know how much I love her. But the closer I got the farther she went. It didn't matter how hard I tried or how tight I gripped her hand, she always slipped from my fingers.

"I miss you," she whispered. "But it's not time yet."

"Mom?" I stretched out my hand, barely touching the tips of her fingers.

She laughed. "Always so persistent *figlio*. I said not yet." Her scolding tone brought a smile to my lips.

"But—"

"But nothing, Lorenzo." For the first time, she stepped forward. "One day we will meet again, my little warrior, and until then… fight for her, love her, and live a life full of love and happiness, like your father and I once did. I love you, Lorenzo."

"I wish you were with me, Mom."

"I always am." She stepped forward, placing a kiss on my cheek, and then leaned into my ear. "Wakeup Lorenzo."

And like a slap to the face my eyelids flung open. The bright lights burned my eyes, my entire body felt the pain from my chest and everything came racing back.

Charlotte.

I needed to find Charlotte.

Forcing my aching body, I tried to get up, ripping off the tubes and wires that were attached to me. Lights and alarms went off on the monitor bank beside me, but I couldn't care less. All that mattered was finding my *amore*. Ignoring the pain, I pushed my body when the door flew open.

Dante, Alessio, and a nurse came running in. The nurse went straight to the monitors and worked on the alarms, while my cousin and friend came at my side trying to get me to lie down.

"Enzo, relax." Dante tried forcing me back down.

"Let me go, Dante. I need to—"

"Enzo, you almost died. You need to take it easy." Alessio tried to help Dante, but I kept fighting them.

"I don't care. Where is Charlotte?" The last thing I could remember was hearing her screams and a very distant memory of her voice telling me to not leave her.

"She's—"

"Resting, no thanks to you." We all turn toward the door where Colton and Julian, who wore an arm sling, stood, both throwing looks like daggers my way,

Dante wasted no time blocking their entrance, growling, "Come any closer, and I'll—"

"You'll what?" Colton steps up to my cousin, ready to fight him. This is the last thing I need right now. My only concern is for Charlotte—not being a referee to her brothers and my cousin.

"Dante, leave us." He didn't make an effort to move until I glared at Alessio, who then gave Dante's shoulder a squeeze.

In a few seconds, I was left with Colton and Julian alone. Neither of her brothers appeared inclined to break the tense silence, so I blurted, "How is she?"

Julian scoffed, but Colton stepped up to the edge of my bed. "Considering what she's been through, she is good, lucky to be alive,:

I eased out the breath I'd been holding.

"But don't think for one second that we've forgotten the danger you put her in," he added.

Julian stepped up next to his brother, spitting fire. "She would never have been kidnapped if it wasn't for you."

I opened my mouth to speak, when the TV on the wall behind them got my attention. "What the fuck?"

The TV was on mute, so I couldn't hear what the reporter was saying, but the headline scrolling across the bottom read "Breaking News: Bust on the two biggest drug lords in the city."

"What did you do?" I snarled. I saw red and my mind raced to the danger my family was in.

Julian crossed his arms and smirked. "Exactly what I had to do."

"Do you have any idea what you've just started?" He might be Charlotte's brother, but I wanted nothing more than to kill him in this second. "That's my family you've just messed with!"

"And you messed with ours!" Colton snapped back.

"Charlotte is my family!" I yelled sitting fully up despite the escalating pain. "Despite what you think, I love Charlotte and I intend to make her my wife whether you two like it or not."

Both brothers clenched their jaws, but I didn't let them get a word in.

"I don't give a rats ass who I have to kill in order to protect her. Charlotte is mine, and I will die before ever letting anything happen to her. So again, when I say you messed with my family that includes her! And anyone that messes with them will have to answer to me!" I was breathing heavy by the time I finished, unable to fully catch my breath. It felt like I had just run a marathon. But I was so consumed by rage that my veins felt the kick of adrenaline coursing through them. "I will ask this one more time, Julian. What did you do?"

I was fully aware that the minute he told me that he had blown the lid on my family was the minute I would have to kill him, despite him being Charlotte's brother.

Staring them down, I waited for Julian to answer.

Instead of speaking, his lip curled, and I fisted my hands while Colton stood up taller beside him. After a minute, Julian stepped toward me. My eyes stayed trained on him as he made his way to the bedside table, picked up the TV remote control and hit the unmute button.

Instantly, the room was filled with the voice of the young blond reporter.

"In this warehouse behind me, two notorious drug lords allegedly met and fought over territories and drug trades. Both parties opened fire on each other, resulting in the deaths of many…"

I clenched my fists, giving Julian the death stare.

The reporter continued in a serious, professional voice, "Authorities arrived on scene during the shoot out and found themselves in the midst of it all. Fortunately, only one officer was injured during the chaos, but the two heads of the organizations were killed. Antonio Bocci and Roberto Greco…" My head snapped back at the mention of the two rats. "What?" The reporter was still speaking as Julian turned the volume down.

"Still want to kill me?"

"Yes." I gritted. Then I frowned as I struggled to put it all together. "Maybe just a little less now."

Julian snorted. "I feel the same way. But just so we are clear, I risked my career for my sister, not for you. Even if you did—" Cough. "Take a bullet for me."

"*A* bullet?" I lifted a brow. "More like three or four."

"Details." He waved me off. "So let's talk about some changes that need to happen."

"Changes? There will be no changes." I almost laughed. What did they expect me to do—go straight? Ha! When hell froze over—hell, not even then! I'd just put on a winter coat and say let's go.

"There will be if you want to stay with our sister," Colton intervened.

"I already told you, I'm not letting her go no matter what you two say. Plus, no one tells me what to do."

"Well, this shit can't happen again!" Colton roared. "Because if it does I'll kill you myself."

"Are you threatening me?" I yelled back.

"No, I'm warning you. We might not be able to keep her away from you, but I sure as fuck will make sure you protect her. You have money, guards, extensive resources to keep her safe."

I scoffed. "What makes you think I wasn't already planning on doing just that?"

"Oh, we know, but we want to be part of whatever security you're planning for her. We're her brothers, her only family since our piece of shit parents left. So we want to know who you're hiring," Julian said.

At that I laughed. "I don't think you will like my hiring process."

"What? Does involves torture?" Colton chuckled, but at my grave expression he stopped. "Seriously?"

"Look, I don't need to explain myself to you. Just know that she will be safe from now on."

"How are you so sure?" Julian asks.

"You have my word."

"Your word?" They asked at the same time.

Then Colton continued. "This isn't a game. How do we know we have your word that this shit never happens again?"

"Because if there is one thing that my family takes seriously, it's our word." I had no reason to make them promises, listen to their concerns, or take their opinions into consideration. Except... they were Charlotte's brothers. I knew what it meant to her.

Like they said they were the only family she had left, and she was all they had.

Yes, I might be boss, but family was important to me, and I could tell these men in front of me felt the same way or else they wouldn't be standing there making threats, knowing what I was capable of. And… they had covered for me, hidden my involvement in this whole mess. This was a hard pill to swallow and was guessing it was for them as well.

Julian was a man who believed in the justice of the law, and Colton was a standup soldier. Both saw the world as black and white.

Good and bad.

Whereas I saw it as gray. There was really no good or bad in the real world; it was blended. Sometimes you had to do bad things to do some good. Yes, my family sold drugs, but we controlled what was sold, and to whom, and the money from that allowed us to help others who needed it.

Maybe my next action wasn't the best idea in other people's eyes, but I needed to show Charlotte's brothers that despite my deals, my values were the same, we just had different methods of dealing with the people who hurt us.

"Dante!" I called, knowing he was right outside the door.

He came in wearing a stoic look, probably ready to kill them if that was my request.

"Knife." I held out my hand and everyone looked at me confused. "Now," I snapped.

Everyone spoke at once. "You can't be serious," Dante gritted

"What fuck you want a knife for?" Julian asked.

A string of curses slipped from Colton's lips.

I gave Dante a nod. "Knife." After a few curses of his own, he pulled his switchblade from his pants pocket and stood by me.

"What are you going to kill us now? After what I did for you!" Julian stepped forward. "Are you seriously—"

"Shut the fuck up!" I bellowed. He opened his mouth to

speak but was stopped when I lifted my hand and ran the edge of the blade against my palm.

"You wanted my word, well here is how we give ours…"

FORTY-FOUR

Charlotte

Beep. Beep. Beep.

I heard the sound of the monitor and some whispering.

My brothers?

"Lor-enzo?" Blinking a couple times, I opened my eyes, and in moments my brothers were at my side, each taking a turn hugging me. Julian one-arm hugged me a little longer. He had sacrificed his life in order to save me and then his career saving Lorenzo's. "What you did, I will never—"

"Important thing is that you're okay." He pressed a kiss to my head.

My eyes watered. "Is... he um..." I couldn't bring myself to ask. Because I didn't know what I would do if the answer was one I couldn't live with. My chest felt tight and tears fell just at the thought that he might be gone.

Julian sat next to me grabbing a hold of my hand, and the fear I'd felt earlier hit as I curled into his embrace. "He's alive."

Snapping my head up, I stared at Julian as he gave a small smile.

"He is in the next room. Actually, he woke up hours ago but said he wanted to let you rest."

"What! How long have I been asleep? I need to see him!" Throwing the cover off, I let out shriek at the searing agony in my arm.

Colton rushed to me. "Easy, your body went through a lot. They had to sedate you because you wouldn't stop screaming and crying. You've been asleep for almost a day."

"What!" Then I winced—briefly remembering fighting off doctors and nurses. I thought I punched Nurse Tina. I had tried taking my IV out but was stopped. "I swear, Colt, if you try to stop me again I will punch you in the throat."

Next to me, Julian chuckled.

"That goes for you too, brother. No one is stopping me from seeing Lorenzo." My brothers gave each other a look, and I balled my fist. I wasn't joking.

"Okay, Rocky, relax." Julian stood and went to look for a nurse. After a few minutes I was unhooked, given another hospital gown to cover up and a pair of slippers. With my brothers at my side I pushed through the soreness in my body to Lorenzo's room.

He sat up the moment he heard us. "*Amore.*"

I let go of Colton's hand and ran to his side.

"Charlotte, you shouldn't—"

I cut him off by pressing my lips to his, reveling in the warmth of his touch.

"I am so sorry, *amore*. I never—"

"It wasn't your fault. I'm here, and you're alive." Tears ran down my cheeks. I thought I had lost him forever.

He wiped my cheeks with his thumbs then held my face between his hands, pulling me in for a kiss.

Julian cleared his throat. Heat flooded my face, I'd forgotten they were still there. Colton had his fist clenched as he subjected Lorenzo to a harsh staredown. "You know our conditions. We have your word?"

Word? What the hell? I opened my mouth but got cut off.

Colton crossed his arms. "It happens again—"

"You have my word." Lorenzo lifted his wrapped palm. My brothers both nodded and did the same. Why did they have the same wrap on their hands? I looked between them, confused as my brothers just turned around and walked from the room.

"What was that, and why are your hands bandaged?" I turned to Lorenzo.

Lorenzo grabbed my hand and kissed the back of it, sending a tingle throughout my body. "Just your brothers looking out for you. Hey, I didn't know they were Patriots fans."

"Yeah, big ones." I shook my head, refusing to allow the change of subject. "What deal?"

"Later. Right now, I just want to hold you in my arms." He started pulling me toward him.

"Lorenzo, be careful you've just been shot."

"Don't care. I came close to losing you."

I placed my head gently on his chest. "And I came close to losing you."

"I love you, Charlotte."

"I love you, Lorenzo Rizzi." I ran my fingers over his hospital gown where his family crest was. "Monster and all—always and forever."

"Always and forever," he repeated, pulling my chin up with his thumb. He planted a soft kiss on my lips, and I opened my mouth, enticing him in so our tongues came together as one. When he pulled back, his eyes glittered. "If the bullets didn't kill me, I swear your mouth will."

I nipped his lip, feeling his erection growing against my leg.

He chuckled. "My gravestone will say, 'And he died with a fuckin' smile on his face under the sexiest woman alive.'"

Giggling, I leaned back. "Not until you heal."

"Great, now I'm going to die from blue balls." He looked heavenward then back at me acting hurt.

I rolled my eyes.

"Oh now you've done it." He slapped my ass.

I laughed—after I had been kidnapped, beaten, stabbed.

After I came close to losing him.

We lay in that hospital room where we had found each other again.

He had been my high school crush.

Now he was the man I had fallen in love with, killed for, and would die for.

My soulmate.

My savior and monster in one.

Mine.

Always and forever.

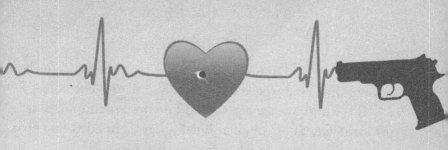

EPILOGUE

After a couple days at the hospital, we spent the better part of a week at Lorenzo's, wrapped up in each other's arms, well at least when my brothers and friends weren't over or when he wasn't working. Even after everything there was still a big mess to handle.

Not to mention my own battles.

The events from that day still haunted me, all except Roberto's death. He deserved no mercy, and I would have killed him ten times over if it meant saving Lorenzo and everyone else.

It was the torture I had endured that was traumatizing. Sometimes I woke up in a panic, dripping sweat, screaming for help. Lorenzo always held me until I stopped crying and finally fell back to sleep. But I hated what it did to him. The pain his eyes revealed every time it happened or the hours of sleep he lost just to stay up watching me, making sure I was safe—it all took a toll on him.

My life would never be the same. A mafia boss was the last person I had ever expected to fall in love with—but I did.

This world was dangerous and Lorenzo feared I might face the same fate as his mother, but I always reminded him that no one's life was to be taken for granted. Our next day, or our next minute was not guaranteed. I could be walking down the stairs, trip, hit my head, and die right there. And maybe that was the worst example ever because for two days after I said that, he carried me down and up the stairs—and he was still recovering! But I proved my point...he would do anything to keep me safe.

Love was a risk, and it all depended on if we were willing to kill for each other or not.

Never thought I would ever utter those words.

But what can I say? Mafia.

Others might look at me like I'm crazy and wonder how it was possible for me to accept my new reality so easily, so willingly. Want to know my response? I did struggle but my love for Lorenzo outweighs it all. And no, it wasn't infatuation, lust, or for all the riches he had. It was true, honest, fate bidding kind of love.

I believed that our fates were sealed that night eight years ago. That it was fate that made me work the night I was supposed to be at home digging into the tub of cookies and cream ice cream. I was meant to find him in that hospital room, even if he was an ass. Our fates were destined from the beginning and there was nowhere else I would rather be than by his side. Protecting the family... our family... at all costs.

Others on the outside looked at it as something evil, only capable of causing harm, but what they didn't see was that the mafia was evil in order to protect their own. That at the end of the day, they were just human. Fighting for love of family and their own. Blood wasn't spilled just because someone walked in front of them and pissed them off.

If you bled, they bled.

If you hurt, they hurt.

My blood for yours was what Dante said to Lorenzo when he saw him hurt but was grateful he was alive.

Family was sacred and was put above all else.

Something my brothers and I came to respect because when it came to us, we would do anything to keep each other safe. Julian risked his career for us and after arguments, stare downs and many, many drinks… Lorenzo gave them a small inside look into the Rizzi organization.

And maybe it was all the alcohol or maybe my brothers felt a sense of loyalty. Something they both experienced in their lines of work and something they could trust and fight for.

Now they are all working together.

Weird?

Maybe.

I was just glad they were getting along.

Colton had made a new plan of security for Lorenzo, and together they locked down a plan that kept us safe and made sure to sniff out any disloyal associate. His contract was coming to an end with the Army and he was already thinking of starting a security business so helping Lorenzo was a perfect start. Julian being more of an extrovert, a UFC fanatic and having fought illegally in high school helped Dante with the underground fights. Yes, my brother the detective had a past, one that, had not been for Katy's father, would have landed him in jail at sixteen. He changed his ways, and became who he is today but ever since finding out Lorenzo controlled the rings, my brother offered to help. Hell, he even made friends with one of their best fighters, Crew. Turned out the three of them bonded over motorcycles one day.

It wasn't anything we imagined for ourselves, but we were family, and we found another family who took the same vow of protection, like we did ,seriously.

"Five more minutes." Lorenzo caged me in with his body.

I giggled. "Fine but then I have to leave. Bella is waiting, and I need clean underwear." We had come straight here from the hospital, and while Lorenzo's clothes were comfy, I wanted some of my own. Plus, I had promised Isabella I would finally stop by today.

"I like you better without any." He licked down my neck, to my boob, down my stomach until his head was between my legs.

"Ahhh, Lorenzo!" I pulled his hair. "Oh, that feels…" I felt him smile. With a groan, I yanked his hair hard, which only ignited a fire in him making me moan harder, tremble, and scream out his name. Probably God's as well. But could you blame me for praising the God for creating a man with an insane amount of beauty and tongue skills?

Halle-freakin-lujah!

It ended up being a hell of a lot more than five minutes, and even then, he still tried to distract me from leaving. It wasn't until Dante came by and practically begged him to deal with Rizzi Energy that he released me.

Dante hated Rizzi Energy, said his skills were better used for family business; even more so now that Bella had started working at their company. He avoided the office like the plague and usually came home drunk, bloody, or both.

"I have a little surprise for you," Lorenzo said as he opened the front door.

My jaw hit the floor.

There in the middle of the driveway with a big giant red bow was a brand new shiny white G-wagon with big black matte rims and tinted windows.

"You're kidding, right?" My eyes went wide, and my eyebrows lifted so high they were probably lost in my hair. "You bought me a car? And not just any car, but a $100,000 one!"

He shrugged. "You needed a new one and it was more like $180,000 give or take."

I choked. That was like buying a house and way, way more than I made in a year! "I'm sorry, what?" I asked after I was done choking on air.

"You deserve the best. Oh, and it's bulletproof. So no driving any other car that's not this one or one of mine. After everything, I'm not taking my chances with something happening to you." He put the key fob in my hand.

I opened my mouth to assure him that even after everything that happened, I was still here, a little different but alive, but the man from the office a few weeks ago approached, the giant.

"Just in time. Charlotte, this is Aaron, your new bodyguard."

"My what?" I didn't know where to look; at Lorenzo, the giant bodyguard, or my new car. My head snapped back so many times I for sure whiplashed myself. "Is this a prank?"

"Nope, your brothers agree. The car and the bodyguard." He gave a casual shrug.

Great, so now there was basically no fighting him on it since my brothers were on board. But to be honest, after being kidnapped, a personal bodyguard didn't sound like a bad idea. "Aaron, follow her in the SUV along with Kane and Axel. Anywhere she goes, you go, you don't let her out of your sight, and if need be, you take a bullet for her. Anything happens to her Aaron, and I'll test my new gun on you. You got that?" Lorenzo was all boss mode.

"Understood, sir."

So, I guess this was my life now. Surrounded by bodyguards who were willing to give their lives for me.

Normal, right?

"Alright, stop threatening my bodyguard and get to work. Aaron, we will leave in a minute." With a nod he turned and walked over to the SUV where the other two were waiting while I turned back to Lorenzo. "Thank you for my new car. I love it. I'll thank you later." With a swipe of my tongue on his lips I turned and got in my new G-wagon; loving the way the black leather felt. Stretching, I closed my eyes and drew in a deep breath then let it out slowly.

Lorenzo chuckled at my reaction and leaned in the open window. "I'm glad you love it. But you know what makes me even happier?"

"What?"

His hand on my cheek he smiled. "That fate brought you back to me. I love you, *amore.*"

I didn't think it was possible for my love for him to grow, but somehow in that moment it multiplied by ten. My eyes watered at the sight of his chocolate brown eyes. The same ones that enchanted me when I was seventeen and promised me he had me.

"I love you too." I smiled before feeling the soft touch of his lips. Bringing life to my soul.

That single kiss from him was an electroshock to the heart. Something I will never tire of.

I watched him as he pulled back, smirking, swiping his

thumb over his lip as he walked to the house, looking like every inch of a mafia boss in his burgundy dress shirt with the top few buttons undone, showing off his tattoos and a gun tucked into his black dress pants.

I loved seeing the power in him knowing that with me he was different, softer but passionate. That the ruthlessness was reserved for his men.

"Hey," I called out just before he turned to go inside. And right as he turned I lifted my white long sleeve, flashing him my white lace bra. "A little preview of my thanks." I winked and took off. Through the rearview mirror I could see his face, and it was priceless.

On my way home, my brothers called, I barely got a hello in when they were already asking how the new car ran and if I liked my bodyguards so far. Apparently, they all had "interviewed" Aaron and his guys for the job. My ass they interviewed them… more like threatened them.

But according to Julian, Aaron had been with the family for years in Chicago and was one of their best men. He had been one of Dante's younger sister's guards until Lorenzo's dad sent him to Boston to help.

"We'll wait here Miss. Frizzell," Aaron said as we rode the elevator up to the apartment.

"Please call me Char, and I am going to be here for a while. There's no need to wait."

"The boss doesn't want you going anywhere without us so let us know if you need anything." We approached the front door where he and Kane took guard.

"Umm…okay then," was all I could say as I went through my front door.

I might have to talk to Lorenzo about this.

My eighty-year-old neighbor might have a heart attack when she walked out and found two giant gorillas with guns and knives strapped to their chest right outside her door.

Removing my Nikes at the door, I walked toward the living room, looking for Bella. "Hello, I'm home." I saw that her bedroom door was ajar so I stepped in looking for her. "Bella?"

The bathroom door swung open.

"Hey, there you—" I stopped when I noticed the paleness in her face. "Isabella, what's wrong?"

Tears started running down her face and I quickly made my way to her, freezing when I saw the white plastic stick in her hands. "I-Isabella is that—" I gulped.

"I'm pregnant," she breathed, right before her eyes rolled back, fainting right in front of me. Barley catching her I looked down at the test that had landed on the carpeting.

Positive.

What. The. Fuck?

Thank you

for reading Charlotte and Lorenzo's story.

Want to read Dante and Isabella's story?

Undeserving

Book #2 coming early 2022

ACKNOWLEDGMENTS

Wow I honestly don't know where to begin…

This story came to me one day and I fought it off for a while, thinking I was crazy. I mean ,who was I to write something like this? Hell, even a story… a book? I am just a regular girl who never finished college, was in the middle of finishing up a medical assistant course and had absolutely no experience in writing. Well, except for essays from school lol. But aside from that, I had zero experience. But I simply picked up my laptop one night (after a glass or two of wine if I might add) and started typing. I can still clearly remember the first words I typed… "Why in the world am I doing this ?" Funny how the words I first typed were the exact feeling that was running through me at that very moment. Yet I kept typing away, wrote three chapters that night; finished at 2am and sent it to my best friend, Ale. She was the very first person I confided in and let read my words. She screamed—well that's what I assumed she did since it was over text but I swear I heard her voice in that message. She said, "keep writing" and I did.

And well, here we are months later, releasing my words out into the world for you guys, to enjoy.

But this book couldn't have come all on its own. Like I said I knew nothing when I started this. And when I mean nothing, I really mean... NOTHING! Thankfully my all-time favorite author, Rachel, led me to some amazing people when I nervously reached out to her and confessed to her that it was her who inspired me to write. She's amazing and the people who she recommended were just as amazing.

Jill, I can't thank you enough for everything you helped me with. Pretty sure you had better things to do than to help out a silly girl like me. Who bombarded you with millions of questions and hundreds of concerns, but you did, and I couldn't be anymore thankful. And can I just say, amazing job on the formatting! Like wow! Kay, my amazing editor, I don't know what my story would be without you, thank you! Jen, the cover you created was even more than I imagined it could have been, and I am in so love! Ale, my best friend, thank you for reading everything I sent you and proofreading it all.

And please, let's not forget C.A. Mariah.... we started this writing journey together. When I found you, we each had just started something that was completely crazy to us. But together we helped one another, asked each other's opinions, made edits and so much more. Girl, I am grateful for you! Can't wait to release so many more stories with you. Also thank you to all the amazing authors I have met along the way like V.Domino and Natalie Lourose who gave me so much amazing advice and motivation.

Also my family… Mom, Dad, Cecy, Aunt Sindy and Grandmas (Mami Estela and Mama Blanca); thank you for not laughing in my face when I told you about this. To Gustavo, for letting me live out my dream and not killing me after so many late nights I kept you up with my typing, editing or research. I love you babe!

Well, I think I might end this here because this might be 20 miles long if I keep going lol.

This story comes from the heart. I poured my heart, soul, tears (maybe even a little blood, just kidding, maybe…..) into this story. I hope you guys enjoyed it and are ready for more because now that I have started, I can't seem to put my laptop down. So, expect more from me and I can't wait for you guys to see what's next.

I love every single one of you and thank you for taking a chance on me!

ABOUT THE AUTHOR

*S*elena Gutierrez has always loved to read and was always coming up with crazy romance stories in her head. Always kept them to herself up until recently when one day she thought she would write them down and found her love for storytelling. She wrote her first story, Amor Fati and now she can't seem to stop. Always writing down a new idea, and probably has about three stories started. She is a coffee addict, a lover of wine, music is always blasting and when she isn't writing, she is usually with family or friends making memories. You can always find her on social media posting her daily pics and laughing at the latest tiktock videos.

Made in the USA
Coppell, TX
21 September 2021

62742977R00204